The Broken Red Road

Book One
of the
Havelock Emerald series

© Copyright 2020
by

Tom Frye

Published by Storm Haven Press

Although this is a work of fiction, many of the places and the events in this story are real. However, names and characters are the product of the author's imagination. Any resemblance to actual persons, living or dead is entirely coincidental.

Copyright 2008 © Tom Frye. All rights reserved.

To Evan Bowers-Davis
my greatest
Ambassador
who shared
my books
with his
friends and family.
I could not
have asked
for better support.

Chapter One

Hooting like a mad owl, the grungy rider's chopped hog roared over the hill like a black streak of motorized lightning. Clinging to the ape-hangers of the big 1200, fierce winds clawed at 17-year-old Jack Holland, threatening to pluck him from his seat. He cut in and out of both lanes, on a collision course with the school bus coming down the highway in the opposite lane. The kids riding the bus that Friday afternoon stared in terror at the crazed Harley rider speeding toward them. Bus driver, Ben Black Bull, cranked the wheel as the rider swerved in front of the bus then crashed his black iron horse in the ditch beside the road.

Clawing at the wheel, Ben sent the bus crashing into a pond in the pasture beyond the highway. At the back of the bus, thirteen-year-old Rain Nelson latched onto his little brother as the bus dipped down into the pond. Wild tangles of black hair trailing over his shoulders, Rain did a face-plant on the seat in front of him. When his vision cleared, he saw his little brother writhing beside him in pain. "Rain," Jessie cried, "my arm's broke!"

Staring down at the bone sticking out of Jessie's left forearm, a sick feeling swept over Rain as he removed his brother from the bus. Blood leaking through the strands of Jessie's dark hair, Rain took off his flannel shirt. As blood speckled the orange Harley Davison emblem on his black T-shirt, he used his flannel shirt to dab at Jessie's head wound.

"Jack Holland!" Jessie whispered as the drunken biker staggered out of the ditch. Rain turned to see the son of the president of the Elder's Den moving toward Ben. Jack snarled, "Damn you, Chief! Should have let that dog fight! You interfered in Den business!"

He stumbled across the road, his eyes locked on Ben. He reached inside his leather jacket and pulled out a bottle of whiskey. Removing the lid from his bottle, Jack took a swig, his cheeks puffing out with the whiskey inside his mouth. Ben reached out to steady him, and Jack spat whiskey all over him, drenching his shirt with the liquid.

"Now," Jack said, "you are one drunk bastard, Bull."

Ben latched onto the bottle and tossed it to one side. Jack bent down and removed a knife from his boot top. Ben executed a palm strike that connected with Jack's chest. The blow catapulted him off his feet and went flying backward. Jack clambered up from the ground, lunging at Ben with his knife. Seeing that Ben was in trouble,

Rain snatched up a Coleman thermos bottle from the debris scattered behind the bus. He focused on Jack and let fly. The bottle struck Jack in the center of his forehead. The kid staggered back, the knife falling from his grasp. Jack turned and vanished into a nearby cornfield, a silver cigar tube landing on the ground behind him.

Rain walked over and picked up the metal tube, sliding it into the top of his left boot. "What was that?" Ben asked him, curiously.

"If I'm lucky," Rain said, "a Swisher Sweet cigar."

Staring at him silently, Ben said nothing.

Sheriff Mike Tory brought his cruiser screeching to a halt on the highway beside the pasture. Mike was a big man, whose beer-gut stretch-ed his brown uniform shirt to the max. He sported a buzz cut and had a craggy face. As he heaved his bulk out of his cruiser, he growled, "What happened here, Bull?"

Ben said, "I'll explain that after we get these kids up on the road."

Sirens wailed, piercing the country air as the ambulance raced toward them. Several seconds later, the ambulance skidded to a stop behind the patrol car. The driver switched off his siren and a paramedic climbed out of the vehicle. As he assessed the injuries, thunderous rumbling came from Sprague just down the road as a Harley came roaring toward the place of the accident. "Chase," Big Mike said. "He'll know who was riding this bike, won't he, Rain?"

Rain ignored him as his little brother was led away by a tech to the ambulance. Chase Nelson, father of Rain and Jessie, pulled his bike up behind the cruiser. At thirty, Chase was tall and lean, with long dark hair that fell past the collar of his black leather jacket. He sported a neatly-trimmed beard and his blue eyes missed nothing as he inspected the mangled hog in the ditch. "Do you know who that Harley belongs to?" Big Mike asked.

Chase said, "Not a clue. Do you, son?"

"No," Rain said, lowering his gaze. "Jessie got a busted arm. He's headed to Crete in an ambulance. We best drive him home in the old wagon, Dad."

The sound of more thunder filled the air as a large bike flew past the ambulance on its way to Crete. Daws Holland rode his Harley up behind Big Mike's cruiser. Daws, father of Jack and president of the Elder's Den, was a large man in his early thirties. He had blond hair and was built like a tank, with broad shoulders and muscular arms. Daws and Chase had once fought. In the end, Chase had dislocated Daws's jaw, and after delivering such a brutal blow, the President of the Outlaws had left Daws where he had fallen. Dazed and in pain, Daws barely managed to kick his bike over and weave his way out of Sprague.

Daws killed his bike. He put the stand down and dismounted. Staring at the mangled bike in the nearby ditch, he walked over to Bobby Morris, looking down at his broken leg. Ben said, "Best not move this one. This is a bad break."

"Shut up, Bull!" said Daws. "I'm not touching him."

Rain said, "A maniac on that bike swerved in front of us."

Daws asked. "What club? Did you see his colors?"

"Colors?" Rain said, trying to play dumb.

Daws moved so fast that Rain had no chance to dodge his meaty hand as the big biker shoved his slender frame up against the side of the car. Rain shook back the long strands of his dark hair and glared back at him. "Whoa," said Chase, "turn this down a notch, Daws."

Daws said, "Got a call from my son, Sheriff. He spotted this wreck and drove to a farmhouse to call in for help. Jack claims the Indian was swerving all over like he'd been drinking."

"Oh, hell, too!" burst from Rain's lips.

"Rain?" came from Chase. "Shut your mouth."

"But that just ain't true," Rain said.

Daws focused his attention on Ben leaning against the patrol car. "Should be ashamed of yourself, Chief. Not a lot of folks around here take kindly to a drunken Indian putting their kids at such risk. I'd say you've got a lot to answer for. And you smell like a tavern."

To sit there and listen while Daws convinced Sheriff Tory that the bus crash had been due to the fact that Ben had been drinking, caused Rain much distress. Daws crossed the ditch and picked up the whiskey bottle, and said, "We got to fish your bus out of Miller's Pond all because you've been drinking in Whiskey River, Ben!"

Chapter Two

Seated behind his dad as he throttled the Harley, Rain was regretting the fact that he had so boldly defied Chase. He had no doubt that Chase would deal with him later. Rain had known Ben ever since he'd started school in Crete back in first grade. He knew him as the first friendly Native he had ever met. Ben had such a way about him that he put Rain at ease with his soft-spoken words.

When the Lakota was not driving the bus for the Crete district, he worked at his dog rescue ranch west of the small town of Sprague. The past summer, Rain and Jessie had seen the magic of Ben. He had spent his life around dogs back on Pine Ridge and had learned the secret of working with the most challenging dogs. The two brothers considered it an honor that the Lakota shared his secrets with them.

As soon as Chase pulled up beside the Sprague general store, Rain leaped off his dad's bike and strode over to the dusty porch. While the thunder of the Harley slowly faded, Rain planted his butt on the rickety wooden bench situated there. He looked squarely at his dad. Chase slipped his kick stand down, dismounted his Harley, and walked over to the porch.

Rain shook back his raven hair and stuck out his chin in a show of obstinance. "You gonna hit me for not backing down from Daws?"

Chase said, "I am gonna hit you for not shutting your mouth when I told you to."

He let loose with a swift round house, his palm slamming into Rain's startled face. Staggered by the blow, his boots slid out from under him and Rain landed hard on his butt. Chase froze as a voice came from beside the porch, "Rain got the point. Now, back off."

Chase said, "You're a wise ass, Beef Tory! This is club business!"

Fifteen-year-old Beef flicked his long, blond bangs out of his eyes. "But Rain doesn't even belong to the Outlaws yet. Pummeling him, would not sit well with Pops, Chase."

Chase was president of the Outlaws, and not one of the sixty members ever defied him. He was clearly drawing a line in the sand for some odd reason. Rain knew there were reasons his dad kept his cool with Beef stepping into club business. Chase and Beef's father had grown up together. Big Mike was the Sheriff of Gage county and he didn't like domestic abuse one bit. "You're just worried," Beef said, "about the dog, ain't you? Calling off her fight has all the clubs on edge. Outlaws. Elder's Den. Gladiators. Screaming Eagles."

Chase looked over to the female Pit bull waddling up beside Beef. She was a brute, with her stocky chest, thick muscular legs, and her Brindle markings covering her bulky head. The Outlaw president said, "Keep her hidden in the barn. Word gets to the Den that we've got Molly, her and her pups are dead. You two take Molly back to the barn. I'll get the wagon to pick up Jessie from the ER."

Rain waited until Chase kicked over his bike before wiping blood from his bottom lip. He didn't want to give his dad the satisfaction that he'd hurt him. He forced a grin at Beef with his split lip.

An hour later, Chase dropped Jessie off in front of the General Store. Before driving away, the big bear of a biker president shook out two pain pills and offered the little kid a swig of his soda to down the pills. Jessie thanked his dad, then turned slowly due to the cast on his right arm. He joined Rain and Beef on the dusty porch.

A storm washed over the small town. The three boys waited it out on the porch of the general store. Sheltered by the overhanging roof and lulled by the falling rain, Beef and Rain smoked cigarettes, watching puddles swell in the streets on either side of them. Jessie groggily leaned against Rain and fell asleep, the medication kicking in. "The rug rat's asleep," Rain said. "If Dad saw this he would say, 'How gay.' Chase is hard that way."

"Right," Beef said. "Me? I've always been proud of the fact that you never pick on Jessie, unlike Chase who always picks on you. Jessie ain't built like that. He cries if your dad even looks at him wrong. Besides, I think your dad likes it when he sees you being cool to Jessie. Just probably not like this. If Chase seen this, he would definitely make a fag comment."

The two of them sat there listening to the patter of the rain on the shingles above them. Rain looked over at his friend, his face illuminated by his cigarette's bright cherry. Rain said, "He got hurt way back when his first and second wives ran off. Teresa, my mom, took the Nelson name, but Jessie's mother, Krystal Dalton, never made their marriage official. That's why we are always explaining that we are brothers with different last names. Losing both wives hurt him, but my dad's carried another pain for a long, long time."

He flicked away his cigarette butt so that it flitted through the air like a firefly. Rain said, "My dad's little brother was gay. Dad beat him up one night in an attempt to change him. Two nights later, Josh took their dad's gun out behind their house and put a bullet in his head. Now you know what sorrow plagues Chase Nelson.

"At 19, he started the Outlaws in Sprague, then they branched out with chapters in twenty small towns throughout Nebraska. Chase rode solo into Guardian territory up in Omaha to have a sit-down with the president. Chase asked him to leave Sprague and Crete out of his network, arguing that coke, heroin, and acid posed a danger. The president of the Guardians wouldn't agree.

"So, Chase contacted Billy Connors, owner of the Emerald Pub in Havelock. The leader of the Irish granted that the two small towns would be deemed a no-man's land for the sale of these stronger drugs. But the Guardians told Chase one more interference with drug deals, they would send some maniac down here to shut the Outlaws down."

Changing the subject, Rain withdrew the cigar tube from the top of his boot. "Check this out. Jack Holland lost it today when he caused our bus to crash."

Beef took the metal tube, removing the cork sealing it at the top. He removed a badly yellowed page that had been rolled tightly to make it fit into the tube. "A map. Looks like something valuable is buried at Quarry Oaks outside of Lincoln. Those words say Indian artifacts. To a relic collector, ancient artifacts are worth millions. What in hell would Jack be doing searching for Indian relics?"

Rain rolled the map up and slid it back into the cigar tube. "Don't know, but finders keepers, losers weepers. As far as I am concerned."

Chapter Three

Chase drove the Chevy Impala station wagon toward the town of Sprague, population 110. The town's business district consisted of five buildings, three on the main street, the other two sitting on two adjacent corners. The hub of community activity took place at The Bar, where the locals jawed about the war being fought in Viet Nam. Bob, owner of the tavern, had a black and white TV above the bar, and the moment a news announcer came on its screen, patrons would listen to reports about the war taking place thousands of miles away.

Chase said, "George Kramer, Rusty Hicks, and Hob Nash all had sons drafted into that war. George and Rusty were proud fathers, too, bragging up their sons fighting for the US Marine Corp. Hob, however, does not condone a war that has nothing to do with America. He was not pleased that his son was being made to serve in the jungles of an Asian country. Thirty-thousand lives so far, and for what?"

Chase gunned the old wagon. The rolling farm fields passed by in a blur. With summer fast approaching, those fields were dotted with farmers planting seeds on their John Deere tractors. Chase passed by the place of the accident. The school bus had been hauled away and someone had hauled Jack Holland's mangled Harley out of the ditch. Rain figured that the Den took it to repair the damaged beast.

Five miles down the road they passed by the Bluestem, a favorite fishing spot for most locals. Rain and Jessie had camped out there many weekends during summer breaks. The lake made Rain think of his little brother. "You should have seen Jessie. He hardly cried at all with that bone sticking out of his arm. It hurt him something awful."

Chase said, "Big Mike locked Ben up in jail for being drunk."

"No, Dad!" snapped Rain. "It was Jack Holland who caused that wreck! Ben lost control when he tried to avoid running him over! Jack attacked Ben with a knife. Before he disappeared in Miller's field, he poured whiskey all over Ben to make him smell like he'd been drinking."

Chase said, "Keep that to yourself. If Jack is to blame, Daws is gonna be gunning for anyone who can testify against him. Outlaws have enough trouble. Hell, one wrong word to the Guardians of Omaha, and the Elder's Den will crush the Outlaws. Keep quiet about Jack. I know that Indian taught both of you boys a lot about dogs. But I've always thought Ben strange the way he talks to dogs while breaking them."

"He doesn't break them," Jessie said. "He repairs the wild in them, inviting them to reinvent themselves, using powerful medicine to still the whirlwind within them."

Rain said, "Oh, I get it. Let the drunk Native take the blame because everyone will believe that story! That just ain't right!"

Chase slowed as he approached the road into town. "Biker protocol demands silence. Ben is facing some serious charges! Motor vehicle homicide. The Morris boy? The one who broke his leg? The bone in his leg pierced his artery and he bled to death."

Rain felt dizzy. The same sick feeling that overcame him back on the bus when he'd seen Jessie's bone sticking out of his arm stole up over him. Chase snapped his fingers, causing Rain to lean back in his seat, out of the range of his dad's fists. Rain admired his little brother then, for Jessie dared getting smacked when he snapped, "What the hell, Dad? Last summer you wanted us to work with Ben, and now you're refusing to help clear him of any wrong-doing?"

Chase stopped the car in front of their house. Rain climbed out of the car, opening the front door for Jessie, being careful not to bump his cast on the door as he exited the front seat. "Do your chores," Chase said. "I'm heading to the pit to prepare for church tonight."

Rain said, "Dad, could we sit in?"

Chase said, "Church is club business."

Chase then drove the car into the driveway and continued down into the open field beyond. As Rain joined him on the porch, Jessie said, "That was ballsy, asking about us attending church, my brother."

When they entered the kitchen they found Molly and six of her pups sprawled on the floor next to Jack Holland, who aimed a .22 pistol down at Molly. Jack said, "You both need to keep your mouths shut. That Morris kid died. Ben's gonna be nailed for it. Don't hang this on me."

Rain glanced up over Jack's shoulder. Jack glanced back, alarmed by the look in Rain's eyes. Rain snatched up the cast-iron frying pan from the nearby stove. He brought it around, catching Jack in the side of his head with the heavy pan. Jack collapsed in an unconscious heap in the middle of the kitchen floor.

Leading Molly and her pups outside to the front yard, Rain took them over to the barn, placing them in her kennel. He then led Jessie to the field where the council fire burned brightly. The two managed to remain unseen as they took cover behind a stockade fence. There, only twenty yards from the fire, they found peep holes in the boards and looked on as the Outlaws attended church. Chase stood between the fire and sixty club members seated in lawn chairs.

He said, "There's a cold-blooded psychopath stalking us on account of a contract on us put out by the Elder's Den. They call him the Nomad. Some say he's striking down members of clubs across the country. Others claim he is a hired assassin, who has killed over sixty bikers in his career. We don't need him here."

Loud thunder came from the road leading into town. Hidden behind the fence, Jessie and Rain peered in alarm at Daws Holland and a dozen bikers coming up the road. Daws and his Den members killed their engines. "I am looking for my son," Daws said.

Chase had just opened his mouth to respond when suddenly from inside the house there came a loud thump. Chase wheeled around to see Jack hobbling toward the front screen door. He gave one clumsy lurch forward, and the screen exploded out onto the front porch.

Chase growled, "What are you doing inside my house, Jack?"

Jack stood frozen as the Outlaws closed a tight circle before him. In desperation, Daws said, "Chase? You best call off the dogs!"

The twelve Elder's Den placed their kick stands down, preparing to back their president. Things were about to turn ugly. "Stand down!" Chase thundered. "Let Jack walk off that porch!"

Daws sighed in relief as his son wove his way in between the enraged Outlaws. As Jack mounted up behind him, Daws said, "I want that map that my son lost. Does your boy have it?"

Chase shook his head. "Don't have a clue what you are talking about, Daws. Now would be a good time for you to leave my town."

Seconds later, Daws led the Den out of Sprague, the thunder of their bikes loud.

Chapter Four

At the end of that week, Chase let Judge Riley know that Rain and Jessie testified as hostile witnesses. It was on account of their testimony that the judge dismissed charges against Ben Black Bull. Both boys swore that Jack Holland caused the wreck in which the Morris boy had died. Although grateful that the boys had exonerated him, the Lakota dog handler decided to move away before suffering hostile repercussions due to the bus wreck.

He asked Chase that he be allowed to thank his sons before moving away from his ranch.

Rain, Jessie, and Beef approached Ben's home on his dog ranch outside of Sprague. As the three boys reached the steps, two children emerged from inside the house. The first was a young Native boy of ten, his long black hair finely braided and hanging down his back. He said, "Welcome to my father's home. I am Benjy Black Bull."

Jessie shifted his cast about awkwardly so that he could shake the boy's hand. He said. "I'm Jessie Dalton and this is my brother—"

"I know," the 13-year-old raven-haired girl said. "I'm the Black Rose, daughter of the Irish Godfather of Havelock. My dad's ancestors are Saints from the Emerald Isle, but Billy Connors is the Devil."

Benjy smiled. "Despite biker protocol to never talk to cops, you sure did help clear my dad of serious charges. For that, I thank you."

Jessie said, "We just told Judge Riley the truth."

Rose said, "Ben's moving at the end of the week to a rescue ranch outside of Havelock. The place has an appropriate name, since he's going to be rescuing some of the most angry dogs on the planet. In the 1800's there was a Lakota camp there. One of the braves stole horses from the Pawnee. When he returned to the Lakota camp, he fell dead at his mother's feet, riddled with many arrows. In memory of her son, this mother insisted the camp be called, *Wounded Arrow.* It is there that Ben shall rescue dogs."

Rose and Benjy followed the boys inside the house. Ben was seated across from them near a wood stove in the center of the floor. He pointed at a pile of thick buffalo hides, indicating that they should seat themselves before the stove. Ben said, "One of the greatest meteor storms took place over the United States in 1833. The skies were lit up by thousands of shooting stars every minute for four hours. It was marked by several nations of Native Americans. Abe Lincoln spoke of it. Founder of the Mormons, Joseph Smith, believed the falling stars were a sign that Christ was coming back. It was big medicine.

"The Night the Stars fell from the Sky a band of Cheyenne marked a peace treaty on a white buffalo robe. The Treaty of 1833 marked on this robe was a turning point for the Cheyenne. My people, the Lakota, joined them during Red Cloud's War. Comanche, Kiowa, and Apache became allies of the Cheyenne at the end of the Indian wars. When such fierce enemies suddenly find peace it is also big medicine.

"The Nomad came to the Den this last week. He's a Creole Indian and enforcer for the Memphis mob. He sold a map to Daws, claiming it would lead to ancient Indian relics, namely a white buffalo robe. Also a .50 caliber Sharps rifle used by Buffalo Billy Cody when he killed 4000 buffalo. And a Colt .45 pistol used by Custer at the Little Big Horn. During the Battle of the Rosebud, the Cheyenne retreated, leaving behind the wounded Chief Comes in Sight on the battlefield. 15-year-old Buffalo Calf Road Woman carried him to safety. She was at the Little Bighorn.

"During that fight, Custer was shot in the chest by White Bull. Buffalo Calf rose up out of the grass and struck the blow that knocked Custer from his horse. Fearing a gruesome death by torture, Custer raised his pistol and shot himself in the temple. The Colt pistol is worth three-thousand. The Sharps three times as much. Both are cursed and need to be destroyed. The robe and the war-club of Buffalo Calf Road Woman are worth ten million and change."

He paused, then added, "If I had that map, I could return the white robe and the war-club to the Cheyenne."

Rain, Jessie, and Beef remained strangely silent. The Lakota man did not press them on the matter. A short while later, he dropped them off in front of the General Store back in Sprague. Ben waved as he drove away. Rain responded by nodding politely. "Why didn't you give that map to Ben?" Jessie asked. "Native artifacts are sacred."

Rain said, "Quarry Oaks is what is written on this map. That's near Lincoln. We just need to find out which tunnel the stuff is hidden in."

Jessie said, "Let's just help Ben recover those artifacts."

"Gold fever," Beef said, "won't let him. He won't be free of that until he finds those relics. And when he retrieves those two cursed guns, a demon will take over him and he'll be royally screwed."

Rain said, "Demons? Ghosts? Geis? Curse? Get real."

At the sound of a Harley rumbling along on the highway a block away from the porch, the boys turned to face the Harley Davidson coming up the street to the General Store. The biker had the tattoos of twin stags inked on his shiny skull. He killed his engine and stared at Rain. "I'm the Nomad. Jack lost something the day of the crash. Do you have it?"

Rain said, "No. What did he lose?"

The Nomad said, "In 1876, a buffalo hunter killed a white buffalo in Texas. Big Medicine was born in Montana. Medicine Wheel was born on Pine Ridge. He escaped his pasture and was shot by a tribal cop. Spirit Mountain Ranch donated a herd of white buffalo to the World Peace Church. I could take one of these hides and fabricate that peace treaty that the Cheyenne marked on that robe in 1833, but that would be a fraud. I want the real deal, the white buffalo robe of the Cheyenne."

With a wild laugh, the Nomad started his bike. "Do not lie to me, Son of Rain. That map belongs to me. Lies will only bring you pain."

He then went roaring down the street and out of town.

***

The next day, Rain found Chase sprawled on the front porch a Bowie knife driven into his chest. It appeared he'd just sat down, his chin resting on his chest as if he were asleep. "Dad?" he said. "Dad?" Jessie burst through the screen door and stood there staring at Rain kneeling down next to their dead father. He reached for the knife. Rain latched onto his wrist, keeping him from drawing the knife out of the wound.

Beef discovered them there, so grief stricken that neither could talk. Jessie bawled openly while Rain sobbed quietly. Unable to console the two brothers, Beef ran down the street to get Pops.

Big Mike Tory called the sheriff in Crete and reported that Chase had been murdered. Days after Chase was killed, Mike took the two boys into his home. Two months later, he moved them and his son, Beef, into Havelock, an Irish Catholic suburb of Lincoln, Nebraska. Despite all of Mike's efforts to keep the three boys from reconnecting with the club, Rain at 19, formed his own chapter. Jessie became VP. Beef served as warlord. The three of them worked for the Irishman Billy Connors, owner of the Emerald Pub in Havelock. Billy had been a gun-runner, supporting IRA patriots. But when he lost his wife to a drunk driver, the Irishman took a hardline to those bringing drugs into Havelock, and he paid the Outlaws to enforce his law. Rain married Rose, Billy's daughter, and had two sons. It was the map, however, that led to tragic events that Rain could not help but stumble his way into. Rain had hidden the map for these past years. It haunted him that his last words with Ben had been about the map. He wished that he'd told the truth about finding it.

His conscience finally getting the better of him, on the night of his twenty-sixth Birthday, Rain rode out to Quarry Oaks to meet up with Ben to give him the map.

When he entered the mine shaft designated by the map, he found Ben gunned down by Daws Holland who stood over him, his shotgun still smoking. He said, "Black Bull is on his way to his happy hunting ground. Unless you want to join him, give me the map!"

The shoot-out that followed left Daws dead. Rain fell with a gun shot wound to his chest. Minutes later, Big Mike entered the quarry, where he found Rain badly wounded. Later, Rain was sentenced to ten years for the shooting of Daws Holland. While he served time, Big Mike met with Billy Connors, owner of the Emerald Pub.

Mike wanted to give the map to Benjy Black Bull, Ben's son. Billy claimed Benjy was too young to be in charge of such valuable Native relics. He suggested meeting with Cheyenne elders of the Wind River reservation on the matter. After a heated debate over the map, Billy placed it in a safe inside the Emerald, to be kept there until Rain was released from prison.

Out of sight, out of mind, as far as Billy was concerned.

Chapter Five
Five years later

Reason Nelson was nine when Nate Holland shoved a gun in his face. Two heads taller than Reason and outweighing him by at least ninety pounds, Nate yanked a .22 pistol from the waistband of his jeans.

Scrawny little Reason snarled, "Do it! Shoot me, Nate!"

Seated on his bike nearby, Vince said, "Just let Reason go. I'll tag the Emerald Pub, okay?"

Nine-year old Vince Young had tried to get Reason to tell Boone about Nate, but Reason knew that nothing he did would eliminate the threat he posed. Not until he did as commanded in order to join his small mob of wanna-be-gangsters. Nate was the president of the little thugs who called Havelock home. His dad's beating of a drug dealer in T-town had sent Jack Holland to prison, leaving thirteen-year-old, Nate, a mean and angry kid.

Small, shaggy-haired Reason's mouth got him punched on a weekly basis. His defiance disorder kicked in, and all the meds in the world could not fix his problem when it came to his mouth.

Vince looked over to the playground sixty feet away. A dozen little kids from Saint Pat's school had all stopped playing. Their teacher, Sister Valerie, heard Reason say, "Take this gun off my face!"

The collision of two human disorders could only result in one outcome. Neither boy was wired right. During conception, both had been rendered a few genes short in their DNA. Reason's defiance disorder had caused him plenty of trouble in his earlier years. He also had ADHD to jump-start his bad behavior. But with Nate's sadistic nature keeping his rage in overdrive, he and Reason were bound to clash. The bullet exploded from the muzzle of the gun, zipped past two kids from Saint Pat's, then plowed into little Katie Brant's chest, killing her instantly.

In the silence that followed, Sister Valerie freaked out. Screaming at the kids she was in charge of. Screaming at Nate who stood there frozen. Screaming at the fatally wounded Katie. Screaming at God, who seemed to be a million miles away.

Fleeing from the park, Reason and Vince rode double on Vince's moto-cross bike to the Nelson house, four blocks from the park. As they pulled up next to the front porch, Vince skidded to a halt, dumping Reason off the handlebars. A few seconds later, Reason's sixteen-year-old brother, Boone, stepped out onto the porch. Tall and dark-haired, Boone had never been in trouble with the law. He had become a father-figure to Reason since their father had been sentenceed to prison five years ago. If he wasn't playing the heavy when it came to his problem behavior in school, he was keeping him in line when it came to taking his meds.

Boone said, "Those sirens came from the park. Do you guys wanna head down there and check it out?"

Reason and Vince remained rooted to the yard. They knew Boone would grill them, and while Reason could lie his way out of anything, three minutes into Boone's grilling, Vince would spill his guts.

An hour later, a police cruiser pulled up to the Nelson house. Officer Beef Tory was a large man. Reason knew that he once rode with the Outlaws. Beef had a falling out with his dad for some unknown reason. Instead of riding with the club, he had joined the Lincoln Police force. Beef said, "There was a shooting at the park. A little girl was killed. Sister Val said a blond-haired boy was trying to shoot a little scarecrow of a kid with wild strands of shaggy hair. This doesn't have anything to do with HVK that Nate Holland has been recruiting for, does it?"

Reason glared at Officer Tory. If he found himself boxed in by his mom, his brother, or even cops, he could divert their attention and put them off their game by defying them with a snide glare. He had learned how to manipulate his way out of tight spots in the past. But Beef was no rookie. Five years at Youth Aid and he could outsmart most deviant delinquents. He said, "Code of silence, right? Perhaps, someone could call Crime Stoppers to solve this little girl's murder."

The two boys watched him walk slowly back to his cruiser. As he drove away, Reason said, "That was easy."

Vince muttered, "He'll be back."

***

Nate struck Reason in the center of his chest. He snarled, "If you talk to anyone about this, I'll come and put bullets in you! It'll be your funeral they'll be holding down at Saint Pat's! Understand?"

Reason stood there watching as Nate kicked Vince, sweeping his legs out from under him there on the playground of Havelock Park. Nate said, "None of this would've happened if you would've tagged the Emerald! If anyone calls Crime Stoppers behind my back, I swear when I get out on bail, I'll come hunt them down!" Nate gestured at the backpack beside him. He used one meaty hand to reach deep into the pack and pulled out a can of blue spray paint. "Reason? Vince? Go down to the Emerald and spray HVK!"

"But," Vince protested, "what if old man Connors finds out?"

Nate grinned wickedly. He then walked Vince and Reason down to the Emerald Pub. Reason sprayed a big capital H on the white bricks of the Emerald. Vince sprayed the V, and Reason finished with the K. When they were done, the three letters were two feet tall and covered a wide area on the front of the pub. Reason knew Billy Connors was a gunrunner for the IRA. He'd once snuck into the pub to look at the award above the Emerald's fireplace. It came from the Irish Republican Army given to Billy for him sending them guns.

Tonight, both boys knew they had crossed a line. If Billy Connors ever learned that they had dared to tag his place, they were dead. Both young boys cringed when they turned and found themselves facing four of Havelock's Misfits ambling down the sidewalk toward the Emerald. Nate said, "Who the hell are these clowns?"

Reason said, "Newt, with his flashy suits and his gaudy hats, was in a car accident that altered his brain. He makes train whistle sounds up and down Have-Ave. At Ballard ball games he makes loud farting noises with his mouth. Newt is king of the Oddballs."

Behind Newt came Franco. Reason said, "Franco is an Italian who scrounges in garbage cans and snags the stubs of cigarettes left behind in sand traps of butt-cans lining the business district. Franco came home from the war to find his wife sleeping with another man. He stabbed them both to death with a butcher knife and ended up exiled to America."

Coming up behind Newt and Franco were two dwarfs. Reason said, "George and Louie live above the mortuary. Most days they can be seen standing on their corner watching cars go by."

The four odd men noticed the boys' handiwork and gawked at it, muttering in dismay. Nate snatched a paint can out of Reason's hand and began to spray them with wild raking motions. George hid behind Louie. Newt backed up against the Emerald and ended up with paint all over his backside. "Holy Mary, Mother of God!" gasped Franco. "What's wrong with you, boy?"

Uncertain how to deal with the old Italian man confronting him, Nate laughed wildly all the way down the block, disappearing into the mouth of the next alley.

The next day at Havelock elementary school, Reason blew up. He tossed over his desk, threw a chair across the room, and proceeded to pummel a girl classmate senseless for making fun of his drawing. Miss Taylor, his fourth-grade teacher led him away to the Quiet Room. Reason resisted, going ape. "Damn!" he yelled. "You're a real stinky hag, Miss Taylor!"

"Reason?" came a voice from down the hall behind them.

"Go to hell, Boone!" ranted Reason, breaking free of Miss Taylor's grasp. When Reason swung at him with his right fist, Boone latched onto his wrist, and with the grace of a martial artist, he spun his little brother around. "Got him now," Boone said.

Miss Taylor smiled gratefully and moved toward her classroom. Boone had grown up on the mean streets of Havelock, and while most of his friends were getting high, he volunteered his time at juvenile court. He not only dealt with his little brother's problem behaviors, he had been assigned five adolescents who were struggling with their own behavioral issues and drug addictions. Boone served as a truancy tracker to these five problem teens. He also spent time working at *Outreach* down at the local detention center.

He was a controversial figure, with his long, dark shoulder-length hair and his uncanny ways of dealing with some of the more troubled kids. Rose, the mother of both boys, who ran her own drug and alcohol group at Saint Pat's church, once told Reason, "Boone is like that horse-whisperer, who knows how to tame even the wildest horses. Only Boone is the Kid-Whisperer."

Lately, due to Reason's increased aggression at school, Boone had been doing his volunteer work for the court at Reason's school. Teachers welcomed his intervention when the Typhoon Kid went out of control. And Boone, a three-year student in the Sho Rei Khan dojo, was able to apply all the martial arts restraint moves he could muster to keep Reason from hurting himself.

By the time they reached the door to the Quiet Room, Boone had Reason in a basket hold. The only thing Reason could do is head butt him. But Boone leaned into him, keeping his arms pulled against his sides, using the side of his body to absorb the impact of his striking head. Boone then used his left leg to sweep Reason's legs out from under him, taking him down to the floor on his rump. He came crashing down too stunned to realize Boone had removed his tennis shoes. Tossing the shoes outside the Quiet Room, Boone shoved

Reason forward, exited the room, pulling the door closed behind him. *Ka-wham! Ka-thud! Bang! Thud! Thud!*

Reason vented his rage on the solid wood with his fists. He had already broken a toe earlier that year when he'd kicked it. So he knew better than to rail at the barrier with his feet. After a fair amount of pounding, he planted his butt against the door and reared back into it. All the while, Boone stood just outside the door, silently listening. It took thirty minutes for Reason to wind down.

By then, he was exhausted from keeping up a constant barrage on the door. Boone opened the Quiet Room door to find Reason sprawled on the floor. Boone held out his hand.

Swatting his hand aside, Reason skulked down the hall in front of his brother. Before entering the classroom, he sullenly took back his shoes and slipped them on. Reason joined the circle of kids seated on the reading rug as if nothing had happened earlier. His classmates risked nervous glances at him. It never occurred to Reason that they sat around the dinner table in their homes, talking about the whacked-out kid in their classroom. It never dawned on him that his behavior was anything out of the ordinary.

Chapter Six

Rose Nelson showed up after school that day. This was the seventh violent episode Reason had since school started in September. It was now mid-October, and if something wasn't done about Reason's outbursts, he would have to be sent to a behavior modification school. Rose sat in conference with Beef Tory, resource officer of Havelock school. A slender lady with cascades of wild raven hair, she was dressed in faded blue jeans and tie-dyed T-shirt. At thirty-years-old, Rose gave off the impression that she was still deeply entrenched in the biker culture.

Beef said, "Diagnosed with ADHD and Oppositional Defiance Disorder, Reason might be Bi-polar."

Rose blurted, "It seems you've run out of disorders to place on him, because now you're coming up with ones I've never heard of."

Beef said, "We're just trying to ascertain where this aggression is coming from. He does take his medication daily, correct?"

Rose nodded. "For his impulse control, he takes those meds at night when he's not so cranky. Mornings are different. I let him and Boone fight it out over him taking his doses after breakfast. I tried repeatedly to enforce the taking of his meds, but he fights me, until Boone steps in and gives him an ultimatum."

"Which is?" Beef asked, curiously. "Violence?"

"No," Rose said. "Boone has never struck Reason. Boone has this thing he does which drives Reason nuts. He goes silent on him for hours at time. He refuses to acknowledge him. This seems to work, too. Because Reason is afraid of being left out of his brother's life."

Beef said, "We're just trying to stay on the same page. His episodes here at school have escalated. Any particular reason why?"

Rose sighed. "Not a clue. We ground him each time he has a bad day here, but that doesn't seem to have much impact on him. He just throws one of his tantrums."

Beef said, "Reason just doesn't seem to get it, does he? We have exhausted our behavior modification techniques. Have you considered institutionalizing him for an evaluation? Any chance he's dry-firing his meds?"

Rose said, "Reason still objects to taking his meds. Of course, that comes from me saying that some doctor is not going to practice on my son like a guinea pig. I've adjusted my thinking now that I've seen the calming effect meds have had on him."

Beef shrugged. "Perhaps a med adjustment is needed. Perhaps after being on the ones he's been on for the past several months, he's become immune to their desired effect. Without the meds, we'd be fighting a losing battle. You have a challenging boy, Rose. He's a little ringmaster who manages to run the show, but we need to stay on top of him, so that he doesn't spoil the circus, for us or for him."

Rose peered out the window to see Boone attempting to lead Reason home. She shook her head as Reason swatted Boone's hand aside. Reason continued to mouth off all the way home. He was in complete denial about blowing up in school. That he called his teacher a hag. That he deserved being locked in the Quiet Room.

Once back at home, Boone snapped his fingers and pointed at the porch. Reason snapped his own fingers, mocking him. He snapped his fingers again, raising his hand up to Boone's face. At which point, Boone latched onto his skinny arm, and placed Reason in a wrist lock, something that his sensei had shown him.

When Reason became angry, he would throw himself around, not hurting anyone but himself. But lately, his aggressive outbursts included throwing punches at anyone who got within range. Boone had learned how to move offline when it came to a frontal attack by a raging little whirlwind. Reason always tried to knee Boone in the groin to inflict critical damage. Thanks to his martial arts training, Boone had saved himself from taking one of Reason's upraised knees to his privates many times, and with the wrist lock, he'd learned to take control of the ranting bundle of sticks and bones.

Twisting around, Reason proceeded to plant his teeth in Boone's forearm. Boone yanked his arm out of range, and in the process he lost the firm hold he had Reason in. Reason turned completely around and threw himself bodily against him. Off balance, Boone toppled over backward and sprawled on his back, cushioning Reason's fall. Reason planted his teeth in Boone's chest and bit down hard, his jaws closing just below his left nipple.

He managed to free himself from the painful bite and turn him so that he was facing forward. He then sprang up, looped an arm around his neck, and placed him in another restraint hold. Boone firmly planted him on the porch.

"Reason?" came a voice from inside the house. There, standing beyond the screen door, was eight-year-old Collin Young. His white-blond hair hung just below his ears while his scraggly bangs dangled into his catlike green eyes. Collin, a year younger than his brother

Vince, was a permanent fixture at the Nelson house, since his own home was in constant chaos due to his older brother's behavior. Logan hadn't been to a full day of school since he started tenth grade. Collin's parents enlisted the help of Boone to keep Logan in line, shamelessly admitting they lacked the parenting skills to deal with their older son.

Reason snapped, "He thinks because our dad got sent to prison, he's got to be like a stupid dad!"

Collin said, "You're lucky. Me? I got a brother who's so busy keeping himself in trouble, he never has time to keep me in line. I wish Boone was my brother. Did you hear about the Oddballs? Someone spray-painted them with blue paint. Crime Stoppers is paying a reward for information leading to the arrest of who painted the Oddballs."

Silence reigned on the porch as a black Pontiac pulled up in front of the house. The huge guy driving the car was bald with the dark green image of a dragon tat dominating his skull. He was dressed in a sleeveless black vest. His chin was covered by a thin beard, and he had cold dark eyes like a shark. The man climbed out of his Pontiac and walked toward the porch. "I'm Jack Holland. HVK stands for Hell's Viking Kings. My son, Nate, told me you did the tagging. In two days' time I want all the HVK's removed from the thirty places you tagged."

Reason folded his thin arms before his chest, trying to look tough, although his stomach felt like a million butterflies were flapping their wings inside of him. Both brothers looked past Jack to see fifteen-year-old Logan Young standing beside the Pontiac in front of the house. Logan casually ran his lock-blade knife through the strands of his long, black hair. Collin's older brother offered Jack a big grin as he leaned down beside the Pontiac, jabbing his lock-blade into the right rear tire.

There came a garbled curse from Jack as he sprang from the porch.

Logan laughed and zigzagged his way down the street and directly into the nearest alley.

Chapter Seven

Back inside the house, Boone said, "Viking Kings? I best call to Beef to find out if these symbols are violating any type of gang rules."

A few minutes later, Logan stepped out of the kitchen, sweaty strands of his black hair plastered to his face. "I lost the guy down at the park. Beef Tory and old man Connors just pulled up."

Reason sprang up off the couch, clawing at the front door. Logan latched onto Reason and pulled him back from the door. "Leave this to Beef to sort out. If this is a gang thing, there is proper protocol."

"Proper what?" Reason asked, squirming to get free of Logan.

"Protocol," Logan told him, hauling him over to the couch and plopping him back down. "All these gangs have rules they live by. Bikers. Gangsters. Mobsters. They have certain laws that you just don't break."

Reason glanced down at Logan's wrist, thinking about sinking his teeth into his flesh. But Logan followed his gaze and popped him on the arm. Reason collapsed on the couch. "Good choice," Logan said.

Beef wore his police uniform and did not look much like a member of Reason's father's biker club the Outlaws. Billy Connors, who greatly resembled Mark Twain, with his snow-white hair and his thick gray mustache, nailed Reason as he stood there holding a stare down with the cantankerous old Irishman. Beef said, "You might think HVK reps Havelock, but the Hell's Viking Kings have been around a long time."

Billy tucked long strands of his snowy hair behind his ears. "Beef, pay him for the tire Logan slashed. Tell him the Irishman wants peace with the Den. Not to start a war. And Reason, you've got a lot of cleaning up to do, lad. I'm buying two gallons of paint for you to clean the HVK off the Emerald Pub. You tagged HVK in bright blue letters on the Joyo Theater, May's Cafe, two shelters at the park, and the concession stand at Ballard park!"

Reason said, "Why did Nate tell his dad that I did the tagging?"

Billy said, "Jack would kill him if he did the tagging."

A moment later, Gypsy came through the front door. Reason was amazed that a tough guy like Gypsy seemed to like Boone. As he sat there watching the big bearded biker, he figured that if Boone hadn't been a youth worker, he would have been riding with the Outlaws. Gypsy, a former member of the club, eyed Beef for long moments. Reason studied the two ex-Outlaws.

Gypsy reminded him of a panther, his long, black hair glistening. Beef reminded him of a bear, brawny and bearded. "Listen up, Reason," Gypsy said. "Jack demands that you paint over HVK on the places you tagged. But he made threats against you. It has to do with your dad, Reason. Before he went to prison, Rain interfered in a business transaction of the Elder's Den and Jack Holland."

Reason asked, "Did Dad screw up one of their drug deals?"

Gypsy's words came out in a soft rumble, "No, little man. This is about ancient artifacts. There was a shootout at the quarry. Daws was killed. I told Jack that business ended long ago. Rain's boys know nothing of the relics. Jack says Rain stole a map leading to these relics. He wants it back."

***

When Nate appeared beside Collin's garage there in the alley, he punched him in the nose with the Maglite he held. His vision blurred by tears, Collin stumbled on down the alley, Nate's flashlight poking him in the back. When they arrived at the entrance to the Havelock tunnels, Nate used the flashlight to prod his captive into the storm sewer. Dazed and disoriented, Collin didn't know how far he walked before Nate produced a pair of handcuffs. Collin cried out when the cold metal enclosed his skinny wrist and Nate fastened the other end of the cuffs to the iron rung halfway up the wall. Collin wept, "Please let me go!"

Nate chuckled. "Pleeeeaaasssee! You should have never narced me off for killing that Brant girl! You'll have to gnaw through your wrist like a raccoon does in a trap! Gnaw! Gnaw! Gnaw!"

The yellow glow of Nate's flashlight moved back down the corridor, leaving Collin in total darkness.

***

Vince tried to calm Reason down as they walked through Havelock Park. A loud burst of thunder rumbled across the dark sky above them. Then lightning zigzagged across the billowing banks of angry clouds. Reason snapped, "You called Crime Stoppers! Snitch! Now Nate has done something to your little brother because of you!"

Vince said, "I did what I thought was right, Reason."

Reason lunged forward, but Vince dodged aside. He wheeled around and locked in a violent embrace they toppled over to the ground. They grunted and tussled, clinging to each other as they

23

struggled. With rain falling steadily now, the two boys squirmed on the ground, their fight taking them directly into the wall of the playground. When Reason struck his head on the wall, Vince sprang up. He met Reason's flying tackle.

Once again, they toppled over into the soft, wet sand. Reason landed on the bottom, his breath exploding from his lips. Vince straddled him. Reason sucked in air and reared up. But Vince came back down, his knee slamming into Reason's chest. Wrenching his shoulders free of Vince's grasp, he twisted, then snaked his way out from under him.

As Vince tried to latch onto him, Reason head-butted him in the face. Blood sprayed from Vince's nose. At the sight of the bright red blood, Reason swooned and fainted.

When he came to, he was seated against the fireplace in the north shelter. Nate pointed at Vince's bloody nose. "What were you guys fighting about?" he asked.

"Nothing," Reason said. Thunder rumbled overhead. Rain began to fall. "Here," Nate said, handing Vince the key to the handcuffs. "Go get your little bro out of the storm sewer before he drowns."

***

Deep in the middle of the storm sewer, Collin sat huddled in two feet of rising water. Thunder boomed above him and he knew that whenever it rained for more than four hours in Havelock, the storm sewer flooded. He had tried repeatedly to free himself from the cuff pinning him to the iron rung connected to the wall, but his wrist was now bleeding from tugging on the iron band. He remembered the night Mike Truax had fallen into the drain culvert. Mike had slipped on the rain-slick cement and plunged into the madly rushing water. He was sent down into the flooded sewer, with barely room to keep his head above the water. The tunnel was nine feet deep and ten feet wide, and Mike floated through the darkness, struggling to keep his nose out of the deep water.

Kids talked about how fast Mike must have been traveling when he reached the last three blocks of the storm sewer, where the ceiling dropped down three feet and the tunnel became a five-by-five round shaft until it ended at the Burlington yards. Mike claimed he had been forced underwater for those three blocks. He didn't remember sucking in air to hold his breath but the whole trip had gone by in a flash, he had been sucked through that culvert in seconds.

It took them ten minutes to run down to the entrance of the Havelock storm tunnels. Vince slid down the rain-slick embankment and followed Reason into the knee-high water swirling around them. "Collin?" Reason cried out. "Collin? You there, bud? We're coming to get you!"

A mad rush of water came surging through the tunnel entrance. Reason and Vince were swept off their feet. "Holy crap!" Vince cried, clawing his way back to his feet. Reason clambered to his feet. He then removed his flashlight from his back pocket, watching the yellow orb of light bouncing wildly over the walls. They soon turned down a corner which led to a straight corridor. Collin cried out when he spotted the glow of their light. Vince sloshed through the water. "Got it!" he said, pulling the key from his pocket.

There came a roar from the tunnel, and water came pouring down the corridor, swamping Collin and rolling over his head. Vince dove beneath the water. He blindly felt along the metal cuff, until he felt the indenture for the key hole. He slid the key into place. He turned the tiny key and the metal ring popped open.

All three boys were then struck by a three-foot high wall of surging water. Vince resurfaced in between Reason and Collin. He dog-paddled frantically to keep his head above water. Clinging to each other, the three boys picked up speed, when a shaft of light shone down from the ceiling ahead of them, Reason cried, "Jesus!"

"No," said Boone, "but I'm the next best thing!"

Boone scrambled down the ladder leading up to the open manhole. He clung there with one arm, while using his other to latch onto all three boys. And then Logan was there. Boone scooted Reason up the rungs ahead of him. Vince clambered up next, and Logan carried Collin up to the opening above.

They collapsed there on the wet grass, the gaping hole of the manhole only a few feet away.

Chapter Eight

Boone used both hands to guide Vince and Reason down the sidewalk running through the park. Vince kept crying so he was finding it hard to see clearly through his tears. They were almost out of the park when Boone spotted a cardboard box in the center of the middle shelter. When the box suddenly moved, Boone released the two boys and walked over to investigate. Boone kneeled down there in the shelter and scooped up a skinny little runt of a German shepherd pup.

"Hey," he said, cradling the little guy in his arms, "looks like you had a bummer of a time, pup."

The pup began to whine. Boone stood up, taking off his flannel shirt to wrap around the shivering puppy. He handed the bundled pup to Reason, and as they walked, the puppy fell asleep in Reason's arms. When the boys arrived home, Rose took one look at the runt of a shepherd.. "No," she said, "we're not keeping him!"

Boone sat in the recliner, sulking. Reason sat on the floor, playing with the feisty little scrapper. The puppy was playfully nipping at his fingers, sprawled on his back, his tiny legs wind-milling in the air, completely oblivious of the fact that Rose was talking about him. "We'll just call Animal Control and have them come pick him up. He is so skinny he probably has worms! Reason, quit putting your fingers in his mouth! He might even have rabies!"

The telephone caused Rose to pause. Boone leaped up to answer it. He paced around in a circle while listening to the caller. When he stopped and stood very still, Reason noticed his brother's stance. "Yeah," Boone said, glancing back at Reason seated in the middle of the floor with the pup now sprawled in his lap. He hung up the phone. "What was that all about?" Rose asked, curiously.

"Beef," Boone said. "Nate is still on the loose."

Rose held the pup up by its shoulders. The pup's big dark eyes locked on her face. He didn't squirm. He didn't so much as move a whisker. To his credit, he seemed to know the matron of this house held his life in her hands. It was quiet there in the living room for long moments. Moments later, Rose said, "If Nate is still running wild on the streets, Reason, you are grounded until he is picked up. Besides, you've got to spend tomorrow taking care of this fleabag."

Reason was so mad at being grounded to the yard that he didn't quite catch that last part. It wasn't until Rose asked, "What shall we name him?" that he came out of his angry funk.

Rose took the pup in her arms. "He's the most wretched, little runt I've ever seen. You have to help clean up after him. Feed him. Water him. Walk him. But first? A name. King? Bandit? Outlaw?"

"Bummer," Reason said. "It's what Boone said he'd been through when we found him. So let's call him Bummer."

***

While Bummer curled up on the back porch in the afternoon sunshine, Reason, Vince, and Collin proceeded to use their ball gloves. After about an hour of tossing the ball to each other, Reason went over to the porch and scooped up the bat. "Wanna see me put one over the house?"

Vince threw the ball. *Thack!* Reason's bat connected and the ball went flying up through the open window of their tree fort situated in the oak tree near the alley. *Crash!* The boys heard the sound, followed by the *plinks* of shattered glass raining down on the floor inside the fort. They raced each other to the boards nailed to the tree.

Once inside the tree fort, they discovered the baseball had struck Reason's dad's award. It had knocked it off the wall where Reason had hung it two years earlier. "Crap," he said. "I hung that there in memory of my dad. My dad got that award for a charity run where the Outlaws raised money for kids to go to police summer camp."

Reason kneeled down, studying the paper that lay behind the award. He picked it up. "What is this X? It's marking a missile silo next to Quarry Oaks. Dad and his club used to hold church in these abandoned silos! They go three-hundred-feet down. They used to hold missiles, like in case the Russians attacked. The Outlaws used to prowl around in them. Neal Hopper was crossing a beam stretching across the open floor of one of them. Hopper fell straight down to the bottom and died."

Vince and Collin turned to follow Reason out through the door. They were met by Nate in the yard below. Reason folded up the scrap of paper. Nate snatched it out of his hand. "Did your dad send this from prison?"

Rooowooff! came from the tiny mouth of Bummer as he ran up beside Nate. He continued to bark, his hackles raised. *Yoowrap!* exploded from Bummer's small mouth as he darted out of the path of Nate's foot. Bummer scampered over to Reason, whimpering in fear. Reason bent down and scooped him up in his free hand. Juggling the puppy with one hand, Reason stepped back too fast and tripped over

27

a skateboard laying there in the yard. Bummer fell from his grasp. Nate offered him a fierce grin and moved toward Bummer. Still mad about the older boy leaving him to drown, Collin threw the baseball at him with all his might. *Thwack!* came the sound as the ball struck Nate on his nose, causing blood to spurt from his nostrils.

All four boys then froze in alarm as Jack Holland pulled into the alley in his black Pontiac. Jack stepped out of the vehicle and walked toward the boys. He reached down and snatched the paper out of Reason's hand. The rumble of a Harley filled the air, making it obvious the bike was approaching the Nelson house. With the sudden slap to the side of his head, Reason saw bright stars whirling before his eyes, and Jack shoved him into his car. Reason glared defiantly at the biker.

Jack said, "We are going on a treasure hunt. Quarry Oaks is where your dad's deal went south. He never found the lost relics."

When Gypsy pulled up on his Harley in front of the Nelson house, he spotted Jack driving away with Reason trapped in his front seat. Wisely hanging back some distance from the black Pontiac, Gypsy's bearded features were creased by a deep frown. Jack had no business kidnaping the boy, and the biker suddenly realized he was the only one who knew he had Reason with him. He became determined to see that no harm came to the youngest son of his former president, Rain Nelson. The large biker maintained a good distance from the dark car, yet he continued to follow them out to Quarry Oaks.

A short while later, Reason and Jack stood there, peering at an old army trunk. Jack opened it to discover it empty. "After gunning down my dad," Jack said, "Rain planned on coming back here to reclaim those hidden relics after serving his time."

Reason's brow furrowed deeply. "Mom forbids Boone and I from ever visiting Dad. She refuses to see him herself."

The rumble of a Harley could be heard outside the quarry. Jack drew a pistol from the waistband of his jeans. He ran to the entrance of the cavern and fired off his gun in rapid bursts. Someone outside the entrance to the quarry fired back. Hot lead pinged off the walls around the tunnel entrance. A bright burst of red blood spurted from Jack's left shoulder, and he staggered away down the corridor even as Gypsy appeared at the entrance to the tunnel, a pistol in one hand. He checked on Reason, his bearded features filled with deep concern.

Gypsy raced to the entrance of the tunnel, dragging Reason with him. At the bottom of the stairs, he scooped him up and carried him to his bike. Gypsy kicked his 1200 to life, pulled Reason onto the seat behind him, and asked, "What was that about, Reason?"

"This," Reason said, handing the paper over to the big biker. "Jack thought it would lead to some Indian relics out here at the quarry."

Slipping the wrinkled paper into his jacket pocket, Gypsy took them flying down a country road, heading back toward Havelock.

Chapter Nine
Four years later

Thirteen-year-old Reason Nelson shouted, "It's a bust! Seconds later, a company of cops stormed the party house. As they smashed through the front door, the sound of splintering wood echoed like thunder in the room beyond. At once, a swarm of terrified kids fled in all directions. Two kids slammed into a table, sending a keg crashing to the floor. Two others trampled over a pole lamp, plunging the room into darkness.

In the far corner of the party room, Reason sprang out of his chair. The long-haired little kid knew he had to flee, and yet he simply stood there. Reason's black shirt and jeans blended well with the shadows there in the corner, but as flashlight beams shimmered through pot smoke drifting before him, one beam flickered across the white Harley emblem on his chest. It was this logo that attracted the attention of private detective Jessie Dalton moving across the room. The moment Jessie spotted the shaggy-haired kid, chaos erupted.

In the mass confusion, partiers scattered like a flock of swallows changing flight in midair. Cops and kids slammed into each other and went sprawling across the floor. Two boys laughed like lunatics as they plowed into a liquor cabinet, sending it crashing to the hardwood floor. In the wake of the thunderous explosion, they trampled over the cabinet's broken bottles. Glass shards crunched beneath their feet, sounding like gunshots. Startled by the loud pops and convinced that the cops were shooting at him, Reason snatched up his black leather jacket and fled down a hallway.

Three strides later, he kicked over a case of beer, spilling cans across the floor. Beer cans spinning beneath his feet, he looked like he was performing a bizarre version of Riverdance. His long hair flying, he stomped through the hissing cans and collided with Jessie and a large black man. Reason's jacket flew from his grasp.

"Brooks!" Jessie shouted as he grappled with the pistol Brooks raised. Reason snatched up what he believed to be his leather jacket. He darted into the kitchen. Swinging the jacket up and holding it like a shield, he hurled himself through a screen door and tumbled off the porch beyond. He landed in front of a Rottweiler chained to a doghouse. Gasping in alarm, Reason threw up his hands to protect himself. The huge dog continued to gnaw on his bone. Reason latched onto the jacket and crawled into the doghouse. Behind him, Brooks passed through the mangled screen door. The Rott lunged at him, grazing his crotch with his teeth. Brooks aimed his gun at the snarling dog. Reason yanked on the chain, pulling the dog back through the doorway. The Rott sniffed at the long strands of his dark hair and Reason sighed in relief as Brooks raced away into the night.

When certain he was gone, Reason gently pushed the dog out of his way, and crawled out through the door, dragging the jacket with him. He entered the nearby alley. Shivering in the chill night air, he slipped on the leather jacket. The leather jacket he'd taken to the party fit him perfectly. The one he now had on was three sizes too large. He slipped out of it, wondering whose jacket he'd picked up. He searched the pockets, hoping to find money in them. In the second pocket, he found a small blue key.

As he glanced back at the green Thunderbird pulling into the alley behind him, Reason fumbled and dropped the key. He cursed as it bounced in the street and vanished into the mouth of a nearby drain sewer. Leaving the jacket where it had fallen in the shadows, he - swiftly ran away, setting his sights on the ballfield of Ballard Park ahead of him. Tires screeched from the street behind him. Reason ran the length of the field and scaled the chainlink fence blocking his path on the opposite side. He plummeted to the ground as the Thunderbird screeched to a stop in the parking lot in front of him.

Blond, beefy Nate Holland sprang out of it, whipping out a pocket knife. Nate planted the tip on Reason's left cheek. He snarled. "I served three years in detention because you snitched on me about shooting that little girl!"

Nate froze as a blue Continental pulled up beside his Thunderbird and a black man with dread locks stepped out. Nate wisely walked back to his Thunderbird and drove away down the street. Grinning, the black man walked over to Reason. "Little white dude, your name Reason Nelson? I'm JR Brooks. Ever heard of me?"

Reason said, "Kids say you're the biggest dealer in T-town."

"Oh," Brooks said. "Do I look that threatening to you?"

Reason said, "No. Maybe. I don't know. Why?"

Brooks said, "Were you at Nate's party? During the bust, I lost my jacket. In all that chaos and craziness our jackets got swapped."

Reason said, "Any chance of a finder's fee?"

"Finder's fee?" Brooks said. "Yeah, fifty bucks."

Alarmed by the hostility in the man's eyes, Reason froze when a bike roared into the parking lot. Brooks spat in disgust as Jack Holland parked his Harley beside his car. Reason waited until Brooks began talking to Jack, he then ran, whispering, "He's after that key!"

He ran back to the party house, picking up the leather jacket he'd dropped there beside the manhole. Trying yet failing to lift the heavy manhole cover, he spotted 13-year-old Vince Young riding up on his dirt bike. Slender as a reed with long, shoulder-length dark hair, Vince stared at Reason as he told him about his encounter with Nate and being rescued by Brooks. "He was at Nate's party. I ended up with his jacket. He's offering fifty bucks. But what he really wants is that key I dropped in this sewer. We need to nab it. Once we do, we'll negotiate a better deal. Let's get us a crowbar to lift this thing."

Setting his sights on the tall, stone Celtic cross ahead of them, Vince pedaled them past Saint Pat's to the two-story Nelson house half a block away. Reason sobered up quickly, his mother the director of *Haven Outreach* financed by Saint Patrick's church, could smell alcohol a mile away. Rose, a former user herself, ran the NA support group. To keep herself clean and sober, she served as a sponsor to others to see that they remained free of addictions.

Bailing off of Vince's handlebars, Reason grimaced as his brother stepped outside. Tall and slender, nineteen-year-old Boone Nelson wore his black hair in a long, braided tail. Most folks assumed that he was a biker or a stoner, but he didn't own a bike and he didn't do drugs. In fact, Boone took it upon himself to supervise Reason. If he wasn't scolding him about skipping school, he was cutting off his supply of weed. He was always confiscating Reason's bags.

As far as Boone was concerned the Nelson house was a drug-free zone. He asked, "How did you get that cut on your cheek? Vince, grab a wet washcloth from the kitchen."

Vince followed the two brothers into the house. Tossing the jacket on the couch, Reason sat down in a chair. When Vince came back with a washcloth, Reason grimaced, but remained silent as Boone used the damp cloth to gently dab at the cut on his cheek. Reason wilted under his stern gaze, and though he failed to mention the key, the rest of the story came spilling out. The bust. Hiding in the doghouse. Nate poking him with the knife. Brooks chasing Nate away. The arrival of Jack.

Boone snapped, "What if you'd been busted? One more arrest your probation will be revoked! You violate your terms now, you just can't use your sad smile and your big blue eyes to broker a deal for pardon! You're taking advantage of Judge Sully's second chance!

Last time in court, remember how I tried to convince Sully that you're not a hardcore delinquent? I claimed you needed to be rescued, not punished. But Judge Sully didn't see it that way! Not after the last prank you guys pulled! Don't blame Vince for that! You've been blaming him ever since you were little.

"In second grade when you were expelled for that fire extinguisher fight at school. In fifth, when I caught you smoking that joint. In sixth, when I caught you with a six-pack of beer. It's always Vince! After you boys were arrested for breaking into the Emerald, Vince lucked out with probation while you were sent to detention. While detained there, counselors there nailed you with hard facts, reminding you that at ten years old you'd been charged with egging a police cruiser and stuffing an M-80 in a toilet at a skate rink. Convinced that you had a substance abuse problem, the counselors recommended that you remain confined to undergo treatment.

"Despite their evaluation, you begged the judge to let you off with probation. Later, despite Sully's pardon, once you returned to Havelock you continued to get into trouble."

Reason was saved from Boone's lecturing by Bummer as he entered the living room. The German Shepherd plopped down at Reason's feet. "Can we take Bummer with us?" Reason asked.

Boone said, "No, if he bit Nate, he'd likely get listed as a vicious dog. I'm just gonna set Nate straight. Poking you with a knife is serious. I can't just let it pass."

Chapter Ten

They ran to Havelock Park, four blocks east of the Nelson house. Sprinting across the green lawn beneath the towering pines, they entered the stone shelter on the north side of the park and were greeted by Logan 19-year-old brother of Vince. Logan, whose black hair fell loose about his shoulders, was the only one of Boone's friends who had ever worn handcuffs, ridden in a police cruiser, and spent a night in the drunk tank at city jail. He was notorious for his fierce temper. He and Boone both belonged to a Mixed-Martial Arts team that represented Havelock in a three-state region, and though Logan was a sloppy fighter, Boone actually had earned several titles, coming close to turning professional.

Boone said, "I made some calls. Nate's playing in a pool tournament at Madsen's. He's got backing from the Elder's Den. The Kid, the Brothers, and Tiger will back us if we go hunting this clown. They're pulling duty tonight as bouncers for Old Man Connors, but Billy let them off so they could help us."

They headed for Logan's blue El Camino parked in the street. Logan climbed into the driver's seat, and Reason and Vince piled into the open back end. As Boone approached the vehicle to take shotgun, a drunken grin plastered on his face, Logan clumsily fumbled with the keys. There came a commotion from the edge of the park. His eyes open wide in amazement, Reason told Vince, "Boone's old boxing team! Legends! The Mendoza brothers won the Golden Gloves award! Tony *The Tiger* Menefee once fought in a nationally televised match! Doug *The Kid* Kaluza had over a dozen knock-outs in his ten-year career!"

Vince said, "Nate Holland is a dead man walking!"

Tall, blond-haired Doug checked Logan's condition. After words with him, he plucked the keys out of his hands and tossed them to Tiger. While the Mendoza brothers helped Logan into the back of the El Camino, Tiger climbed into the driver's seat. He popped the clutch and sent the vehicle squealing away down the street.

They drove to Madsen's, but did not find Nate there. While Boone went inside the pool hall, Logan crossed the street and bought a bottle of vodka from a liquor store. Shortly after nine o'clock they pulled into the parking lot of Cassidy's across the highway from Havelock. The arcade was frequented weekly by hundreds of kids donating thousands of quarters to video games. Boone poked Logan in the chest. "I don't need trouble. Stay out here."

Logan stared sullenly at Boone and the Kid as they entered into the arcade. Reason and Vince stepped up to the arcade's door, but before they went inside, Logan slipped a tan pill from his shirt pocket. "You guys wanna take one and see what happens?"

The two younger boys entered the arcade. Snorting at their rude behavior, Logan swallowed the pill and the horse tranquilizer exploded within his system.

Reason and Vince passed through the large swarm of rowdy teens gathered inside Cassidy's. By the time they reached the pool tables, Boone and Doug had selected sticks from one of the wall racks. Ten minutes later, they were in the middle of a game, when Tiger barged through the arcade's front door and started shoving kids aside to clear a path to the pool table. "Boone!" he said. "Logan's wigging out! He says he's gonna jump off the old railroad bridge!"

Outside in the parking lot, Boone raced toward the railroad bridge above Havelock Avenue a block away. There, on the overpass twenty feet above the street, Logan clung to the bridge railing, shaking his fist at the sky. Barging through a crowd of kids already gathered to watch the show, Boone ran to the steep incline beneath the overpass. Logan shouted, "I'm the Birdman!" He leaped off the bridge, hurtling down to a cement pylon ten feet below. There he lost his balance, slipped off the pylon, and plummeted eight more feet to the street.

By the time Boone reached his side, Logan was biting into the palm of his right hand. As sirens wailed in the distance, Boone yanked his hand out of his mouth, sending drops of blood flying from his severely mauled palm. He sighed in relief as a patrol car pulled up, and two cops exited the vehicle. The cops cuffed Logan and led him to their cruiser.

Boone turned as Vince skidded to a stop, nearly running into him. He and his team listened as Vince bawled out his message, saying that Nate Holland was dragging Reason into a car in HP's parking lot. Boone led his old team toward the street.

When they reached the parking lot, Tiger confronted two beefy bikers trying to run interference for Nate as he tried to shove Reason into his Thunderbird. Tiger jacked one of the bikers up. As the second biker lashed out at him, Doug the Kid pummeled him senseless. Boone raced past the El Camino, sending a fist flying into Nate's face. Holding Reason by the back of his neck, Nate spun around, and

Boone struck him again, sending him down on both knees. Backing up Nate, the angry mob of rowdy drunks all members of the Elder's Den, moved toward Boone's old boxing team and attempted to swarm them under. The Mendoza brothers collided with the bikers, causing the nine-man crew to scatter and fall back.

In the chaos that followed, Boone drove another fist into Nate's face. Doug hammered one beefy biker into oblivion. Tiger took out another with a stunning right hook. The Mendozas held off four more long enough for Boone to lead Reason away from the crowd.

By the time they piled into the back of the El Camino, Boone gunned the vehicle, sending a barrage of gravel at the angry drunks scrambling across the parking lot toward them.

***

Reason lay sprawled in his bed, looking over at Vince sleeping soundly next to him. He grinned, suddenly reminded of their younger days when overnights were so much fun. Staying up late to watch spooky movies. Drinking so much pop they thought their bladders might burst. Playing prank phone calls on girls. Ordering pizzas for teachers they didn't like. Impressing each other with gut-wrenching belches or thunderous, jean-ripping farts. Yeah, spending the night together when they were kids was quite a blast.

In those days things were so simple, too. Going to a Saturday matinee at the Joyo Theater. Riding skateboards at the park. Shooting BB guns down at Stephen's Creek. Playing Army. Flag Football and *Do or Dare* and *Run like Sixty*.

But now Reason realized they were no longer innocent little kids. Their transition from childhood to adolescence had been a rough one. Breaking laws. Skipping school. Violating curfews. Smoking too much pot. Being placed on probation. From kid to teen, they'd traveled into dangerous territory. And now because of the bust of Nate's party, they had strayed into even far more treacherous regions.

"Vince!" he whispered. "Wake up! We gotta go get that key!"

Vince hastily dressed while Reason retrieved an aluminum base-ball bat and a flashlight from his closet. Once outside, Reason and Vince zipped up their sweatshirts, while Bummer peed on a tree. The air was nippy, numbing the ends of their noses. Far above them, stars dotted the sky. The moon's radiance trickled down through overhead branches, casting shadows on the street. Both boys leaped nimbly from space to space, making a game of not placing their feet on shadow lines. When they reached the sewer on Kearney Avenue, they pried the heavy lid off the manhole.

Suddenly, a yellow cat ran past them. Bummer bolted after the cat. The moment he did, a bald man appeared out of the nearby shadows. He said, "You the kid who stole Brooks's jacket?"

Reason noted that the man had the tattoo of a dragon on his shiny skull. It suddenly occurred to him who he was. "It's Nate's dad," he whispered to Vince. "Jack Holland, President of the Elder's Den."

"Did you lose something down there?" Jack gruffly asked.

Reason whispered, "Let's get the hell outta here!"

Vince followed him through the manhole, clambering down iron rungs to the storm sewer's floor nine feet below. Swinging his flashlight from left to right, Reason searched the floor. He then aimed his light at a graffiti-covered wall to illuminate a drainage shaft in the ceiling above them. They looked up to see a foot appear through the moonlit opening. Vince slammed the bat down on Jack's foot, causing him to scramble out of the manhole opening.

"Got it!" Reason said as he scooped up the key, slipping it into the pocket of his jeans.

They raced down the tunnel for nearly three blocks, splashing through puddles of water and skidding through patches of mud. They skidded to a stop on a ledge overlooking a cavernous chamber intersected by a channel of water three feet below. Pointing down at the wooden beam spanning the water, Reason watched the water shoot past him. Dropping the baseball bat on the floor, Vince grabbed onto Reason's belt. Reason inched his way out over the channel.

Taking a deep breath, he tottered from side to side, the soles of his tennis shoes squeaking on the wet wood. Vince snatched up the bat and stepped onto the bridge. Reason snagged onto the bat. Connected by the bat, they wavered back and forth. Finally, Reason darted into the tunnel beyond. Vince sprang forward into the tunnel, dropping the bat. They fell to the floor, watching the aluminum bat slide off the ledge and vanish into the chamber behind them. Reason aimed his flashlight at the tunnel on the opposite side of the channel. Seconds later, Jack came charging down the tunnel, unaware of the drop-off in front of him. Blinded by the light, he plunged into the water six feet below. The two boys ran to the entrance to the tunnels down beside Ballard pool, where Bummer sat waiting for them to return.

Reason gave his dog a hug, and they headed for home.

Chapter Eleven

Boone joined the boys at the table as they ate breakfast. "Rumors about you narcing on Nate's party are still circulating. You can go along with us, but you're grounded to the yard when we get home."

Reason asked, "Where we going? Where is Logan?"

Boone said, "He is in the State Hospital."

"The looney bin?" Reason blurted. Vince turned and walked outside. Boone glared at Reason and followed Vince. Placing his bowl on the floor beside Bummer, Reason patted him on the head.

By the time Reason reached the driveway, Vince had already planted himself in the front seat of Boone's blue Ford Falcon. Reason climbed in back without claiming shotgun in the front seat. When they arrived at the State Hospital they entered a large brick building. Once inside the visiting room, Boone and Vince joined Logan seated at a table.

Reason stood there, staring at the stuffed monkey in Logan's hands. He tossed the monkey up into the air. He laughed as the monkey slipped from his grasp and landed on the floor. He then began rocking back and forth. One second he frowned in sorrow. The next, he grimaced in anger. A moment later he was wide-eyed with fear. Logan then looked at Reason and cackled like a psychotic witch.

Logan said, "Told you I was Birdman. Million dollars is coming to me! They owe me a million dollars! I played guitar on the Zeppelin album. I wrote the lyrics to 'Stairway to Heaven.' I wrote songs for KISS and Ozzy, too. They know the Birdman. PCP mixed with vodka is a cocktail from hell! See, we all have a spirit inside that wants to connect with unseen powers. Or demons who poke holes in our soul! God said that Jesus wept last night when I wounded my spirit."

Tears streaming down his face, Vince leaped up and bolted out of the room. Logan stared at him in dismay and slammed his bandaged right hand down on the table, sending an ashtray clattering to the floor. Two men in blue uniforms ran into the room. It took them several minutes to restrain him, and as they led him away Boone and Reason exited the room to find Vince huddled in a chair, badly shaken by his brother's outburst. Reason couldn't seem to get Logan's words out of his head: *Jesus wept last night . . .*

When Boone dropped them off back at the Nelson house, Vince sat down on the porch swing. Sitting down next to him, Reason decided some kind of distraction would work best to get Vince to quit stressing out about his brother's condition. Determined to help, Reason slipped a small pack of rolling papers from his shirt pocket and pulled a metal container from his sock. Opening it, he took out three pinches of grass and began to roll a joint.

Reason then gently rolled the papers, licked the ends, twisted them together, and held it up to study his handiwork. He said, "Remember the first time I rolled a joint? I used seeds and all, ripped the paper twice, and thoroughly soaked it with saliva. It took nearly an hour to dry out! I was disappointed that I didn't see fireworks going off inside my head. But I did cop a buzz. Unlike you, who hacked up a lung!"

Slipping a lighter from his back pocket, he offered Vince the joint. Vince raised his hand to brush it away and their wrists connected, sending the joint sailing across the porch. "Give it a rest, Reason!" he snapped.

Puzzled, Reason didn't even bother to pick the joint back up. He sat there baffled. Vince left the porch and headed down the sidewalk.

****

Seated on the front porch, Reason eyed the nattering black squirrels in the branches above him. Bummer sat at the foot of the porch, unfazed by the angry scolding of the fidgety little beasts. Reason tried to relax as spring breezes swept the long strands of his hair over his shoulders. Although the leather jacket lay there beside him, the key remained in the coin pocket of his jeans. He would hand over the jacket for fifty dollars, but he was still determined to scam Brooks out of more money for the key. Reason headed to the backyard. He climbed up the boards nailed to the trunk of an oak tree near the alley.

After fiddling with the combination lock on his tree house door, he climbed inside and slid the key into a pack of playing cards. He then exited the tree house, locking the door behind him. Upon returning to the front porch, he saw a brown Nova stop in front of the house.

A white guy with long dark hair exited the car. A smile creased his beard as he said, "My name is Jessie Dalton. You and Brooks and I had a collision at Nate's party. I went to that party to track down Brooks. Next thing you know, the bust went down."

Reason said, "I don't go to parties. I don't even do drugs."

Jessie took a step forward, but Bummer growled a warning. Hearing the commotion, Rose stepped outside. Rose Nelson was an attractive lady with wild tangles of black hair. Reason could tell that the man assumed she was a bad mother. Reason saw him checking out her faded blue jeans and red, tie-dyed shirt. *He probably thinks she's a pothead,* he thought. *She hasn't touched drugs since Dad went to prison!*

"Reason," Rose said, "this is private investigator, Jess Dalton. Back in the day, he used to ride with your dad's club, the Outlaws."

"Didn't give me time to introduce myself, did you?" Jessie said.

Reason rudely said, "Gosh, you're such a cheerful fellow. What did Mom do? Offer you a dozen donuts?"

"Reason," Rose warned, "don't be such a smart mouth. Come on inside, Jessie. We can talk in the living room. I'm sure Boone is going to want to hear this, too."

As Rose led them inside, Boone joined them, saying, "Reason, show this man some respect."

As they took seats in the living room, Jessie took out the joint that Reason had dropped on the porch earlier. "This," he said, dropping it on the coffee table, "could get your probation revoked, right?"

Reason thought, *If he demands I pee in a bottle the THC in my system will send the pot-testing machine off the Richter scale!*

Jessie placed a photo on the table. "Kelly Drake worked the streets as an informant. She was young and attractive, and as a narc, she used her charm to set up dozens of dealers in several major busts."

They all looked down at the young, blond girl in the photo, then Jessie put a second picture on the table. "Jack Holland," he said, pointing down at the bald man with the dragon tat. "Six years ago, Jack robbed a drug dealer in T-town. He had Brooks run the man out of town. Curious as why they had partnered up, Kelly went to Jack, inquiring about a job. Jack hired her and began robbing an entire statewide narcotics operation. When it came time to take Jack down, Kelly was to be a star witness. She had a meeting in the outdoor café of the Emerald Pub. There, someone shot her, leaving her dead in the pub's café. Later that same night, some mystery player broke into the pub. The pub's security system had recorded her murder. He confiscated the DVD and set a blackmail plot in motion. But things took a strange twist on the night that Brooks and this mystery player met to make the exchange of the DVD. In fact, word on the street is the disk is locked in a safe-deposit box at a local bank. Someone had the key to this box, and Brooks went to Nate's party to buy it from him."

Reaching behind his chair, Jessie picked up the leather jacket Reason had left behind on the porch. Jessie took his last photo and placed it on the coffee table. Reason peered down at the statue of an angel kneeling beside a grave, a sword in one hand and a plaque in the other. On the face of the plaque were the words, *Kelly, gone but never forgotten.* Jessie said, "A reward is being offered for information leading to the arrest and conviction of those involved in Kelly's murder."

Jessie crumpled up the joint and slipped it into his pocket. He stood up to leave. Boone said, "A private detective telling us about a murder is way past serious, Reason."

Boone looked to Jessie. "A year ago, I walked away from the MMA. Instead of going pro on the fight circuit, I went to work for *Outreach*, a youth agency. I was assigned ten state wards. I became a truancy tracker. An advocate in juvenile court. Having dealt with my little brother's defiance disorder, I used all my tactics that worked on Reason, applying them to other troubled kids. Havelock is a rough suburb. Our great-grandfather would roll over in his grave if he knew the park was now a party haven. He helped build the town in the year 1891, when Havelock was a train depot between Lincoln and Omaha, and it was placed on the world map by Irish railroaders, whose descendants now own the pubs in Havelock: *Misty's. The Isles. Castles. The Emerald.* As far as drugs go, back when Reason was ten, he smoked up. After getting busted for breaking into the Emerald, he was sent to detention. There, he heard every speech about the c-hemicals in marijuana—"

"THC is a powerful intoxicant," Reason said, mockingly. "It damages brain cells and controls my thinking process. THC accumulates in the microscopic cells in my brain . . ."

Jessie held up his hand to stop Reason's prattle. "Do you have the key, Reason?"

"Nope," Reason said, looking anywhere but into Jessie's eyes.

Jessie offered him a sad smile as he exited the house.

Chapter Twelve

The next morning, Rose greeted Reason as he stepped out of his bedroom. "How," she said, "did your meeting with Boone go last night? Did he talk you through your amnesia?"

With a mouthful of a cold Poptart, Reason mumbled, "Amnesia?"

Rose said, "Don't play dumb with me, my wild child. Did Boone speak of the key that Jessie Dalton believes you have?"

Reason noisily slurped his orange juice, then belched before saying, "Nope. It never came up."

"I see," Rose said. "Well, you are still grounded for going to that party, so when you finish up here, stick around home."

"Yeah, Mom," he said, waving at Rose as she left. Seconds later, Reason slipped out the front door and walked down to Havelock Park. He had just taken his stash container out of his right sock, when Nate stepped out of a nearby alley. Reason wheeled around and - bolted, hearing nothing but his own labored breathing for another two blocks. He darted across the playground of Havelock school.

Reason continued on across the playground and slipped into an alley. Sliding on loose gravel, he scrambled toward a narrow opening in the stockade fence bordering the alley. He squeezed through the gap between two boards and fell to the ground. When he finally reached his driveway, he tripped over a skateboard near the porch. Reason stumbled up onto the porch. Pulling the door open he ran inside and shoved the door closed.

Nate pounded on the door with a fist. Inside the house, winded from his run, Reason collapsed on the couch. He heard a loud voice from the porch, and Nate stopped his pounding. When he opened the door, Nate was gone, yet Brooks stood there. "You have the key?" he asked. "There's evidence in that deposit box that connects dozens of dealers to a city-wide investigation. If word spreads that you have the key, those dealers will be coming after you. I'm trying to save you from that grief, kid."

Reason said, "As soon as I have it, I'll look you up."

"Reason?" Rose called from inside. "Who are you talking to?"

With another frown offered to Brooks, Reason silently held up his index finger, and quietly closed the door.

Reason sulked in his room for the next thirty minutes, trying to figure a way to get Boone off his case. When a knock came from the front door, he bolted past Boone in the hallway, and spotted a boy with pale, elfin features encased by wild strands of long, blond hair, standing on the front porch. Twelve-year-old Collin Young stood there dressed in faded jeans, scruffy tennis shoes, a red T-shirt and a ragged, dark blue military jacket. Although it nearly swallowed his thin frame, the jacket belonged to his older brother, Logan, who his folks had sent to a military academy. One night after a violent altercation with their dad, Collin's older brother had hopped on a train at the yards.

During the two years of his brother's absence, every time he heard the horn of an evening train passing through the Burlington yards, he would ride his bike down there expecting to see Logan return. With several trains passing through the yards each night, Collin had ended up at the yards three or four times a night. Reason could never hear a train horn echoing from the yards without thinking about the sadness that constantly plagued Collin Young. Small and scrappy as he was, unlike his two older brothers, he wasn't a doper. He didn't need drugs to get high. His high came from simply being himself.

Reason recalled what Vince had once said about the little kid. "When you talk to Collin, it's like what you're saying is the most important thing in the world. Time slows down when you're talking to him because he actually cares about what you're telling him. My little bro is cool."

"Bummer!" Collin said, dropping down to one knee. "Give me a kiss!" Bummer happily licked his chin. Collin whispered, "Vince told me about this trouble you're in. I talked to old man Kelvie about safe-deposit boxes. Could I see the key?"

Seconds later, Reason climbed up the boards that led to the tree house. He quickly spun through the combination on the lock and opened the door. He snatched up the pack of playing cards, only to find that the key was gone. "Vince!" Reason said.

When the boys approached the California Lunchroom, they were greeted by railroaders heading back to the Burlington shops across the street. Still furious with Vince for taking the key, Reason said, "Why did Patsy name this place the *California* Lunchroom?"

Unfazed by Reason's foul mood, Collin said, "When Patsy was a girl, her father planned to move their family from Chicago to Cally.

But unfortunately, they only made it as far as Nebraska, so he opened up the California Lunchroom, a memento of broken dreams."

They were greeted warmly by Patsy, the eighty-year-old owner of the popular eatery. Collin gave the spry old lady a hug, but Reason simply blurted, "Patsy, have you seen Vince?"

"No," Patsy said. "But Boone stopped by. He looks more like a Harley-riding biker than a truancy tracker. I'd never skip school if I had a truant officer like him. Are you still mad at him for revoking your truancy contract. Strange, but after that, *someone* spray-painted the image of a long-haired man and the word NARC on Boone's van. Probably some kid he ticked off. One night he confiscated Kenny's bag of weed. Another time he made Kyle pour out a quart of beer. He preaches to potheads like he's the Patron Saint of Havelock's Stoners! Funny, since the image on his van was supposed to resemble him but actually looked like Jesus."

Collin said, "Patsy, speaking of visitors. Did you ever tell Reason that Charles Lindbergh used to land his plane at Arrow Airport, then visit here! Knowing that Charlie sat here, makes me feel connected to the world beyond insignificant Havelock."

"Insignificant?" Patsy said. "I once visited a pub in Dublin, Ireland. I found a map of Nebraska tacked to a wall, and someone had crossed out Lincoln and marked Havelock as the capital! Havelock isn't even listed on a Nebraska map! Who in Ireland would even know about us?"

"Billy Connors," Reason said. "Owner of the Emerald. My mom claims he was a gun-runner for the Irish Republican Army. He has a plaque in his pub that the Sinn Fein gave him for sending them guns! A house in Havelock blew up one night! Firemen discovered an arsenal of guns in the smoldering ruins. Billy planned to ship them to Ireland. Too bad that old fart didn't get blown up. I've hated that codger since he caught me stealing pop off his loading dock! On Saint Pat's Day, Billy gets spruced up in his green suit and greets guests at the Emerald as the Lord Mayor of Havelock, claiming green beer flows in his veins!"

As the boys left the Lunchroom a full moon hung above the park's pines. There in the shelter a fire burned in the fireplace. Faint pops and hisses came from the fire. Wood smoke drifted in the air. An owl hooted from a nearby tree. A dog barked in the distance. A train horn drifted through the countryside beyond. Collin said, "Nothing like the haunting sound of a train horn. Those tracks at the yards connect us with thousands of people beyond Havelock. And yet those same tracks took my brother away. Train horns make me feel *lonely* and *connected* at the same time."

Suddenly, brilliant bursts of green light appeared in the sky. "Wow!" Collin gasped. "Seven falling stars! Good omen! Wish upon a falling star, God will make your wish come true."

"Wishes," Reason said, "only come true in fairy tales."

Collin asked, "You don't believe in God, Reason?"

"Sure I do," Reason said. "He just doesn't believe in me. When I see a falling star, it leaves me feeling lonely. The same when I see a sunset. Fireflies on a summer night. Mist on an autumn morning. Snow on a winter's night. He might be out there, but I don't think God gives one whit about me. Falling stars are supposed to remind us that there has to be someone out there in the universe. But, what if we're really nothing but a bunch of dust motes floating around on a giant dust mote on the back end of the universe, and God doesn't even know we're here?"

Chapter Thirteen

Reason stopped inside the stone shelter at the park. Before him, a slender, young girl with long, brown hair followed Vince to the shelter. Reason had been attracted to Jenna Kane since fifth grade. And yet, after he was busted for shoplifting at Ben Franklin's Five and Dime two years ago, Jenna had claimed she wanted nothing to do with a delinquent. Instead of smacking Vince for taking the key, he had to keep his cool around Jenna. Vince sheepishly handed him the key. "Sorry I took it to Kelvie the locksmith to find out how deposit boxes work. See those tiny letters? Kelvie says the key opens a one lock box, which means you don't need to go through a bank official to snag that disk."

"But you're in for a grilling," Jenna said. "Boone came snooping at Kelvie's. Vince and I had to sneak down the alley in the back."

Vince said, "Logan came home this morning on a day pass. He had on a trench coat, claiming he's a special agent for the Feds."

Trying not to grin, Reason said, "Agent Double O Logan!"

"Not funny, Reason," Vince said. "Logan claims he's the Head of the Havelock drug task force. I had to go get him out of the bank. Just past the customer counter, I located the security cameras mounted in three corners of the lobby. They are trained on the center of the lobby, not on the safe-deposit boxes in a small chamber ten feet away. But there is an armed guard seated before the chamber. We need someone innocent looking to get past him. The whole time we were in there, Officer Lard Ass didn't budge from his post!"

As Reason slid the key into his pocket, Collin said, "You guys can't nab that evidence. There's a good reason Boone is searching for you, Reason. He's trying to act like a dad. Ever since your dad went to prison, Boone looks after you. Remember his lecture about having no dad the night you trashed the pool table at the Emerald?"

Reason nodded. "I was smashed on Mad Dog. After I puked my guts out in the pub's bathroom, I ripped the lid off the toilet, then hopped up on the pool table, holding it like a steering wheel. I claimed I was racing away from the demons. Officer Tory came to the pub to arrest me. I told him I needed to talk to *Father* Nelson. Thinking that I wanted to talk to the parish priest, Beef drove me over to Saint Pat's and woke up Father Witt, who had no clue what was going on. Tory drove me over here to the park and turned me over to Boone! And talk about demons. Ever heard of Wild Bill Morris?

"Wild Bill stopped by the park that night, too, and when he heard Boone lecturing me, he pulled out a knife. He even tried to stab him. Now that was a wicked fight! Boone let loose with these punches that left Bill reeling like a drunken sailor. Boone beat the snot out of Bill."

The twelve o'clock whistle blew in the yards. Jenna accepted an escort home by Vince and Collin. As the three of them left, a cat fight broke out in a nearby alley. Bummer took off running toward the horrid screeching sounds. Reason cried, "Bummer, get back here—"

His words trailed off as a Native man with long raven hair stepped into the shelter. Reason stared at the Native in disbelief and said, "Ben Black Bull? Daws Holland killed Ben."

"Benjy," Ben said. "His son. Your dad and I met when we were kids. I run Wounded Arrow Dog Rescue Ranch. Do you have the map? If I had it, I could return valuable relics to the Cheyenne of South Dakota."

He paused as if listening to the breeze, his head cocked to one side. He said, "Many enemies from the Unseen Realm stalk you. In my own battle with these demons, I have two spirit guides, a bear and a buffalo. Nothing like being lectured by a wise old buffalo. In Irish folklore, familiars were spiritual guardians that protected those who practiced magic. Familiar spirits manifested as an animal. Most were defined, as opposed to ghosts with their smoky forms."

A strange thing happened then, one that would impact Reason's life in a positive way. Up until that point, he had experienced a lot negative consequences for the choices he made. This mysterious encounter would prove to be a turning point in the boy's life. A black wolf stepped out of the shadows beneath the park's trees.

Big and buff, his chest and shoulders rippled with muscles, he moved through shafts of moonlight, his black fur contrasted sharply in the silver moonshine. He peered up at Reason, his startling blue eyes fixing him in a curious gaze. Yet suddenly, his glowing eyes narrowed as the form of a hooded figure sprang out from beneath the trees, his sharp claws extended toward Reason's chest.

The wolf intercepted the creature's attack on the boy, sinking his fangs into the thing's breast. The wolf then erupted into a storm of fangs and fury, sending the thing shrieking away into the darkness. The wolf finished his battle, turned and vanished beneath the trees.

Ben said, "You are one lucky boy, Reason Nelson."

Later that night, Bummer slipped inside the open door of the Emerald pub. Following him inside, Reason studied the pub's rustic woodwork, its white walls, enormous oak beams, high-back booths, and tall stools situated before a bar with brass foot rails. A red banner with three black lions wearing gold crowns hung on the west wall. The Emerald resembled an old Irish pub with a massive fireplace with seven deer mounted above the mantle. Strands of tiny, green lights wrapped around the antlers of the noble bucks resembled fireflies. Reason peered at the wooden plaque beneath their chins.

Billy Connors stepped up beside him. Tall and scarecrow thin, his snow-white hair trailed back over his ears, his white mustache was thick and full. The old Irishman wore an expensive suit and in his blue eyes a dangerous rage roiled.

Reason asked, "Is that the plaque the Sinn Fein gave you? Mom says you're the Irish Godfather of Havelock."

Billy snorted, "Do you know your history? Nelson means Neal's son, which is derived from Niall, once High King of Ireland! You've got the blood of kings in you, lad! Your ancestor founded a powerful dynasty. Niall's raids into foreign lands resulted in a young lad coming to Ireland in the third century. Your ancestor brought Patrick to Ireland. Now *you* live one block away from a church named after the great saint, yet you fall short of what you could be. It's tragic.

"Many kids so desperate to find relief from their pain, have trouble coping and turn to drugs to self-medicate. They're not wired for dealing with stress. They turn to a temporary fix to eliminate pain. But eventually, the powerful chemicals they use, leave them with a craving, they become addicted. Small towns. Big cities. Users in each! A major epidemic. The drug trade is like a demon that divides itself into a million parts to get through our borders. We stop it in one place, it slithers through in another. As long as there are users, there will always be suppliers. Victims end up in treatment centers, prison, or the grave. Dealers make a load of cash if they don't get arrested. In fact, the evidence in that safe-deposit box would help Jessie solve a young girl's murder. If only he had that key."

Reason was quick to change the subject. "Ben Black Bull came to me tonight, asking about some map, Billy."

Shaking his shaggy head in puzzlement, Billy said, "Ah, the white buffalo robe with the Cheyenne treaty marked on it? The warclub of Buffalo Calf Road Woman? Bill Cody's Sharps rifle? George Custer's pistol? The map will supposedly lead to those relics. Your dad found the map when Jack Holland caused Ben's dad to crash the school bus he was driving. Right now, that is none of your business. Now, get yourself home."

Chapter Fourteen

The next afternoon despite being grounded, Reason snuck down to Havelock Park. He removed his stash container from his left sock and rolled a joint. He had only taken two tokes, when Jenna entered the shelter. Reason snorted, "Here. Take a hit."

Jenna pushed his hand away. "I don't get high, Reason."

After releasing his breath, he said, "Smoke up with me."

Jenna said, "No. I don't do that."

"Suit yourself," Reason said, then took another hit. He then told her the entire story regarding the key. The evidence in a deposit box that would solve a murder. Gently, she reached over and took the joint away from him. "Not everyone accepts getting high as a way of life, Reason." Watching her flick his joint into the nearby bushes, Reason sat there listening to her. Jenna spent the next ten minutes asking him questions about Kelly's murder. All the time she talked, he was thinking, *She could walk into the bank and that guard wouldn't suspect her of anything.*

Reason leaned forward and placed his lips on hers. It was a little difficult, since he had shut his eyes, but he was relieved when Jenna kissed him back. Reason sat back, gently touched her hand, and asked if she would go to the bank with him

Jenna pulled away. "Is that what the kiss was for?"

"No," Reason said. He spent several minutes telling her that getting involved in his troubles was the last thing she needed. But the more he downplayed wanting her to become involved, the more questions Jenna started to ask. By the time she was ready to leave, Reason pressed his luck and nabbed one more kiss from her before she left the park.

Ten minutes later, Reason called her. Using a ploy, he apologized for even suggesting she help him, and promptly hung up. He was pleased when Jenna showed up a few minutes later. Before leaving the house, Reason scooped up a gallon-sized wine bottle filled with thousands of pennies. He knew they would serve as the perfect distraction at the bank. Upon entering Havelock Bank, Jenna crossed the lobby and joined two women standing at a table with their checkbooks. Several moments later, Reason and Vince walked in and joined a line of customers in front of the teller counter. They waited anxiously as the line dwindled in front of them. Trying to appear as innocent as altar boys, they both eyed the beefy guard stationed before the corner room containing the safe-deposit boxes. Long moments passed as bank patrons made their transactions. The lady ahead of the boys finished her business. Vince nodded at Jenna across the lobby.

The moment Jenna moved toward the safe-deposit boxes the guard stopped her. "Miss, I need to see some identification." It was then that Reason stepped up to the teller counter, fumbled with his bottle, then dropped it. The large bottle hit the linoleum floor and shattered, sending pennies and shards of glass flying. Alarmed by the commotion, the guard moved away from his post. Jenna darted into the small room and used the key to open box thirty-one. She reached down and picked up a small blue backpack. Slinging the pack over one shoulder, she retrieved the key and closed the box, then walked out of the noisy bank.

Totally oblivious to what had taken place, the guard escorted an older lady away from the broken bottle while Reason and Vince caught up with Jenna in the alley beside the bank. Jenna and the boys took off running down the sidewalk to Havelock Park one block to the south. Jenna said, "There's Logan over in the park!"

Carrying the pack, Reason noted that Logan had slicked back his hair and braided the dark strands into a ponytail. He also wore dress slacks, a black trench coat, mirrored sunglasses, and looked like a special agent. He said, "That backpack? You guys went to the bank, didn't you? Hand it over unless you want to be arrested!"

Reason laughed out loud. "Secret Agent Man has flipped his lid."

Logan proceeded to follow them back to the Nelson house. Vince tried to get him to leave them alone, but Logan insisted that they give him the backpack. As they entered the house, Reason shut the door on Logan, locking it so that he could not follow them. He turned around and dropped the pack on the floor. Bummer nosed it and Vince reached inside the pack and pulled out a pearl-handled .22 Ruger pistol. Reaching into the pack again, Vince pulled out a DVD and a small bottle with shiny blue pills inside it. Carefully plucking it out of his hand, Reason looked past him to see Boone mounting the porch steps outside. "We best just hide this for now."

Reason gathered up the items and stuffed them inside the pack. Jenna got up and unlocked the door for Boone. He offered the three kids a suspicious scowl. Keenly aware that the backpack was on the floor beside his chair, Reason tried to distract his brother by brushing past him and stepping outside. He could feel Boone's eyes on him as he looked to the street to watch a black Harley stop in front of the house. A young man climbed off the beast. Tall with broad shoulders, his thick mustache curled down to points at the base of his chin, his long, raven hair was held in place by a black bandana.

"Stone Holland," Reason said, "warlord of the Elder's Den. The Kid kicked your ass in the ring up in Omaha."

"Not me," Stone said. "My older brother was defeated that night, for this Kaluza Kid is a good fighter."

Reason said, "What happened to his threat of a rematch?"

"My brother's last fight," Stone said, "was with cancer. There will be no rematches for him."

Boone stepped outside. Stone said, "You are Reason's brother? I have a younger brother, much like yours, Nate. As older brothers, can we rescue them from their own stupidity? I've gone through treatment. I've been clean now since Kelly was killed. Jack and Nate are determined to get all the evidence you took from the bank."

"Reason?" Boone asked. "Did you use that key at the bank?"

Stone glanced over at Reason, "If you find pills in that evidence, don't be stupid enough to sample them."

"Why not?" Jenna asked as she joined them on the porch.

It became silent for several moments. Stone and Boone exchanged curious looks. Neither one missed the look that Reason shared with Jenna and Vince. Stone said, "Sky Rippers are a new drug produced by bathtub chemists. They have a rippling effect. The chemicals once introduced into a person's system ripple through nerves, veins, the lungs, the brain, and explode with the kick of a windstorm. Rippers were the new drug Kelly was trying to bust my dad on. It was the reason she was killed."

Reason asked, "What color are they?"

"Reason," Boone whispered, "what have you done now?"

Chapter Fifteen

Stone left them, warning about the dangers of the synthetic drug. Reason followed Boone inside. He exchanged alarmed looks with Jenna and Vince as they looked down to the empty spot on the floor where the pack had been only minutes ago. Shooting a panicked look at the back door, Reason knew immediately who had taken it. "Damn it!" he snapped. "Logan made his move!"

"No!" Boone said, latching onto him. "Sit yourself down!"

Reason let loose with a string of heated cuss words that got him grounded for the rest of that day. Feeling a bit uncomfortable with Boone being so angry at his little brother, Jenna and Vince quietly left. Vince called later to tell him that Logan indeed had confiscated the backpack. He told him Logan planned to sell the evidence to Nate that night.

Two hours later, Reason snuck out of the house, and he found Logan making his way through the park with the backpack. He planted himself directly in his path, demanding that he turn the evidence over to him. Smiling, Logan said, "I just love summer. Soon sounds from the Ballard ballpark will fill the air. Shortly before sundown, the ball games will begin. The voice of the announcer on a crappy PA system will echo through the air. The umpire shouting! The crack of a bat! The crowd going wild when the bases are loaded and the batter hits a homer! Makes me wish I was a kid again."

Reason said, "Sadly, you are deliberately moving away from the innocent days of your boyhood. You're as lost as the evidence we took from the bank. Do you know the trouble you will be in if Nate gets it? What's the penalty for interfering in a police investigation? Jessie Dalton warned me several times what would happen to me if I did not cooperate. If Nate—"

"Nate offered me two-thousand," Logan said. "He's meeting me at Danny Kane's party. Once he steps into my trap by giving me the money, I will arrest his sorry butt."

"Arrest him?" Reason blurted. "You ain't no secret agent, Logan! If the Den gets that evidence, they will destroy it."

Logan shook his head. "Not if I arrest Nate first. Hey, back my play and maybe I'll give you cred with the Feds."

When they arrived at the Kane house, Reason and Logan were greeted by Jenna's little brother Danny, a small kid with long, black hair. Loud heavy-metal music blared from the speakers on the front porch and a large crowd of kids milled about the front yard. Danny scooped up two cans of beer from a nearby cooler. Logan stood outside drinking his. Soon, Reason tossed away his empty can, picked up a full one, and followed Danny into the house. In the front room several kids gathered around a keg, filling their mugs with beer. Others sat on a couch, a bong on a table in front of them. Reason took a swallow from his second beer. One young girl passed him a pipe. He raised it to his lips and inhaled deeply. He released his breath and passed the pipe back to the girl. An older boy handed him a bottle of tequila. Reason took a long swallow that caused him to cough and splutter. Dizzy from the alcohol coursing through his system, Reason stumbled as he passed through the crowded living room to reach the front porch.

There he found Nate. When he spotted Reason, he laughed wildly and said, "I'm ripped on rippers, man! I snuck them from Dad. When I get the evidence from Logan, my old man will be happy-happy. Have you seen him?"

"No," Reason said.

"Then," Nate said, "what good are you, fool?"

Nate let loose with a right hook that caught him above his left temple. Dazed by the cheap shot, Reason landed near the porch and passed out.

When he woke up he found himself sprawled in a chair in the Kane living room. Still groggy, he sat up. "Are you okay?" Jenna asked. "You blacked out. Danny's friends chased Nate away by throwing cans of beer at him. Danny's been in the bathroom drunkenly blubbering about Logan leaving before Nate got there. Vince is out searching for him. I'm going to join him. You stay here, you still don't look so hot."

Reluctantly, Reason settled back into the chair, watching a wretched-looking Danny fidgeting for nearly ten minutes before clambering out of his chair and running into the bathroom. There, he lifted the toilet lid and a stream of projectile vomit came shooting out of his mouth. Reason said, "I bet you wished you hadn't chugged so much beer."

Ten minutes later, Reason left the house. He spotted Vince in front of Arnold's Tavern on Havelock Avenue. He was peering in through the window, his features illuminated by the giant, neon beer mug above the tavern's door. Peering in through the window, Reason saw Logan seated at one end of the bar. The place was packed with workers from the Burlington shops and the Goodyear plant. Many of the patrons were seated at tables or booths. Others gathered around the shuffleboard and the pool table. Willie and Waylon blared from a jukebox. Pinball machines buzzed. Glasses clinked together. Peals of laughter echoed across the room. The sudden *crack!* of a break came from a pool table. Cigarette smoke hung thick in the air.

Reason approached Logan at the end of the bar.

He slapped Logan on the shoulder and a silence passed through the crowded tavern. A pinball machine in one corner gave out a last dull ring. *Whiskey River* faded from the jukebox. In the center of the room the puck on the shuffleboard table spun to a rest in a pile of sawdust. Sighing in frustration, Reason snatched up Logan's mug from the bar and dumped the cold beer over his head. Reason and Vince raced toward the front door. They ran the entire four blocks to the Nelson house. Once they entered the backyard, Reason darted to the oak tree near the alley. He began climbing up to his tree house. He had almost reached the door when Logan grabbed onto his ankles. Reason tumbled to the ground. He caught a blurred glimpse of Boone placing Logan in a full-nelson. After a brief struggle, Boone escorted him away down the alley, while Doug Kaluza and Tiger led Reason inside the house. "Boone," Doug said, "is trying to recover that stuff from the bank. He asked us to keep an eye on you."

Reason shrugged. "Can I go outside to my tree fort?" he asked.

"No," Doug said. "We're supposed to keep you here."

Due to his two bodyguards, he angrily stomped into the kitchen, where he sat sulking until Vince joined him. The two quietly slipped upstairs, where they opened a window and climbed out onto a small patch of roof. Years ago, Reason had gone up there to retrieve a frisbee one night, only to discover that the upper walls of the two-story house formed an L-shaped enclosure. It was a perfect spot for a secret nook. He claimed the high haven as his own private sanctuary and named it the Loft. The two boys looked down to the backyard, and there at the edge of the trees, the huge, black wolf appeared, his blue eyes fixed on Reason. "Whoa!" Vince gasped. "Is that a—"

"Yes," Reason said. "He's my spirt wolf. When he attacked this demon seconds before it attacked me, he broke into a furious storm. I think I will call him Storm. He is looking out for me."

The wolf let out a long, mournful howl, then turned and was gone.

Chapter Sixteen

The next morning, Vince and Reason discovered Logan carrying the backpack on his way over to Nate's house. Logan said, "Last night after I missed Nate at the Kane party, Nate sold Danny two bottles of Sky Rippers. Reason, just be glad I didn't tell Boone you took this stuff from the bank. Help me set Nate up on conspiracy charges?"

Reason and Vince both said, "No!"

"Why not?" Logan asked. "Things are already in play. I called Officer Tory and told him Nate has more of these."

He reached into the pack and pulled out a bottle filled with blue pills. Five blocks later, Logan walked up to Nate's door. Reason and Vince led Bummer over to the bushes beside the house. Hidden behind the shrubs, they watched Nate confront Logan standing there.

A moment later, a patrol car pulled up out front. Logan removed the lid from the bottle, and dumped the blue pills onto Nate's front porch, then took off running, leaving Nate shuffling the pills around with is foot in order to conceal them. Beef promptly placed Nate in handcuffs and spent several minutes gathering up the pills before driving him away.

Reason and Vince guided Bummer away toward the alley. Nate's Rottweiler suddenly poked his head out of his doghouse in the center of the yard. Terrified that a dogfight was about to break out between the Shepherd and the Rottweiler, Reason read the name above the door of the doghouse and said, "Down, Harley!"

Harley made a sudden lunge, but the chain anchoring the dog to the doghouse stopped him in his tracks. Bummer stood there growling fiercely. The massive Rott drug his house with him. Reason stared down at the ground where the doghouse had been. "A trapdoor!" he said as Harley drug the doghouse completely off of the trapdoor. When he reached Bummer, the Rott whined and rolled over on his back in submission. Bummer cocked his head, peering down at the dog. Staring in disbelief at the outline of a doorway sunk into the ground, Vince said, "It's a storm cellar. Lots of folks in Havelock had a shelter in case of tornados."

Vince lifted up the trapdoor, revealing a set of steps leading down into an underground room. Taking out his lighter, Reason moved down the steps, whistling in amazement as the flickering flames illuminated dozens of large trunks stacked in one corner of the underground room. Reason opened one of the lockers, revealing hundreds of small cellophane packets, filled with blue pills. Realizing the dog-house was the same one he'd hidden in the night of Nate's party, he moved back up the stairs.

The Rott began whining as he gave it an affectionate pat. "Now that Nate's locked up, who's gonna take care of his dog? If he can't post bail, Harley will get sent to the pound! Think your mom would let you have a dog?"

Vince said, "No. My Mom's idea of a dog is her snippy little poodle. And I already have to clean up the butt nuggets he leaves behind! Hell, if that tank of a dog came to live with us, I'd get a hernia from cleaning up logs as big as Ponderosa Pines!"

While Reason and Vince shoved Harley's doghouse back in place over the trapdoor, Bummer let out a ferocious bark as a shiny, black Malibu pulled up in the alley. Billy Connors stepped out of the car. The old Irishman lit his pipe and blew out several puffs of smoke. He said, "I checked Danny Kane into treatment today. I'd like to do the same for you. Brooks and Jack have been trolling Havelock like a pair of blood-crazed sharks!"

"Harley," Reason said, "needs a new home."

Looking down at the Rott, Billy said, "Stay safe at home for the next few days. Let me worry about that dog."

"For real?" Reason asked. "You'll find him a home?"

Billy smiled, "Yes, just promise you'll go home now."

The old Irishman man gave them a ride to the Nelson house in quite a hurry. The boys took Bummer outside in the backyard, joining Boone and his old boxing team seated at the fire in the Pit. Stars glistened in the sky above. A full orange moon rose in the east. A nearby dog howled as a train whistle blew in the distant railyards. Down the street, two cats made horrid yowling sounds and the night was filled with blood-curdling yammering. Bummer ran off in the direction of the catfight.

"What's this about?" Reason asked. gesturing to the Thunderbird pulling up in the street. Jack Holland exited the car. "My boy got arrested today," the biker snarled. "I came here for the evidence you took from the bank. And I am stoked for a fight!"

Before Jack could close the distance between himself and Reason, Boone intercepted him. The fight started without warning. Boone fell with a solid punch to the face. Jack then attacked the Mendoza brothers. He delivered two blows to Joe's chest, dropping him to his knees. Jack then rammed Tony in the face with an elbow.

Reason saw the mad rage roiling in Jack's eyes. He thought of the Sky Ripper drug Stone had told them about. He was certain Jack had the chemicals rippling through his system. In his wrath, he appeared to be unstoppable. With a growl, Jack punched Joe in the nose, then threw a swift uppercut into Tony's chin. Shoving the Mendozas out of his path, Jack wrapped his fingers around Tiger's neck, using a stranglehold. Pulling him close, Jack head-butted him, sending blood spurting from his nose.

Jack flung him away from him and wheeled to face the Kid. Kaluza went straight for Jack, blocking a flurry of fists, while side-stepping to throw the huge biker off balance. Kaluza then lived up to his legend. In more than a dozen fights in his career, other boxers claimed that the Kid's left fist came from out of nowhere. It was an phenomenon, for when his right fist couldn't get the job done, his left took on a life of its own and struck like lightning. The Kid then brutally stopped his opponent in his tracks, sending the poor fool down for the count.

When Kaluza struck Jack beneath his chin, his left fist connected with so much force that Jack sailed back and crumpled to the ground. Only to rise once more, shaking off the damage he'd just taken.

Jack shouldered Kaluza aside, and sent him staggering with a blow to his head. The biker then went for Reason. Jack leaped on Reason and pinned him to the ground. Reason frantically struggled, trying to worm his way out from under the large man. Straining to breathe, Reason looked up as Jack grabbed onto the front of his shirt. A low growl suddenly came from the shadows. Bummer sank his teeth into Jack's upper left thigh. Screaming in pain, he staggered away from the dog, and fled from the Nelson house.

Fifteen minutes later, Jessie Dalton walked up to the fire pit, offering Boone and his four friends a worried look. "Jack just left," Boone told the private investigator. "He bloodied us up pretty badly."

Reason said, "Jack was ripped on one of those Sky Ripper pills."

Boone herded the battered members of his old team into his car to give them all a ride home. He looked to Jessie and said, "See if you can't talk sense into my little brother, will you? Do whatever it takes to get that evidence from the bank."

Chapter Seventeen

Five minutes later, Reason and Vince sat at the Pit in the Nelson's backyard, where Jessie interrogated them about the evidence from the bank. As he addressed them, Collin approached the yard with Harley and Ben Black Bull trailing him. Ben offered Jessie a curious look, asking, "Why am I here, Jess? Why did you call me?"

Jessie said, "Billy told me to find Harley a new home. He told me to find someone who loves dogs. It would prove to Reason he kept his word. For some reason that seemed important to Billy."

Ben kneeled down. "Come here," he gently coaxed the Rott. Harley padded forward and rolled over and offered the Native his belly to scratch. "So, who did this monster dog belong to? Why am I privileged to take him into my custody?"

"Nate Holland," Reason said. "He's been locked up."

Ben sat down in a lawn chair. Harley settled in at his feet. Reason was amused to witness the Lakota dog handler talking to Harley in that rare language that humans revert to when smothering their dogs with affection. He knew then that Billy had made a wise choice. Ben was going to provide a good home for the Rott.

Ben said, "Did you find that map?"

Reason shrugged and went strangely silent.

Jessie nailed Reason with a stern look. "If I had this disk it could put Jack away for good. I have a paternity test that confirms Jack sentenced his unborn child to death. Before she got involved in this mess, Kelly had a meth addiction. She entered your mom's program at Saint Pat's. Rose was her sponsor. To help stay clean and sober, Kelly determined she was going to clean up the streets. But in the end, it was this that got her killed.

"Several years ago, Jack Holland ran a gang known as the Renegade Crew. They stole millions from dealers in the trade. But one night during a raid on a pharm the Crew caused four men to drown in the Platte River. However, one dealer survived, and due to his testimony against the Crew, Jack's entire gang were arrested. Ten members went to prison.

"Jack shot and killed this dealer using a .22 Ruger pistol. After the hit, he began robbing Nebraska dealers. Kelly infiltrated his crew as a narc. Upon discovering her identity, Jack shot her with the same .22 Ruger pistol. At the time, Logan Young was a courier for Jack. That night, after stealing the gun from him, Logan broke into the Emerald to confiscate the DVD of Kelly's murder. During the burglary, Logan and old man Connors scuffled. The gun went off. The bullets struck the wall above the fireplace, leaving two round holes in the award the IRA gave Billy. Ballistics linked the gun to Kelly's murder.

"Logan jumped a train at the yards, but he came back. The jacket you took from Nate's party? It belonged to Logan. He was there at Nate's that night to set up Jack. He was the one who placed all the evidence in the safe-deposit box at the bank. The gun and the DVD."

Jessie's stern look creeped Reason out. "Give me the evidence you took from the bank," he said.

To which Reason responded, "I can't. I don't have it."

***

The next afternoon, Reason and Vince shared with Jenna the story they had heard at the Pit the night before. Jenna shook her head in disbelief. "Kelly was pregnant? Maybe, your mom blames herself for Kelly's murder? Once the girl got herself clean through your mom's program, she decided she needed to do something about the drugs on the streets. As if her becoming an informant made any difference in the scheme of things. But to keep herself from using, she had to feel she was making an impact on others. Your mom works her program, impacting so many others, that it gives her a feeling of accomplishment. Can you imagine how good she feels about herself, to have been a former user, then help others who are where she used to be. Your mom has an amazing career. She has a purpose in life."

Vince said, "Too bad her son can't seem to find his way out of the drug culture. Nothing like a little recreational pot smoking to clear your mind. After all, life ain't complicated enough without all those chemicals bouncing around inside your head. Didn't all that stuff we heard last night, smack you in the face? Logan being Nate's courier? Him being at Nate's party? Jack had a relationship with Kelly?"

On the walk over to Collin's house, Jenna and the two boys passed by the Joyo theater. "The Bum Lords," Reason said, gesturing at the five scruffy-looking men who commonly occupied the corner. "That grizzled old man is Franco. Born in Italy, Franco discovered his wife sleeping with another man, so he killed them both with a knife. Franco was then exiled from Italy and ended up here in Havelock. George and Louie stand on Bum's Corner. Kids call them Opey and Dopey. And that man with the purple straw hat that's Newt."

Pointing at the enormous hulk of a man dressed in blue denim overalls, he said, "Aaron looks menacing, but the only time he ever gets mean is when he's drinking. He's tough on the outside, but on the inside, he floats like a butterfly."

Rose Nelson stepped out of the Catholic Social Service building situated on the opposite corner and approached the Misfits on Bum's Corner. Reason said, "My mom cares about those oddballs. She even includes them in her group sessions down at St. Pat's every Saturday night. Those guys are always three sheets to the wind come Sunday morning. Once, they even got arrested for disturbing the peace when they started singing the National Anthem at the top of their lungs right there on Bum's Corner. At three in the morning!"

When Collin approached them, he had a smile on his face. He said, "Billy Connors outlined his plans for that youth center he's trying to start. He left me with all these flyers to pass out. He only needs like two-hundred residents to sign some petition."

Vince and Jenna took interest in Collin's campaign, but Reason said, "If all those potheads mobbing the park ain't enough to let people know us kids need help, then some stupid flyers ain't gonna make a difference. People will just ignore them, like they do us kids."

Chapter Eighteen

Four blocks away from Havelock Avenue, at the clubhouse of the Elder's Den, Stone Holland raised his shotgun. "Easy, Dad. Keep your hands where I can see them. You bonded out of jail? That was foolish to go after Rain's kid."

Jack asked, "What did you call this meeting for?"

Stone watched him closely, one finger resting on the trigger of his gun. "To let you know Nate and I never betrayed you. You thought Nate placed that evidence in that bank. And we thought it was you. That kid, Logan, played a number on all of us."

Jack said, "In the trade, killing threats is the order of business. Nate? Brooks? Logan? You? You all gotta go!"

Jack raised his pistol. Stone raised his .12 gauge and pulled the trigger. Jack would have taken the blast to his chest, but Stone was hesitant to kill his own father. Jerking the gun to the left as he fired, the close range shot sent hundreds of lead pellets blasting through the front window of the clubhouse. In the next second, Jack hurled himself through the shattered picture window.

Two blocks down the street from the shootout, Vince and Collin stopped in the middle of an intersection, both startled by the sound of the gunshot. "What was that?" Collin asked, squinting to see the bald man running toward a Thunderbird parked in the street nearly a hundred yards away. Having nearly run out of flyers, Vince tucked the last few he had into his back pocket. The two boys stood there in the center of the street, both looking on in confusion as Brooks pulled out of the distant alley in his white BMW. They watched as Jack gunned his Thunderbird and drew even with Brooks speeding down the street.

Vince latched onto Collin.

The two cars slammed together with a horrifying **Crunch!** Tires screeched loudly, and inside the Thunderbird, Jack banged his head slumped in his seat, his car now set on a dangerous collision course with the boys. Shoving Collin toward the nearby curb, Vince was then struck by the bumper of the oncoming Thunderbird. One second, he had been there hurling Collin out of the street. A split second later, he was gone, the flyers fluttering to the ground behind him.

A block down the street, Reason watched in stunned amazement as Vince slammed into a curb, coming to rest in a broken heap ten yards beyond the intersection. Brook's car flew up and over the curb and slammed into a tree. Jack sped away down the street. Finding it hard to breathe, Reason ran toward Vince's shattered form. Dazed, he kneeled down, his left hand coming to rest on Vince's chest. He was barely aware of distant sirens. Reason looked up to see Beef bending over to examine Vince.

"Leave him!" he whispered.

But the cop remained there. Enraged by the senseless tragedy, Reason let out a fierce yell and sprang up, savagely swinging at Beef. The officer latched onto his shoulders. Shouting in protest Reason lashed out, his fists striking Beef in the center of his chest. Beef pinned his arms against his sides and gazed down into his eyes. Reason buried his face against his chest and broke down, crying, "Vince is dead, Beef! Vince, of all people! He's dead!"

***

For the next two days, Reason spent most of his time sulking up in the Loft. The initial shock had passed, but it was replaced by such a deep depression that he refused to talk with anyone. Deeply concerned about him, Collin attempted to break through the sorrow that kept everyone else at bay. "The funeral," he said, joining Reason in the Loft, "will be held in the morning. In the meantime, Vince will lay in state at Roper Mortuary. You should go see him one last time. Brooks is still in the hospital with a concussion. The cops have an APB out on Jack. He's gone into hiding. My brother's death was tragic, but Fate has a strange way of dictating who leaves and who gets to stay. We're all going to die someday. You. Me. Bummer. No one gets out of here alive. A tragedy like this makes you think that our life on earth is like a cloud of vapor on a winter morning. There for seconds before it vanishes. Like walking down a muddy road after a summer rain, you leave footprints, then they fade. You make your mark, then you're gone."

Despite his own sadness of losing his brother, Collin spent the rest of the day with Reason, trying to comfort him, and yet nothing he said helped to cheer him up. Before he left him later that evening, he said, "Reason? I don't want to press you, but if you know anything about that missing evidence, you should let someone know."

That night, Reason and Bummer walked down to the mortuary. After commanding Bummer to stay put in the alley behind the place, Reason climbed in through a window. He explored the building until he discovered the viewing room. Parting the heavy red curtains, he stopped before the open casket and stared down at his dead friend. Vince's features were illuminated by a dim light from the ceiling above, causing him to look as if he were resting peacefully.

Reason reached out, wanting to touch his folded hands, but he hesitated. *What will they feel like?* he thought. *Will they be warm or cold? How will I put them back in place if they fall?*

He placed his hand on Vince's interlocked fingers. They were neither warm nor cold. They were just there beneath his hand, solid and firm. Quietly, he said, "Sorry about the way things turned out. If I could have done anything about the wreck, I would have. I've been wishing for days now that it had been me, instead of you. You were just starting to get your act together. Me? I'll keep screwing up the rest of my life. Remember that night when you pointed down the street at the stained-glass window of Jesus carrying that lamb? You were right. I am lost. It's just that life is so hard. I need to get high. It's too hard to change. If you made it to heaven, put in a good word for me, but remind God how stubborn I can be. If he ever comes searching for me like a shepherd trying to rescue a lost lamb, I'll need clear directions to find my way.

"Vince? There will never be no one else like you. I'll remember our times together forever. Racing bikes at the track. Skateboarding in the culvert. Fishing at Dog Lake. Camping at Stephen's Creek. Riding golf carts into that pond. The fire extinguisher fight at school. Swiping melons from Avery's garden. Sleeping out in the Loft on summer nights."

Tears streamed down his cheeks. For long moments, he quietly wept. Sobs wracked his entire body as he let go of the sorrow that had been building up for the past several days.

***

The next day after Vince's burial service at Fairview Cemetery to the east of Havelock, Reason remained behind at the grave site. Rose and Vince's mom were escorted by the Mendoza brothers. Jenna and Collin walked along beside Father Witt, the priest from Saint Pat's. Billy Connors climbed into his Blazer where Doug Kaluza waited for him. As the cars exited the cemetery Reason looked over at Logan standing thirty feet away in front of an angel statue beside another grave. Logan plucked flowers from a vase beside the angel.

"Logan?" Boone said. "Leave those alone."

"She won't mind, Boone," Logan said. "She's dead." He placed the plastic flowers on top of Vince's casket.

As he pointed at the bronze statue of the kneeling angel holding a sword up in her hands, Logan read the plaque at the angel's feet, "Kelly Drake. It's Kelly's grave."

Chapter Nineteen

That night, at three AM in the morning, Collin came banging on the front door, waking up Reason, Boone, and Rose with his pounding. Bummer began barking furiously. Collin stood there on the porch, out of breath as he said, "Logan started a fire in Nate's cellar!"

By the time Reason reached the alley behind Nate's place, he watched in astonishment as dozens of rockets shot out of the fire blazing in the depths of Nate's storm shelter. Bright bursts of fireworks filled the night sky, their explosions deafening, the percussions of their blasts felt by everyone in the gathering crowd. Three fire trucks and four police cruisers blocked one end of the alley, and six firemen used two separate hoses to douse the flames rising from the opening of the cellar. As they did, Reason looked past them to the park less than a block away.

There he saw Logan on the roof of the north shelter, draping a cloth banner down the front of the low wall running around its roof. The stone safety wall stood three feet high, but the banner covered its surface, and Reason could see what Logan had painted in bright, red letters on the blue cloth: *Havelock Needs a Wreck Center!*

Suddenly a loud roar came from the cellar. Several firemen in the yard were struck by a barrage of hissing rockets. Two of the men took direct hits, causing their hose to spin out of their grasp and thrash around like an enraged snake, sending streams of water directly into the crowd in the alley. In all the chaos and confusion, Reason slipped away from the crowd. Darting between two fire trucks at the end of the block, he ran around to the back of the shelter. There he clambered up the aluminum ladder he found leaning against the park building. Once he reached the top rung, he pulled himself over the safety wall encircling the shelter's roof, and looked up to see Logan, a .22 pistol in his grasp. "What are you trying to prove?" Reason asked.

Logan waved the gun. "Hopefully, a reporter will come down here and take a picture of my banner! When people read my banner on the News, they'll donate tons of money to the youth center!"

He laughed as he aimed the pistol at the transformer box ten yards away. He then cocked the hammer, and slowly squeezed the trigger. The gun produced a dull *Click!* Logan cocked the gun again and fired. "Empty," he muttered.

Reason looked over the wall of the roof to see Beef Tory running toward the shelter. A loud hissing filled the air, and one of the rockets from inside of Nate's underground arsenal zipped off and exploded against a nearby transformer box. A brilliant globe of light engulfed the box and a thunderous roar echoed across the park. The force of the blast sent the large metal box crashing noisily into the side of one of the fire trucks. As firemen scrambled for cover behind their vehicles, sudden bursts of purple light exploded in the air above them, momentarily blinding Logan.

Streaks of lightning rippled across the sky, and the muggy air became thick with the promise of a summer rainstorm. Reason peered at the street below packed with squad cars and fire trucks. A black van stopped and a SWAT team exited the vehicle.

Logan stared in alarm at the top of the ladder leaning against the rear wall of the shelter roof. It was moving. It appeared that someone was attempting to climb it. With a growl of rage, Logan sprang to his feet. Reason leaped up, latching onto him. Muttering angrily, Logan thumbed the hammer back, aiming the pistol at Beef appearing at the top of the ladder. Reason shouted, "His gun is empty!"

Aiming his pistol up at Logan, Beef drew a bead on his head. "Don't shoot!" Reason cried, momentarily blinded by beams from dozens of flashlights brightly illuminating Logan as he struggled to regain control of the pistol. "No!" Reason cried, giving one last pull on the gun, causing Logan to topple over the front of the roof and fall ten feet to the ground. Reason struck himself in the nose with the butt of the gun as he yanked it out of Logan's grasp. Blood leaked from his nose. "Sick!" he gasped, just before passing out.

***

In the morning, Reason had a visit from a local newspaper reporter. Two days later, when the story came out, it spread through Havelock like wildfire. Having a flair for dramatics, the reporter explained why Logan had taken such desperate actions to bring the youth center to the public's attention. The article actually motivated a few local residents to donate money for the center, and Billy received a phone call from an inmate at the State prison who sent him a donation to purchase recreation equipment.

Reason found himself seated on the front porch with Bummer at his feet. "How's your nose?" Jenna asked.

Reason made a face. "I'll live. Logan is back out at the psych ward. I at least kept him from getting blown away."

Jenna handed him the black gym bag she was carrying. "Danny called from treatment this morning. He said that during group therapy there was talk about the incident at the park. After I told him Logan had used the pistol from the bank, Danny told me where to find it. In our garage."

Reason opened the bag to find the DVD inside. He said, "Once Jessie gets it, he'll put Jack away. The city prosecutor wants to cite me for meddling. I best hand it over to Billy Connors. At least that way, the old Irishman might keep me out of the mix."

Night had fallen by the time Reason set out for the Emerald. Bummer ran ahead of him, marking half a dozen trees. Reason kept up a steady pace behind him, his bat in one hand and the gym bag in the other. "This is spooky," he whispered. "Creeping down to the Emerald in the dark to face old man Connors."

Reason stopped and stared at the black van parked in the alley before them. Jack sprang out of the van. He held a gun. Bummer came running back down the sidewalk. Reason dropped the gym bag, saying, "Fine! Take it! Just don't shoot my dog."

Jack turned his head to glance back down the alley as a commotion came from the shadows thirty feet behind his van. There, gathered around a garbage dumpster, were the Misfits from Bum's Corner. Franco the Italian suddenly stood up inside of the large dumpster. He cackled with glee as he held up a gallon bottle of wine. Franco whooped, "Holy Mary, Mother of God!"

"Say, Mister," Newt said, adjusting the wide-brimmed Mexican sombrero he wore on his head, "is that a real gun?"

Upon seeing the gun in Jack's hand, the two dwarfs, George and Louie, slipped behind the hulking figure of Aaron, who stood there, a menacing look on his bearded face. "If it is," Newt said, "you shouldn't be pointing it at us. Someone might get hurt."

Not at all liking Aaron's fierce sneer, Jack raised his pistol.

"Leave them alone," Reason said. "They aren't bothering you. They're harmless. All they are doing is dumpster diving."

Aaron growled, "Mister, if you don't point that gun somewhere else, I am coming to take it away from you!"

Jack fired his gun. A second later, the wine bottle in Franco's hands exploded, drenching the old Italian with red wine. Franco stood there, too shocked to move. Yelping in fright, George and Louie scurried behind the dumpster. Newt sagged against the grocery cart, his sombrero falling to the ground. Aaron scooped up the metal cart and heaved it directly at Jack's van, sending dozens of liquor bottles crashing into the side of it. Reason scooped up the bag. Bummer trailed him down the alley as he ran to the end of the block. On the way home, he expected Jack to come barreling up behind him, but the Misfits had provided a distraction. When he and Bummer came up the driveway, Boone came off the porch, gesturing at the gym bag Reason carried. He said, "Is that the DVD of Kelly's murder?"

***

Two hours after Jessie received the evidence from Reason, he came back over to the house. The two met on the front porch. Jessie said, "Strange story about that pistol. It was used during Kelly's murder. Ballistics proved it was the gun used. The DVD shows the conspiracy that started in the Emerald's outdoor café four years ago. Brooks and Jack are seated at a table in the Emerald's open-air café. The two men look up as Kelly sat down at a table across from them. Jack shot her, then went to Nate's to inform him of the hit. While he was inside, Logan swiped the Ruger pistol out of his car, then broke into the Emerald and confiscated the disk of Kelly's murder. He was trying to fix things by placing that evidence in that deposit box.

"Your mom asked me to conduct this intervention. She thinks it's time you do normal things. Bike racing. Skateboarding. Playing video games. Instead of getting wasted on anything you can get your hands on. Your dad towed a strict line when it came to drugs. Rain was against the club having a thing to do with them. Recovery from addiction starts with accepting help from a Power that's beyond your own strength."

He looked up as seven falling stars suddenly blazed a path through the night sky. "Whoa!" Reason said, amazed.

Jessie said, "Those seven falling stars? Perhaps, an omen from God. Falling stars mean different things to different people. I used to think they indicated how I would die going out in a blaze of glory. But things changed. I realized, yes, they might blaze a fiery path, just remember what eventually happens to falling stars."

"What's that?" asked Reason.

Jessie simply said, "They burn out."

69

***

Seated alone in the park, watching Jessie drive away, Reason was startled by the Nomad approaching the shelter where he sat. "I want that map," the bald man with the twin stags tattooed on his dome said, sternly. "I need to reclaim those relics, kid."

"Storm?" Reason said, staring curiously at the sudden appearance of the black wolf. The wolf moved in front of the Nomad, a low growl coming from deep in his throat.

The Nomad froze. "What the hell is this?" he said.

Very slowly, he backed away, smirking at Reason as he wove his way between the trees.

When Reason turned to thank the spirit wolf, the black beast was gone once more, leaving him shaking his head.

<h1 style="text-align:center">Chapter Twenty</h1>

The humid days of a Nebraska summer slowly passed. September breezes swept in with their gentle rains. With one more summer gone, another year of school began. Reason, Collin, Jenna, and Danny entered Middle school together. All of them unaware that the unseen door of their childhood had closed tightly behind them. And like all the other kids moving down the halls around them, they were all now passing into adolescence. Whether they were ready or not.

Now that school had started, Reason tried to put the tragic events of the summer behind him. But Vince's death kept nagging at him. After constantly struggling with his feelings on the matter, he began to self-medicate and resort to using the vodka he'd stored in his tree house, mixing it with pop. He then got into quite a habit of drinking some before school and drinking more in the evening.

On a sunny day in October, Reason planted himself on the porch swing, pulling a metal flask from his jacket pocket. He unscrewed the cap and took a swallow of vodka mixed with orange soda, when Jenna came bounding up onto the porch. "We hit the paper!" she said, a newspaper in her hand. "An anonymous donor paid for a year's rent on the Goodwill building down on Havelock Avenue."

Reason raised the flask and toasted, "To Havelock delinquents!"

Jenna said, "You can't keep drinking yourself numb to forget about him. Vince wouldn't want that. He thought that all the dope you smoke kept you from thinking straight. I think your problem goes deeper than getting high. When you were a little kid and got in trouble with the courts, you didn't care if it upset your mom or your brother. You are so worried that nobody cares about you, you'll do anything to get noticed. You don't know the difference any more between good attention and bad."

Reason leaned forward, puckering his lips for a kiss. He planted a sloppy kiss on her chin. Pulling her into his arms, Reason clung to her. As she struggled, Jenna slapped him full in the face. She said, "You need help, Reason. Until you quit being so stupid, don't bother wondering whether you've hurt my feelings or not! Because I could really care less about your pathetic need to self-destruct!"

After the incident with Jenna, Reason spent the following two days mentally kicking himself for being so stupid. In an effort to set things right, he remained sober and was determined to stay that way until he made up with her. He asked for Boone's help. Boone invited him to a fire at the Pit that evening. Doug Kaluza came in through the back door. Behind him, followed Tiger who carried a twelve-pack of soda. Boone opened the fridge and tossed him two packs of hot dogs. Doug said, "Boone, did you ever tell Reason why you quit boxing a year ago?"

Boone refused to meet Doug's gaze as he followed Tiger outside to the Pit in the backyard. They spent the next two hours drinking pop, and talking while the crackling blaze ate away at six large logs. Doug entertained them with grisly stories of unsolved murders and ghost sightings. Tiger told them about his midnight encounter with Bloody Mary, and he swore that he'd once seen the Salt Creek Creature out at Pigman's behind Mary's farm.

As Reason listened to the creepy stories, he kept glancing at Boone who remained strangely quiet. And only Reason seemed to notice his brother's brooding as he stared down at the smoldering pile of red coals. Doug said, "Why did you walk away from the fights?"

Muttering angry oaths, Boone started to rise from his log seat. "You afraid," Doug asked, "we'll think less of you?"

Boone sat back down. "I stepped into the ring twenty-three times, and only lost three matches. I quit while I was ahead. Because I just didn't know how I'd live with myself if my career ended in a series of losses. The Kaluza Kid is pretty much unstoppable, right? But Tiger and I were there the night you boxed some fighter from Kansas. You broke your hand on the guy's face. The match was stopped, with the win going to the guy from Kansas. The dude won, but Tiger came out of the sports complex and found the guy standing at a bus stop. Alone. No fans. No friends. No girl on his arm. Just a boxer with a battered face, holding his trophy. Tiger congratulated him, and the guy got all choked up. He won, but nobody noticed. Fighting is bad enough when you lose. But to win like that and get no recognition, left that guy in a sad place. So I quit. Like a bull elephant, who one day loses his place in the herd, and like a lion, who can't be king of his pride forever, there's always gonna be someone badder than me."

***

The next evening, Danny Kane showed up, having just come from a fight with his mom. He said, "Ever since I got on diversion my mom thinks I got emotional problems."

Looking at the little kid, Reason said, "Talk about mental. When I was a little kid, if I wasn't fighting at recess I was hassling teachers

72

or sitting in the quiet room. I still remember what my principal said the day he caught me smoking in the bathroom in fourth grade: *'You've started out bad early in life. If you continue on this road, get used to places like the quiet room. You are heading for a long stay in many more quiet rooms. One day, you'll find four walls surrounding you in prison, for there's no place in society for a wild horse you cannot tame!'*

"The weird thing is that's how I always felt just before I got into trouble, like a wild horse. I'd let all that bad energy out. Get caught. Sit in a cop car. Get a ticket. Go to court. Stand before the judge. Up until he ordered an evaluation on me and sent me to detention, where therapists tried to figure me out. Their reports said: Needs to be noticed. Acts out with no thought to the consequences. Delinquent behavior caused by a poor self-image. After I got released from detention, Boone took me out to the Nature Center and showed me this falcon that can soar at speeds of seventy miles per hour locked in a cage! Boone told me that if I didn't stop getting into trouble, I'd become like a caged falcon. And then he told me this story about a herd of wild horses in Wyoming that was going to be destroyed unless they could be broken."

"And," Danny asked, "they tamed them, right?"

"No," Reason said. "The horses were too wild. Too feral. They had no clue the ranchers were only trying to help them. Strange, but all those people who tried to straighten me out, Mom, Judge Sully, and Boone, they all told me what my problems are. But no one ever told me how to quit being like a wild horse."

Reason and Danny slept out in the Loft that night. Sounds drifted through the evening air. A train horn sounded down in the yards. Crickets chirped steadily from nearby. Down the street, a neighbor's dog barked, wanting in for the night. Two other dogs mocked him, yapping in steady bursts that sounded like laughter. Again a horn echoed from the yards.

Reason dozed off and heard Bummer's sudden bark. He looked down from the Loft to see Danny stumbling toward the porch. Holding up a toilet paper tube and a can of aerosol deodorant, Danny sprayed it into one end of the paper tube, then held the tube up to his face and inhaled. Danny suddenly began gasping for air. He fell backward, his head slamming into the porch steps. Danny lay there motionless, his face pale. He wasn't breathing. A fierce wind ripped Danny up from the walk and he went spiraling through the trees.

Reason then saw Vince wreathed in a bright mist. Long, dark hair trailed over his shoulders and his blue eyes sparkled brightly. Vince sadly shook his head, pulling Danny to his feet and a white mist rolled down and engulfed them.

Upon coming to, Reason felt Danny slapping his hand away as he staggered to his feet. Sucking in great gasps of air, Danny started bawling and ran off into the night.

Chapter Twenty-One

The next morning, Reason woke up to find Rose seated across the room at his desk. A frown creased her dusky features as she held up the empty bottle of vodka he had downed late last night. Rose said, "I've been sitting here wondering if Boone should include this in his next probation report, Reason. If he did, Judge Sully would send you away. I came to invite you to a meeting taking place at the center tonight. I'm speaking there tonight to kids from juvenile court."

Reason looked to the bottle she held. "Is this like a Scared Straight program? If so, not interested. It was optional, right?"

Rose said, "Yes, of course. But, do I really have an option to report this to Boone?"

Rose glanced down at the bottle, letting Reason know in uncertain terms that his probation hung in the balance.

"Collin," Rose said, "suggested I invite you. His older brother was one of my cases when I first started my NA program. Logan was a real pistol. No matter how hard I tried to get him to quit using, Logan just wouldn't listen. I tried during his probation term to keep him clean, but he failed four tests in a row and was on the edge of getting sent to treatment when Logan quit. Just like that. Logan used to write poems in an old notebook. He called his words, seeds. He used to say that after listening to my words for so long, my ideas were starting to grow on him. Like seeds planted in the ground. He used to say my seeds had taken root and brought him to a crossroads."

The main hall of the center was crowded with adults and kids. As Reason sat down behind the crowd, he saw a group of kids taking up the middle section of seats. On either side of them were counselors, probation officers, police officers, and parents. Reason figured each of them had a kid on probation, and now they were there before the eyes of the world, because of their unlawful behaviors. Boone took the stage to get things rolling. "Our speaker here tonight is the director of the drug treatment program offered by Saint Patrick's church. Rose Nelson is here tonight to share her own personal story with you. Mom? The stage is yours."

The audience applauded and Rose took the stage. When she spoke, her green-eyed gaze came to rest on the large group of kids who were attending the meeting at the request of juvenile court. Reason listened, amazed at how she never once talked down to the kids in front of her. That was one thing Rose had a talent for, speaking directly to kids. She called it her Irish "gift for gab," but Reason often thought it was magical the way she could look him directly in the eye and tell him what was on her mind. As she was doing with these kids seated before her now.

Rose gave them all a brief account of how she became addicted to drugs at an early age, and how those addictions impacted her life. She did not gloss over her former life as the wife of the president of the now disbanded biker club known as the Outlaws. Rose only glanced at Reason once during her speech when she spoke of the shooting that had removed his father, Rain Nelson, from their lives ten years past. This talk of her former days as a biker seemed to intrigue the kids, but Reason couldn't help but get a bit emotional when hearing the story about his dad. The sudden sorrow her words caused him, prompted him to leave the meeting. However, as he stood up to do so, Billy Connors entered the center. The old Irishman stood there alone, his eyes locked on the stage where Rose ended her speech.

Reason then heard his mom say, "What is he doing here?"

Curious, he turned to find Rose glaring at Boone as he welcomed Billy to the stage. As Billy stood there before the podium, he greatly reminded Reason of the writer, Mark Twain, with his white hair and mustache. He stared at the crowd, his blue-eyed gaze coming to rest on kids sent there at the request of juvenile court. Billy said, "I'm Will Connors. Seventy-years old. Most of those years I've caused myself shame to have someone I love disown me as her father."

In the back row, Reason followed his gaze, and it appeared that the old Irishman was staring directly at Rose. To his surprise, he saw Rose returning his steady stare with a fiery one of her own. On the stage, Billy said, "I own the Emerald, providing folks with Nebraska beef and a few drinks to help them relax. Not all have a problem with addictions. Difference between those folks and myself is, they can handle it. I cannot. I've been clean and sober for the past seven years. The consequences of my actions led me down a fool's road. You kids who have ingested, smoked, sniffed chemicals, those chemicals build latch onto your brain like microscopic ticks, telling you that you need to keep feeling good. If you can't feel good in life anymore unless it's by a drug-induced high, what the hell's wrong with you? You see, this treatment might keep some clean, but the only real solution to keeping you clean and sober comes down to only one thing: You!

"And I want to tell you about that funny weed you're smoking. The THC in marijuana stays in your brain for months. It's been proven by scientists, that only half the THC leaves your body in a week. Once the potent stuff in the weed gets into your cells, it can't get itself back into the bloodstream. When a toker gets high, chemicals build up in the brain, then the high drops off, and tokers think they're straight, but the chemicals in weed are still active. It's called cumulative. You might feel the high and then think it wore off, but you're still stoned. And after so much smoking pot, a voice in your brain says you need to keep getting high. Marijuana has this chemical in it that touches the pleasure center, telling you that you need to keep feeling good. Before long, that's all that's important to you: Smoking weed to feel good. I have made many mistakes in my life. But the one thing I know for sure, the bottle no longer controls me. I control myself. I can let it burn me out inside, or I can take charge of myself!"

Having heard enough of the lecture, Reason headed toward the door, glancing back to see Billy offering an impish grin to the crowd.

* * *

That evening, Boone caught Reason sitting on the front porch swing, sipping from his flask. He had not had time to ask Rose about what had transpired at the treatment center. She had stayed behind after the meeting to visit with many of her own clients who had attended. Reason was so blitzed he did not even try to hide his flask. Boone asked, "Did you even hear one word Billy said today?"

Offering him a drunken grin, Reason said, "Haven't you heard, Boone? It runs in our family. Mom. Me. Grandpa Billy. How come mom never told us that old Irishman was our granddad? I saw the look he gave Mom when he talked about disowning him as a father. *Her father* is what he said, and Mom shot daggers back at him! If looks could kill, Billy would have been dead!"

Boone said, "Mom has her reasons for . . . disowning him."

"Because of his drinking?" Reason asked. "Or because he was a gun-runner? Or just because he's such a crotchety old bastard?"

Boone said, "You're drunk. When Billy talked about taking control, did you have a clue he might have been speaking to you? Until recently, your consequences have been detention or probation. But now, I'm afraid you're becoming an alcoholic."

He then retreated inside the house. Dismissing Boone's concerns with an angry snort, Reason stormed outside to the tree house and

77

retrieved another bottle of vodka. An hour later, totally ripped on the alcohol, Reason staggered into the garage. When he returned to the backyard, he carried a stool and a length of rope. Walking over to stand beneath the tree fort, he placed the stool under a support board. Climbing up on the stool, he slung the rope over the board, placed a hastily tied noose over his head, and pulled it tight around his neck. Staring down at Bummer seated at the foot of the tree, he said, "I love you, dog, but gotta go now."

Bummer cocked his head, offering Reason a sad stare. Sensing that something was wrong, he began pacing nervously.

Reason said, "See you, dog." He then lost his balance and the stool toppled over beneath him. In that next instant, he suddenly realized what he was about to do. *No!* he thought as he slipped his fingers in between the rope and his neck. He then swung helplessly through the air, spinning around in a circle while the noose tightened, cutting off his air. Bummer began barking furiously. He was just starting to black out, when he felt a pair of arms encircling his legs. The noose suddenly went slack and air slowly leaked back into his lungs.

"Boone!" shouted Rose, struggling to lift Reason higher. Boone appeared beside her, setting the stool upright. He climbed on top of the stool and hastily removed the noose from around Reason's neck. Together, Boone and Rose lowered him to the ground between them.

Bummer rushed up and licked his face, and Reason opened his eyes and sucked in a great gasp of air.

"Am I still alive?" he asked.

Rose and Boone exchanged concerned looks, while Bummer continued to lick Reason's face.

Chapter Twenty-Two

The next night, Reason stood at Vince's grave at Fairview Cemetery on the east edge of town. In the fading light of day, he looked to the western skies in the distance. Tucking tangles of hair behind his ears, he glanced at Rose standing beside him. With the rope burns on his neck reminding him of his botched suicide attempt, Reason figured after his foolish stunt, he deserved to hear what she had to tell him.

Rose said, "Suicide is a permanent solution to a temporary problem. Some put guns to their heads. Some overdose on pills. Some slit their wrists. Some kids hang themselves. Depression clouds their thinking. Instead of realizing how their death might impact those who love them, they check out. Some try to cope by turning to drugs. Many kids become addicted. Why do kids find it so hard to cope?

"I know the kind of sorrow that invades your heart like a demon twisting inside you. Ten years ago when your dad was removed from our lives, I drank an entire bottle of rum. I ended up in the Emerald's parking lot. My father, who had never been there for me once in his miserable life, found me there. During my recovery in the hospital, Billy came to tell me I should never have shut him out of our lives, as if you and Boone would have been so much better off with his drunken guidance. I vowed I would never become my father. That plaque he keeps in memory of your grandmother. She went back to Ireland to plead with the party leader of the Sinn Fein to end his relations with your grandfather. While there, she was killed in an car accident. And Billy quit drinking, but serious damage had been done to our relationship."

The two of them stood there, taking in the silence of the autumn night. Like a regal queen, the silver moon rose in the east, and like sparkling gems upon her crown, clusters of stars shone brightly around her. An owl hooted in a distant tree. An answering call came from nearby cedar trees. Traces of wood smoke drifted on the chilly breezes. Rose gently touched Reason's neck, her sights on the angel kneeling next to Kelly's grave less than twenty feet away. "You've become a casualty in an ancient war. Drugs were used in ancient societies to connect to the spirit world. The Greek word for pharmacy is sorceries. At one time, sorcerers used drugs to predict the future for the kings they served, to connect with the spirit realm. You cannot connect with that realm without being affected. When you step into the world of drugs, you touch upon forces that are unseen, yet their power is revealed in the casualties they inflict. Dads. Sons. Moms. Daughters. And none are safe from their unseen workings."

Giving Reason a hug and a kiss on his forehead, Rose said, "In all the talks you've had with Ben, have you ever heard of the Red Road? I've never shared this story with you on account of your dad's lack of empathy for any race that is not white, but my great-grandfather, Amos Hawkins, was a riverboat captain. I imagined him looking like Samuel Clemens, who got the name Twain from River Jargon. Amos was sailing up the Ohio river during the Ohio floods when he met a Lakota woman, Rebecca Bowers, displaced from her rez due to the floods. Amos married her. They lived in Beatrice, Nebraska. One night, a ten-year-old boy was burned in a house fire. The doctor wanted to amputate the boy's legs, but Rebecca doctored him up using her Indian medicine on him. That boy grew up to be the Fire Marshall of Beatrice, thanks to my great-grandma, Rebecca Bowers.

"She was gone long before you were born. But as a little girl, I used to sit with her while she fed birds and squirrels inside her house. Yet, her legacy lives on. You should embrace your own heritage."

Sadly, Reason muttered, "Right now, I am lost. The Red Road to me is broken."

***

Two months passed by and winter set in. Reason still felt that God was a million miles away beyond the galaxy. Dreams about Vince continued and oftentimes left him more depressed than ever. Rose told him it was part of the grieving process, that in time the pain from his loss would grow less severe. He, however, didn't think he would ever get over Vince's death and he continued to self-medicate.

Despite the fact that Jack might still be stalking him, Reason went to the tree house and retrieved a bottle of vodka. He then headed down to Mahoney Manor. He sat there on the front steps, drinking and watching as huge snowflakes fell down so furiously that he could barely make out the nearby pine trees. He might have sat there longer, but when the midnight whistle blew at the Burlington shops, Reason was beginning to feel the chill of the winter night. Towering above him was the nine-story building of Mahoney Manor.

Reason crawled up the icy fire escape on his hands and knees. When he reached the window on the second floor, he fumbled around until the window slid open. When he reached the roof, he cautiously made his way toward the ledge at the front. There, he quietly said, "Remember how I used to talk to you when I was a kid? Lately, I've kind of forgotten about you. As you can see, I'm messed up. I used to think that you were cool. I sure hope so. I would not want you to get riled because I came here drunk. There are things I don't understand about you. Like for one, how come it had to be Vince that got killed? Vince was just getting his life together. He quit smoking weed and raising hell. So why did you take him? Vince was trying hard to be cool. Me? I don't care about no one.

"How come, if you're so great, why don't you make Logan right again? And why is a little kid like Danny getting all screwed up? And all these years Collin's been stressing about his wild brother. Hell, if you had power you'd fix Logan and the damage he suffered from all of the drugs he used. That's why I quit speaking with you. Because you were being like you are now, silent and distant. So far away. Too hard to figure out. That's all right. Because I got me. I don't need anyone else. I know why you don't give me answers. You probably never even hear my questions. You think I'm wasting my life? Well, I'm only living it up! I get high. That's my way of having a good time. I've got a reputation. I've got to let people know I'm cool."

He then tried to say a prayer that would connect him and forgive him and allow him to feel accepted. But then, his musings were disturbed, and like a rock thrown into a pool of calm water, ripples of doubt spread. He sadly realized he wasn't ready to take the path of recovery. He said, "Why would a God of the entire universe care one wit about me?"

Reason stepped out of the warm manor and was blasted by a strong north wind. When he heard footsteps behind him, he glanced back into the cold, hard eyes of Jack. He shot a straight punch at him. The blow caught Reason just above the bridge of his nose, reducing his world to a hazy shroud. When his senses kicked back in, he looked out through the open door of a car to see a patch of country stretching before him. It took him a few seconds to figure out he was in Fairview Cemetery, for there at the end of the driveway he could see the archway illuminated by blue moonlight. Jack raised his gun. "Come," he said. "Take your place beside her grave."

Reason climbed out of the car, noticing that he'd been made to take this ride in a white BMW. As foggy as his mind was, he moved around to the front of the car, and there he saw a broken grill, proving to him that it was indeed Jack who had struck Vince, resulting in the crash that killed him. Jack thumbed back the hammer on his pistol. The audible *click!* carried far on the night wind. Reason trudged through the drifts of snow, his hiking boots scrunching beneath him. As he approached the madman, his eyes strayed to the prone form sprawled on the ground between the graves. Jessie Dalton looked up painfully at Reason, blood dribbling down the side of his head. His hands were cuffed in front of him. As he struggled to sit up, red drops splattered the snowy ground.

Reason took his place beside the statue of a kneeling angel holding a sword in her two-fisted grip. Jack struck him hard in the chest with the barrel of his gun. Reason landed flat on his butt beside the angel. On the other side of the grave, Jessie struggled to his knees.

Jack snarled, "You foolishly think you make a difference? You think any effort you put forth will stem the tide? You're sticking one finger in the hole of a dike! But all around you, drugs just keep pouring through the cracks! For every thousands of dollars worth that you get off the streets, millions more pour through the floodgates! The drug trade is like a multi-headed snake! You lop off four or five heads, and they grow back! I wanted to carve a piece of the action out of the empire, and you had to send Kelly to take me down."

Jessie said, "What shall I tell your son, when I see him? You knew she was pregnant, didn't you? But you killed her anyway. And all this time you thought it was Stone's kid. It wasn't! It was yours! I've got the proof here."

As Jack leaned forward to see the paper the detective removed from his coat pocket, Jessie used the chain on his handcuffs to entangle Jack's gun hand. Four shots rang out. Two of the lead slugs struck the angel statue, chipping away at her stern face. One tore a chunk of bronze from her stony brow. The other splintered her left cheek, leaving a crease to her mouth that resembled a sorrowful frown. The two men fought over the weapon. Two more shots spat from the gun, whizzing through the cold air. Blinded by the red flashes erupting from the pistol, Reason heard a solid *thud!* directly in front of him: Reason scrambled for the gun. As Jack lunged to retrieve his gun, Jessie gave him one last shove, sending him flying directly into Reason. Jack tripped over him and fell on top of the angel statue, her metal sword driven through his chest.

Reason held up the pistol and aimed it at Jack hanging there, pierced by the angel's sword. "It's over," Jessie said, reaching out with his cuffed hands to remove the gun from Reason's tight-fisted grip. A sound like air escaping from a pierced bike tire hissed through the frosty air, and Jack gave a violent shudder. Jessie was tempted to let him bleed out, but he thought of his brother, Rain, and he knew if he had been left with the choice, Jack would surely have died. But Jessie was not wired like Rain, and he called an ambulance to let Fate deal with Jack.

The Nomad appeared there within the shadows of the trees, twin stags tattooed on his clean-shaven head. Stone Holland stepped up beside him and turned to lift a badly wounded Jack off of the sword. As Stone led Jack stumbling away into the darkness of the night, the Nomad hissed, "Another time, Jess Dalton."

To Reason he said, "And I still want that map."

Chapter Twenty-Three

Jessie drove them to the hospital. Other than a few bruises, Reason was okay. Jessie, however, needed a dozen stitches to close the gash in his forehead. Later that night, his mind in a whirl with Jessie's talk about addiction and recovery, Reason fell asleep, and he dreamed:

He walked up to the Joyo theater. Vince gestured across the street to Bum's Corner. The five odd men occupied the corner. Vince said, "Those Misfits are tragically symbolic of you in the way you just keep missing your mark in life. Franco digs for treasure in garbage cans. George and Louie stand on Bum Corner lost. Newt attracts attention, crying out for somebody to notice him. Aaron, tough on the outside but a butterfly within. Like Franco, you're searching for meaning in the wrong places. Like George and Louie, you've got no map to show you the way out of the juvenile system. Like Newt, you desperately want to be noticed. And like Logan, you've been on a collision course for disaster since you started using. Wasted life is a tragedy that plagues too many young boys. Boys on probation. In foster homes. In reform school. Boys who died of overdoses. Boys who committed suicide. All those boys had one thing in common. They all acted like life was one big game! Let me teach you a lesson."

Reason followed him into the Emerald's pool hall. Vince removed a pool stick from a wall rack. He systematically removed the balls from the table. Soon only the eightball remained. Looking down at the cue ball two feet from the eight, Vince said, "Let's say, it's your shot. I look defeated. You calmly chalk your stick. You look at me, smirking. You'll sink the eight and win the game. You make a jab! There's a hollow thump! The stick strikes the cue ball. It zips across the green and hits the eight. You grin in triumph. I groan in defeat. We watch the eight ball sink into the corner pocket, but then suddenly, the cue ball zips into the pocket behind the eight ball! Game over! If you don't quit scratchin' on the eight ball, your bad choices will cause you to lose in a tragic way. Ain't nothing on that road but dead ends, a dark cell, or a cold grave."

***

That next morning, Reason came to a crossroads. He'd been traveling to that point in time for a long while now, but did not realize he'd reached it, until one afternoon he had started a fire in the Pit in the

Nelson backyard. He'd burned up a bag of weed that Danny had given him, and two pipes and a bong. Reason tossed all three items into the blaze in the Pit. He had made a stand. Drew a line. Committed himself to sobriety. Vowed to say no. And to stay true to his vow, he had burned up anything that had to do with drugs. Yes, he might relapse. And yes, somewhere down the long road ahead, he might stray. But for now, he was done.

Jenna and Collin might not ever understand his need to get high, but they did know what would happen to him if he didn't overcome that need. And if they would be there for him as partners in sobriety, then Reason would accept their help. He knew, however, that the key to staying clean and sober had to do with one thing: Himself.

An hour later, down at the treatment center, Reason looked across the street to see Rose moving past the Emerald. She was illuminated by the giant stained-glass window depicting a dragon blowing red flames next to the pub's entrance. Reason caught up to her and said, "Are you ever gonna forgive Old man Connors, Mom?"

Rose said, "That is between Will Connors and myself. Not your concern. You want to claim him as your grandfather, that's on you."

There came a loud gunshot from inside the Emerald. Rose and Reason entered the pub to find Billy seated at a table, facing Logan, tangles of black, shoulder-length hair swept back from his shoulders. He was armed with a .44 Magnum handgun.

Billy said, "He's pissed about the girl, Rose. He thinks I should have done more to save her back in the day."

Logan said, "You could have run Jack out of Havelock!"

Logan took the gun in a two-fisted grip, aiming it at Billy's face. Billy sat there, stone-faced and calm. Rose said, "Logan, killing him will not bring Kelly back."

"No, Rose," Logan said, anguish in his eyes, "but it will send this old bastard before the throne so he can explain why he didn't call down the wrath of the Irish on Jack before he murdered Kelly!"

Billy said, "I cut my ties with those kind of men long before Jack ever invaded Havelock. That ended on the night I lost my wife."

Billy reached out with both hands, took hold of the barrel of the large gun, and planted the muzzle against his forehead. "Now, you tried this once before, and you failed. I'll make it easy for you."

"Dad?" Rose said. "Don't do this."

"Rosie," Billy said. "I've blamed myself each day of my miserable life since your mom's passing. This would be a welcome relief."

Logan hesitantly backed away, his eyes on Rose. It was his turn to be surprised. "Old man Connors is your father?"

"Yes," Billy sighed. "I'm her rotten bastard of a father. Get it done, son. End my misery."

Logan lowered the hammer and placed the pistol on the table. "Old man," he said. "You live because of her. Only because of her."

Reason sighed with relief as Logan turned and exited the pub, leaving Rose and Billy facing each other.

***

Upon leaving the Emerald, Reason walked home. When he entered the yard, he found Logan starting a fire in the Pit. He remembered Logan when he was fifteen. A tall, thin kid with shaggy black hair, an ever-present smirk on his face. A rebel, always in trouble. He shop-lifted. He burglarized cars. He smoked dope. He drank beer. He had been on probation by the time he was ten. At thirteen, his parents sent him to a Military Academy. Boone had tried to keep him from getting into trouble, but Logan refused to listen to him. He had been a disturbed kid, hell-bent on self-destruction. The night he'd ran away at the train yards, Logan hopped aboard a moving train. His departure from Havelock had a ripple effect on Collin, who loved him fiercely.

Reason, who dragged Collin home from the train yards every time he went down there in hopes of seeing his brother return, was now relieved to see Collin joining them there at the Pit. Logan used his free hand to ruffle Collin's hair. Boone sat in a lawn chair next to Logan. Reason sat on a log before the crackling blaze, and for a long while they talked about growing up in Havelock. Skateboarding at the Culvert. Fishing at Stephen's Creek. Swimming at Dog Lake. Racing at the bike track. Catching minnows at Dead Man's Run. Exploring the Havelock tunnels. Sneaking into Hobbitsville. Camping out at Bloody Mary's Woods.

Then, Collin looked directly at his brother and said, "Sorry it took so long to find your way home. Because we can't ever get those years back. Where did you go when you jumped that train?"

Logan said, "That train took me to Omaha. There, I vowed to come back here to take revenge on those who killed Kelly. After four years, Billy showed up in Omaha to offer me a chance to redeem myself for trying to kill him back when I was fifteen. There's two things in this world the old man hates with a passion. Drugs and the

86

injustice suffered by Mary Partington. As the owner of the Emerald, Billy hired Jess Dalton for security at Mary's place. You would not believe the kids Jess has chased out of her Woods. Before I went on run five years ago, I'd been a courier for Nate. Jack had to go down after he murdered Kelly. Jack is still a clear and present danger."

Hesitantly, Collin asked, "Are you done with drugs?"

"I'm in recovery, little brother," Logan said. "Who knows why kids stoop to such desperate measures to cope? A desperate kid will do most anything to end mental pain. Addictions require you commit to them. So does pain medication and you've got as many kids getting high off their parents' pain pills as kids who smoke dope. Jack is now robbing pharms all over Lincoln. I don't know what it takes to be the head of a drug cartel. I just know that drug lords become rich off the cravings of users. Kids who use their product become casualties in an ancient war. They touch upon forces unseen, yet their power is revealed in the casualties they inflict. It puts my own struggles to remain drug-free in a whole different perspective. It makes me more determined to have power over drugs."

Reason sat there, basking in the warmth of the fire, Bummer sprawled beside him. Gentle breezes ruffled his hair and the faint scent of roses lingered in the air. Boone, Logan, and Collin retreated inside the house, leaving Reason seated beside the smoldering fire. Peering up at the sky, he said, "You know what would really be cool? If you could send a bright star streaking across the sky right now. Like a sign that you're out there. I think that's why I started getting into trouble when I was a little kid. Because I always felt like I was alone. Maybe everyone does, I don't know. It's just once I started screwing up, it seemed I could never do anything right and felt pretty worthless. I used to think, who could care about me? Does it matter to anyone that I'm around? Would anyone ever miss me if I was gone? Is there anyone out there that I matter to? If you're out there, could you just let me know by sending out a shooting star? Just a slight blaze, and then I'll know that I'm not alone."

Watching the sky expectantly, Reason settled back onto his wood stump. He shifted about, almost afraid to blink for fear he'd miss a brilliant green comet soaring through the heavens. When a yawn escaped his lips, he realized he'd been sitting there holding his breath for long moments. Slightly disappointed, he stood up.

He nudged Bummer with one foot, then trudged toward the back door. Following behind Bummer, he glanced once more up at the sky.

Sighing in disappointment, he followed Bummer inside the house, closing the door behind him.

A moment later, a shooting star blazed a path across the sky.

Then faded.

And was gone.

Fourteen-year-old Reason resembled a scarecrow dressed in his black hoody, ragged jeans, and high-top tennies. Long, dark hair trailing over his shoulders, he ran toward the Cosgrove Apartments. It was midnight. Dread locks spilling down about his shoulders, JR Brooks led him up the steps of the complex. Reason was breathing heavily by the time they reached the landing at the top.

Standing in the doorway of one of the apartments, Danny Kane flicked black bangs out of his eyes and stepped out into the hallway. The 13-year-old was bean-pole thin. Dressed in a baggy red hoodie, tight blue jeans, and army boots, the little kid grinned like a weasel. "Reason, meet my business partner, JR Brooks."

Brooks offered Danny an irritated glare. Reason followed Danny through the open apartment door. He closed the door behind them, and joined Danny at a computer monitor. He realized they were staring at the hallway outside, and he could clearly see Brooks and a girl with long dark hair joining him. "Jenna?" Reason said.

Jenna said, "Where's my little brother, JR?"

A man with a shiny bald head dominated by the tatt of a green dragon, stepped up behind them. Jack Holland, president of the Elder's Den, drew out a pistol. The gun roared and red-hot lead tore through the wall beside the door. Brooks raised his hands. It was quite obvious to Reason that Jack was robbing the drug dealer. Jack thumbed back the hammer on the gun.

Jenna shoved him from behind, sending him down onto both knees. Struggling to stay upright, Jack shot Brooks in the chest. Jenna hauled off and smacked him directly in the nose. Jack fell to the ground. Jenna exited the hallway and ran down the steps beyond.

Rushing out into the hallway, Danny and Reason were quick to follow her. When they reached the alley, Jenna said, "You ran drugs for Brooks, so aren't you sad he's been gunned down and killed?"

Nodding, Danny said, "Yeah, sort of. But what I am really freaked out about is you slugging Jack like you did. It's a miracle he didn't shoot you down like he did Brooks!"

Reason said, "I'm telling Beef about this. He needs to arrest Jack for killing Brooks. Also for killing Kelly Drake."

Seemingly unfazed by the shooting, Danny asked, "You still going to Haven that community drug program run by your mom? Hell, you'll be back. Someone will pass you a joint. And you'll blow a whole year's sobriety in three seconds. The drugs I take are for pain relief. I will put anything in my system. I have this need to be blitzed, because something got triggered in me the first time I got high. I like the buzz. I love the dead zone. How many chemicals have I crammed into my system on my endless quest to get high?"

Jenna said, "Thousands of unknown chemicals floating around inside you, feeding off of you in their secret hiding place. If I could scan your system, I could detect where those chemicals are stored at, maybe see if they are doing damage to you as they creep through your system like microscopic ticks. Each one of those chemicals are parasites living off of you, their host—"

"Do I care?" Danny said. "Hell, no, let them cruise around inside of me. Can they really turn my brain cells into worthless mush?"

Reason looked over at him. "Let's get home. I need to call Beef."

***

After seeing the two safely back to the Kane house, Reason cut through the park on his way home. Still shaken by Brook's murder, he suddenly became aware that he wasn't alone. Ben Black Bull stepped out from beneath the trees. "Son of Rain," he said. "Any luck with that map?"

Reason sheepishly said, "Uh, Billy Connors said it was none of my business. Sorry, I don't know where it is hidden."

Ben escorted him to the Nelson house. When they arrived there, the Lakota man said, "My Grandfather from Pine Ridge told me the story of White Buffalo Calf Woman. Long ago, there was famine. A Lakota chief sent out two scouts to hunt for food. On their journey, they saw a beautiful young woman in white buckskin. One of them tried to claim her as a wife. His companion warned him that she was a sacred woman. The man ignored the other scout's advice. The scout embraced the woman, and a white cloud surrounded them. When it disappeared, only the woman and a pile of bones remained.

"The remaining scout was frightened, but the woman said she was holy. She told him to return to his encampment and prepare a feast. The woman's name was PtesanWi, which translates to White Buffalo Calf Woman. She taught the Lakota seven sacred rituals and gave them the sacred pipe the holiest of all worship symbols. PtesanWi then turned into a white buffalo calf that went running off."

90

Ben paused, then added, "Among the hidden relics is a pipe. I must give it to the Morning Star. She will be its keeper. As for that map?"

The Lakota man turned at a slight sound behind him. The Nomad appeared there, a long-bladed knife in hand. "It appears," he said, "we are both seeking this map, Black Bull. Say, kid, how far will I have to shove this knife into you before you give it up?"

His eyes wide in surprise, Reason looked on as Ben withdrew a single feather from beneath his jacket. It glowed with mystical power. The Nomad gasped in pain as Ben shoved the feather into his chest. There came a sizzle of light that erupted from the feather, and from that bright burst, a powerful wind sent the Nomad flying off his feet.

Before he could he rise, Ben wielded the arrowhead he held in his other hand and struck the Nomad between the eyes. He gasped once more and fell to the ground unconscious.

"If you say," Ben told Reason, "that you don't have the map, then so be it. But this man will not give up. He will visit you again, and I will not be there to protect you."

As Reason stood there trying to explain to the Lakota that he did not have a clue where the map was, Officer Tory pulled up in front of the house. In seconds, he had the Nomad cuffed and placed in his squad car. When he returned to the porch, Ben was gone. Still stunned by the display of magic, Reason simply sat down on the porch steps and said, "Could this night get any stranger?"

Chapter Twenty-Five

Reason reported Brook's murder to Beef Tory. The entire story came spilling out, with the exception of what Danny and Jenna were doing at the Cosgrove Apartments. In explaining the condition of the Nomad, he held back, not telling Beef about the mystical force field erupting from the feather and arrowhead. He kept that part of his tale a secret.

The next day, the County Attorney sent Beef to pick up Jenna and Danny to give depositions on what they had witnessed during the murder. Rose, running defense for the two kids, got into it with the County Attorney, warning him of Jack's ties the Elder's Den. She said it was dangerous to put that kind of pressure on kids. One word on the street that they were snitches, they would be in a world of hurt.

Boone voiced his concern when the County Attorney had Reason do his own deposition. He tried to convince the attorney that there was a long-standing feud between Rain Nelson and the Holland clan. He said it was imperative that Reason's name not be released prior to the arrest of Jack. It became clear to the attorney that the lives of three kids would be in danger if the Den learned of their testimony.

When Reason arrived home that day, he passed through the house, listening to the conversation taking place on the front porch. Stopping in the living room, Reason peered out through the screen door to see Boone standing there, his dark hair hung down his back in a braided tail. He heard his brother say, "Reason's commitment to stay drug-free changed things between us. After playing the heavy for all the years I'm grateful I can at last lighten up on him."

Seated on the porch swing, his long black hair glistening in the sunlight, Jessie Dalton said, "Jack is back searching for Native relics. Since Rain started serving time, your mom did not want you boys to meet him until you had grown up. Rain and I are brothers, same dad, different mothers. Our dad, president of the Outlaws, was knifed by the Nomad. Ten years later, Rain ended up at a rock quarry to deal with Jack's father. Daws drew a gun to kill him. Instead, Rain went to prison for Daw's murder. We spent our boyhood together. Hunted at Bloody Mary's. Fished at Dog Lake. Camped at Stephen's Creek. Swam in Dead Man's Run. Rain ran the Outlaws. I was his vice. The day he was arrested, I burned my colors and left the Outlaws."

Although Reason was intently listening to him, he looked up at the rumble of a Harley coming down the street. The rider pulled up in front of the house, killed his bike, and climbed off the beast. "It's time you get to know," Jessie said, "the man your mom has forbidden you to meet these past years. Rain Nelson, recently paroled."

So, this is my dad, Reason thought to himself. *Long hair tied back into a ponytail, a beard close-cropped at the chin, a little more gray than brown in both the beard and the hair, and the man's built with what looks like solid muscle beneath his black T-shirt. Two tattoos on those bulging forearms, an eagle on one, a panther on the other. Reminds me of Sam Elliot from Road House.*

Rain stood before the front porch. He said, "Hello, Boone. Jessie tells me you played so many roles for the kid. Brother. Father. Doing your best to keep him clean. But maybe I have a role to play, too. It's only fair to Reason to consider that. Let the kid and the con have their time. I heard he was quite a hellcat. Caused some trouble and got himself a record down at juvy hall. Kept your Mom on her toes. Heard he changed his ways, though. Is this a calm before the storm? Or is he permanently staying clean? Talk is cheap. Making promises and keeping them that counts. Kids can be so flaky. One minute getting their act together. The next, blowing it all to hell."

Reason stepped outside onto the porch, and met his stare without flinching. For a moment the kid and the con were linked by a silent communication. The con's eyes fierce. The kid's stubborn and resentful. Locked in a stare-down with his son, Rain said, "I've been speaking to Troublemakers. Misfits. Potheads. Delinquents. Most of my audience has been made up of kids placed in detention because of crimes they committed. If any of them would have listened a long time ago to the speech I deliver, most of them would not be locked up now. There's an old philosophy held by some in our justice system that some people are born with a *bad seed;* that from one bad person will come another bad person; that those who end up in prison will breed children who will do wrong. If a father murders, then his son will murder. Habitual criminals have children who are criminals.

"They say some kids have a bad seed, and they can't help themselves. That's a load of bull! Everyone's got free will. Kids make their own choices of right or wrong! No one is a damned robot. There are always going to be kids in our society who mess up. Can it be helped or not? Does the kid who gets into trouble do so because he's unhappy? Rebellious? Not too bright? Needs help? You answer that, and you will answer the question youth workers have been searching for an answer to for a long, long time.

"Reason, you were supposed to show up at Haven last night. A lot of kids received medals for staying straight. There was an empty chair there last night. There was a kid supposed to be sitting in it who deserved one of the medals. It's okay. Jessie found somebody to take your place. I received the medal on your behalf, telling the counselors of Haven that you would get it."

Rain's hands trembled as he held up a fist-sized medal. "This belongs to you, son," he said. handing it to him.

Taking the medal, Reason said, "I might not have ever earned a sobriety medal like this if you had been . . ."

"I know," Rain said. "I failed you, but I am here now—"

"Oh," Reason said, trying to keep the sarcasm out of his voice. "Now, everything is going to be a-okay? Sorry, Dad, it don't work that way. Ten years without you taught us to stand on our own."

He turned to go inside, muttering, "Thanks, Dad."

Chapter Twenty-Six

That evening, as the last rays of the setting sun graced the Nelson's porch, Reason slipped into a silent funk. *Why me? Reason thought. Vince gets killed by a car. Vince's dying left me so bummed I started acting like a damned alcoholic. And now I'm trying to stay clean. God knows I'm trying hard. So why is fate dumping its load on me? And then to have a dad who has been in prison for the past ten years?*

A year of being sober had taught him not to dwell on negative thoughts he had about drinking or smoking dope. Anytime he was tempted to smoke weed or find a bottle, he swiftly shifted gears in another direction.

He tried to do that now. Rose's career as the director of Haven and her work with drug and alcohol addictions made Reason proud of her. Her successful work with some of the toughest cases in Havelock spoke volumes about her character. He wished he could be like her in her stance against addictions.

Two months ago, Danny had stashed a quart of whiskey in the tree house out back. Reason had discovered it. At first, he was going to toss it away. Then he thought about keeping it. He had been sober for nearly three months. But caught between whether to toss it or keep it, Reason made a decision.

He stashed the bottle under the bed that his mother slept in. It was one place where Boone would never look. More important it was a place from which Reason would never take it without feeling guilty. He would have to be desperate before he would go into Rose's room to get a drink. He would feel that not only God was watching him, but he would also see Rose, standing beside him, shaking her head.

He had ventured to her room only twice during two very down times in his battle to remain straight. The first time he had sat down in Rose's rocker, opened the bottle and brought it to his lips. And then, realizing what he was about to do, he began to cry. After draining himself of sadness, he prayed for strength to put the bottle back under the bed. The second time was after a night at Haven. He had come home depressed after hearing some kid bragging about all the dope he had smoked. It had bummed Reason because it reminded him of the way he used to be. He had the bottle in his lap when Collin appeared out of nowhere. He walked into the room, figured out what Reason was about to do then walked out on him, accomplishing more with his silence than any speech Reason had ever heard.

But tonight he longed for a drink. Too many pressures building up stretched him tight as a bowstring. Too many things piling up on him, and him not knowing how to deal with them. Meeting his dad, Rain, had put him over the top. He stood up, determined to go out and get royally blitzed. He stepped over Bummer and slipped out the back door. Slowly, he moved toward the tree house. *It will only be this one time*, he thought. *It will only be for this night.*

Moments later, the black wolf appeared there in the backyard, blue eyes locked on him. The beast let out a long, mournful howl. It then nosed the bottle in Reason's hand. Sighing, Reason poured the contents of the bottle out at the base of the tree. He offered his spirit wolf a sad smile, and said, "I just won another battle."

***

The next morning, Reason found himself seated in the bow of an aluminum canoe, driving an oar into the waters of the Platte River. Jessie had driven him thirty miles from Havelock and had rented a canoe from some old codger living in a trailer beside the river. The next thing Reason knew, the two of them were embarking on a trip. As they cruised along through the waters, Reason looked across the wide river. It branched into two separate waterways with tree-dotted islands in the center. The red blaze of the leaves was spectacular.

A city-kid like Reason had to stop and stare at the passing scenery. Hills lined both banks of the river, and patches of scarlet could be seen weaving their way up into the slopes. Reason was amazed at the towering bluffs. He kept gazing at them as he paddled. It was a new experience for him to just soak up the scenery. Blue sky. Rolling green hills. Bright red leaves. And the green waterway stretched for miles before him. He thought it was cool. Even if his companion was a private eye and his uncle. It was still a good time. He felt at peace with himself. They glided along a waterway with branches forming a leafy canopy overhead. As far as Reason was concerned, the world outside no longer existed. He was alive at that moment, gliding along water beneath red leafy branches. He wished he would never have to go back to the real world with all of the battles he constantly fought. No more Rain Nelson claiming he was his dad. And no more fight to stay free of drugs and alcohol.

Reason found their canoe headed for a sandy bank. Jessie pulled the canoe onto the bank. Climbing out of the canoe, Reason followed

96

Jessie up a series of trails that wound in and out of a deep wooded grove. When he reached the summit of the high hill, he pointed to a clearing below where a rustic old building sat tucked into more trees. "That is the dining hall," Jessie said, "where Rain is speaking."

As they approached the hall, Reason said, "Do you think I'm locked into this thing? Being Rain's son, do you think I'm gonna be messing up all my life? Am I cursed as the son of a con?"

Reason joined dozens of other kids as they filed into a dining hall to get in out of the madly falling rain. As he seated himself at the back of the hall, Rain Nelson was introduced as the guest speaker for the evening. A few minutes later, Rain stood there on the stage of the dining hall, speaking of free will and choices.

Speaking of choices, Reason thought, *what if I admitted that Rain was my dad? I know Boone hates him for abandoning us. What would it be like if I made the choice to accept him as my dad?*

Thunder blasted overhead. Lightning crackled, casting an eerie light across the dark panes of glass in the dining hall. Hail crashed on the roof. Lightning popped and flared like a flashing strobe light.

When Rain's speech ended, he headed to the door of the dining hall. Reason sat watching and waiting, expecting the con to look at him before he exited the place. *Maybe,* he thought, *he didn't know I was here. But that doesn't mean Rain would have to acknowledge me. After all, the last time we spoke, I was pretty harsh with the guy.*

Now regretting his words, Reason watched for some sign that the con knew he'd heard his speech. But Rain walked to the door. And then, just before stepping outside, the man glanced back. Their eyes met. Reason felt a stab of pain shoot through his heart. Rain neither smiled nor frowned. He offered his son an unreadable look that revealed nothing about how he felt about him. It was just a dead look that Reason could not understand, and it hurt to the core of his being.

***

The moment Rain stepped outside of the dining hall, he found himself confronted by Beef and Gypsy. Jessie had invited the two former Outlaws to confront Rain about the matter concerning his sons. Lightning blazed a trail across the sky. Spider webs scrabbled across the sky. The air exploded. Sheet lightning flickered brightly.

Rain's thick mustache and his gray-streaked hair, reminded Jessie of a lone wolf. "You owe it to them," he said. "You are their father."

Rain snapped, "I sure as hell don't need some crusading private dick telling me my kids need their old man. Boone hates my guts. And Reason believes I'm just bad news. Let's just leave it at that."

Beef said, "Every boy needs a dad, Rain."

"Especially," Gypsy said, "a wild colt like Reason. You could step up to the plate on that."

Jessie said, " Jack Holland wants those relics. Find the map. Allow Ben Black Bull's son to claim those relics. You can then be done with them. If you and your sons could reclaim those relics, it would be a win for Reason and Boone, but also for Ben."

Chapter Twenty-Seven
One Year Later

Fifteen-year-old Reason Nelson stood up, peering into the shadows. Brushing back his dark, shoulder-length hair, he picked up a stick and sat back down. There in the realm of the Woods, beside a campfire, he stared at the mist rising above the nearby pond. At that moment, he was a boy, camping out in the country, trying to remain unafraid as moonlight turned the wooded grove into a mystical wonderland. On the other side of the fire, Collin Young slipped long strands of blond hair behind his ears.

The howls of coyotes erupted in the distance. Ghostly shadows gathered beyond their campsite. Reason waited. One second. Two. Three. Four. The coyotes howled again.

Reason said, "They called her Bloody Mary, because she blew some kid away with a shotgun. One blast to the face and he was dead. A serious consequence for a stupid prank. Kids had harassed her for years. Shooting her goats. Hooting at her from their cars. Sneaking up to her house to bang on her windows. Bored kids driving out to the country to scare the old lady. Someone had a real dumb idea that night. Sneaking into her house would be the ultimate prank. Halfway through her kitchen window, the kid froze in terror as Mary pointed her shotgun at him. She then pulled the trigger. The thunder of that blast echoed across Lincoln, and a legend was born. And no one screwed with Bloody Mary after that. Mary had a guardian, though. Some *thing* that stalked the banks of Salt Creek. Two kids on dirt bikes saw *it* one July evening. Glowing green eyes. Gleaming white fangs. The face of a demented baboon. The deformed body of a dog. Rumors spread that it was a beast bred by scientists at Ag. College. It was no longer fun to go near the old lady's house. It was named the Salt Creek Creature, and another legend was born."

Silence settled on the Woods. A light breeze spiraled through the leaves of the trees, causing embers within the fire to whiz through the air like tiny zephyrs. In a nearby tree, an owl hooted softly. Out by the creek, its mate responded with a murmur. The croaking of frogs drifted from the pond at the edge of the Woods. Reason peered down at the glowing embers. In past months, he'd overcome a major problem with drugs and now considered himself recovered. He'd quit using drugs. Collin said, "Flip you for who goes to Traveler's Café to get us a six-pack of pop."

Waiting until the coin was in the air, Reason said, "Tails."

Collin caught the quarter and glanced down at it. "Heads it is," he said, with a smirk. "Hurry back. I'm thirsty."

Mounting his 250 Kawasaki and kicking it over, Reason revved his bike and zipped out onto the service road beyond the Woods. He zipped past the Turn Around, a parking lot to one side of the road. Reason planned to ride another hundred feet, then turn down a side trail that would lead him to the café on Cornhusker Highway. He didn't want to ride too close to Bloody Mary's house. He swerved off the service road and headed up a trail snaking its way along the banks of Salt Creek. Reason clawed at his throttle and sent the 250 Kaw shooting forward like a rocket. Speeding through the S-shaped curve, he whipped the bike through the tight switchback. Far ahead, he could see the trees at the Fat Lady's Nightmare. The trail snaked between a dozen trees, then looped around a deep ravine. Years ago, 16-year-old Bobby Cooper had attempted to jump his bike over the ravine and died sixty-feet below in Salt Creek.

Reason twisted his throttle and sent the bike soaring toward the Nightmare. At the bottom of the steep incline, he slammed into a tree. The Kaw's front tire popped, its headlamp shattered, and Reason flew over the handlebars. He landed at the edge of a pond, skidding crazily across mossy ground, scattering frogs in all directions. Blackness attached itself to him like an anchor and he began to tumble into the murky waters. Suddenly, Reason felt strong hands on his shoulders, pulling him away from the moonlit black waters. When he opened his eyes, fireflies shimmered above him like tiny green jewels. He peered up at into the piercing green eyes of an old woman. Silver hair trailed over her shoulders. She wore a long, snow-white dress.

It was the Lady of the Woods. The legendary Bloody Mary.

Reason fearfully asked, "You going to shoot me?"

A smile creased the ancient lady's weathered face as she patted him gently on one cheek. "Foolish child," she said. "I just saved you."

She then vanished like mist in the wind.

***

When Reason fully regained consciousness, he found himself alone at the edge of the pond. He groaned when he saw his ruined cycle. There was no way he would be able to ride the battered Kaw back to the Woods. The bike would have to be hauled out of there. Baffled by his encounter with the old lady, Reason headed toward the nearby service road. He assumed Collin at the campfire wondered what had happened to him. Minutes later, Reason came in sight of the Woods.

Surprised to see a white Cadillac parked at the Turn Around, he slipped into a row of hedges on the north side of the parking lot. Thirty feet in front of him sat the car. Thirty feet beyond the car lay a ravine lined by dark trees marking the north end of the Woods. He looked to his right toward the service road and Salt Creek. He then studied the open field stretching to his left. To get back to the Woods, he would have to crawl through the field, then climb down into the ravine beyond. He knew that the ravine separating the Turn Around from the Woods was at least twenty feet deep. He was about to crawl out of the hedges, when the front doors on the car swung open and two men climbed out, the cherries of their cigarettes glowing brightly in the darkness. The men walked around to the trunk of the car. One had blond hair and a beard. The other man was bald. Both were tall and built like bears.

Jack Holland, thought Reason. *President of the Elder's Den. And Nate Holland, his vice president. What are they up to?*

As Jack scooped up a bulky shape from the confines of the trunk, Nate joined him. The two men grunted as they moved away from the car and placed their burden on the ground. Jack said, "He's too doped up to do anything but sit there."

Jack stepped back away from the black Labrador sprawled on the ground before him. He then froze as a noise came from the field forty feet to the left. Gray shapes floated toward the Woods, a buck and six does. Hidden behind the hedges, Reason looked on in amazement as the buck plowed into Jack, sending him tumbling to the ground. Nate veered out of the path of the racing does. The herd moved deeper into the Woods. Pulling a pistol from his belt, Jack followed behind the deer herd. Nate followed Jack into the Woods.

Chapter Twenty-Eight

Reason sprang up and ran to the edge of the ravine. Collin dashed out of the Woods. Scrambling up and out of the deep gully, he joined Reason in the center of the parking lot. The two boys approached the dazed Lab sprawled on the ground beside the car. But the dog remained motionless as Reason kneeled down and gently placed a hand on his shoulder. "He still alive?" Collin asked.

The black Lab peered up at Reason with a curious look in his dark eyes. Collin slid his hands beneath the dog's hind end and they lifted the Lab up. The dog attempted to gain his feet but crumpled clumsily to the ground. Reason slid both arms beneath the Lab. Collin kneeled on the other side of the dog and the Lab spastically worked his back legs, then collapsed. Collin swore in frustration. "He can't walk!"

Reason pointed at the raised lid of the trunk. "Keys!" He snatched up the ring of keys. "Let's drive him out of here!"

The sound of gunfire erupted from the south end of the Woods, and Reason hastily told Collin it was Nate and Jack who had stolen the dog. They began pushing and shoving to get the Lab onto the backseat. Reason held the dog against his chest and fell backward inside the car. The Lab raised his head and licked the side of Reason's face. Collin clambered in through the front passenger door. Reason turned the key in the ignition and took them soaring down the road leading away from the Woods.

Steering the Cadillac onto Superior Street at the end of the service road, Reason sent them gliding through the fog drifting out of the marsh to the north of the road. In the backseat, Collin looked down at the dog sprawled beside him. "He's wearing a tag. Tiger, it says."

The boys then heard the distinct whine of a dirt bike coming from behind them. Reason let up on the gas and looked in the rearview mirror. He peered hard at the lone rider moving through the clouds of mist behind them. One second he was rolling toward them, the beam of his headlamp slicing through the fog, then he killed his light curtains of mist engulfed the hooded rider, and he was transformed into an ethereal being.

***

Reason drove them to the suburb of Havelock and parked the Caddie in the driveway behind his house. Turning the car and headlights off, he withdrew the key from the ignition slot and climbed out of the car. Reason guided Tiger out of the backseat and led him onto the porch. Collin reached inside the front seat and withdrew a large envelope. Startled by a sudden noise from the front of the car, Reason saw his German shepherd approaching Tiger seated on the back porch.

Unsettled by the strange dog in his yard, Bummer was not happy. Snarling fiercely, he challenged Tiger. Having grown up around dogs, Reason knew that the second Bummer lunged forward, both dogs would explode into a raging whirlwind. Reason snapped, "Bummer!"

Bummer let out one last rumble then backed off and sidled up to his master. Tiger wagged his tail and lowered his chin to the porch. He *whuffed* and rolled over in a show of submission. The moment their cold, wet noses touched, the Lab and German shepherd nuzzled each other in a friendly manner.

Once inside the house, Reason turned on the kitchen light and proceeded on to the living room. Collin placed the envelope on a coffee table, and the dogs plopped down on a rumpled couch. "Don't mess with that envelope," Reason said. "We'll come back after we ditch the car. Then, we'll look at it."

After parking the Caddie beside Ballard ball field, Reason and Collin headed back to the Nelson house. By the time they reached the front walk four blocks from the pool, the two were jumpy. Reason froze as a light nailed him in the eyes and a police cruiser rolled to a stop in front of the house. In the brief flash of the dome light, Reason could see big, blond Beef Tory. "Is Boone around?"

Reason said, "Him and Mom drove up to Omaha, looking for Danny Kane, who ran away from treatment."

Beef said, "I was hoping to stop Boone from going on a wild goose chase. Heard of Daniel Kane? President of the Bandits. It's his son who went on run."

Puzzled, Reason asked, "Are you saying Daniel Kane is the father of Jenna and Danny? All she ever said about her dad is he lives across town. But president of the Bandits? Why did she keep this a secret?"

Beef said, "Bandits and Outlaws don't play nice together."

He bid them good night and drove away.

***

Bummer and Tiger greeted the boys in the kitchen. Reason kneeled down next to the coffee table. Tiger leaned against him and nosed his chin. Reason draped his arm around Bummer. They spent the next

103

hour looking through documents from the juvenile court system. They were reports on fifteen-year-old Jenna Kane, written by a psychiatrist. Reason said, "This is the deposition that Jenna gave as a primary witness in the homicide of JR Brooks."

Reason narrowed his eyes and read the paper outloud: *"Greetings, Judge Sullivan, Jenna Kane will come before you soon. Basing your decision on reports we've provided, you will sentence her to the Lincoln Regional Center for evaluation. If you comply, arrangements will be made for the safe return of your female dog and her pups. Consider Tiger collateral damage. Do not involve the police. We have you in check, and it is now your move!"*

Collin said, "They're blackmailing Judge Sully?"

"Yeah," Reason said. "That guy hates me! Twice now he nearly sent me to Kearney, but gave me probation instead. Hell, every time I've gone before him, he made me feel like I just taking up space. How does he expect any kid to change when all he does is send them to detention? How is that place gonna make a *bad* kid *good*? Last time I was in court, Judge Sully told me only a heartless kid would keep breaking his mom's heart. He claimed I lost touch with my feelings. Sully thinks I'm a loser. Loser I might be, but I sure did good tonight, didn't I? Wish we could rescue Tiger's mate and his pups. Wouldn't be a loser then."

Reason shook a ring of keys out of the envelope, and they jangled as they fell onto the coffee table. Picking up the keys, he said, "One of these keys has the name of a warehouse stamped on it! Farm Country Storage? Maybe Judge Sully's other dogs might be there."

Reason took the keys and stuffed them in his pocket. As he stood up from the couch, his father, Rain Nelson stepped in through the front door. Flicking long, dark bangs out of his eyes, a frown creased his beard as he said, "Your brother informed me you were camping out this weekend while he is away on business in Omaha. I rode out to the Woods to check on you. What I discovered when I got there, pretty much freaked me the hell out. You need to come with me."

He spun around adjusting his sleeveless jean jacket, openly revealing the colors he wore on the back of the ragged-looking jacket. In red letters were the words, Outlaws MC of Nebraska.

As Collin and Reason followed him out to his red Ford truck in the alley, Collin whispered, "Who is this guy?"

Whispering back, Reason said, "My dad, president of the Outlaws, recently released from prison. I have no idea what he wants, though."

Moments later, they were moving toward the country beyond. Rain remained silent as they turned onto the service road leading back to their campsite. The Woods loomed before them, its black trees standing stark against the starry sky. Parking his truck on the service road, Rain climbed out. "Come on. You need to see this."

Chapter Twenty-Nine

The faint glow of firelight illuminated their campsite. "Holy hell!" gasped Collin as he gaped up at the two sleeping bags swaying above the ground twenty feet from the fire. Jack and Nate had used rope from their camping supplies to form nooses around the sleeping bags, causing them to resemble bodies hanging from the high branches. Rain said, "They shot holes in the tank of this Yamahammer, too."

Collin frowned as he examined his bike, and Reason explained to his dad how they had rescued Tiger from Jack and Nate. He then told him about the blackmail plot involving Judge Sullivan.

Rain said, "Elder's Den are our rivals."

"But," Reason said, "don't you have allies with the Eagles? If you asked, wouldn't they reign down hell on the Den?"

Rain gave him a long look. "Twelve years ago when I was riding out by the Nightmare, I spotted Bobby Cooper's helmet down in the ravine left there after Bobby died. So, I climbed down and got it. When I returned to my bike, these two bikers came down the trail from opposite directions. Both were riding 1200 Hogs and they collided! Moses of the Screaming Eagles. Daniel Kane of the Bandits. That's when Pigman showed up, armed with a shotgun! I heaved Bobby's helmet at him and beaned him on the head, and Kane, Moses, and I booked out of there! My attack on Pigman was legendary, but it did not earn me any loyalty from Moses or Kane."

Rain was now peering at the road beyond the Woods. He said, "Gypsy is heading back this way."

Out on the service road beside the Woods, the cyclist braked to avoid hitting Rain's truck. Spraying rocks behind him, he then headed down the trail leading to the Woods. Gunning his bike, Gypsy swerved crazily, then skidded to a stop beside the fire. Killing his bike, the big rider pointed up at the sleeping bags and gruffly asked, "Who did this? Those Screaming Eagles you met up with at Dog Lake, Rain? You messed two of them up. Get in your truck and clear out, Rain. Their warlord, Knolls, is out for blood."

The steady rumble of seven Harleys sounded like a thunderstorm as the riders descended into the Woods. Slowly then, they rolled past the fire, their headlight beams cutting through the shadows. All seven bikers fiercely revved their bikes before shutting them down. Reason found himself shoved behind Gypsy, while Rain moved in front of the fire to face the bikers. The seven men had that Charles Manson look about them: Long, shaggy hair. Full beards. Glazed, angry eyes. All were dressed in sleeveless jean jackets, ratty jeans, and scuffed boots. A huge, blond, bearded man stepped in front of Rain as he snarled, "Which one of you busted up Bo and Jake out at the lake?"

Rain pointed at the sleeping bags hanging from the branches. He said, "Knolls, I thought some of your guys had harmed my son."

"A reasonable explanation," said a dark-haired, bearded biker stepping in front of the others. Stone Holland, warlord of the Elder's Den, offered Reason a brief smile. "So, this is your dad Rain Nelson, President of the Outlaws?"

"Yes," Reason said, wondering if Stone would keep the peace or pick a fight with his dad. Stone looked to Knolls and said, "I'll sort this out. We've got enough trouble with Kane right now. We don't need *another* war brewing! Eagles and the Den are at odds right now with Kane and his Bandits. We don't need Rain taking sides against us. This ain't over with. Moses will call Rain out for his attack on your guys."

Knolls moved toward Rain. "I say we settle this now."

Rain moved to intercept the big, blond biker. He hooked his arm beneath his, and placed a leg directly behind him, dumping him on his butt. Knolls growled and surged back to his feet. Rain blocked three punches aimed for his face, then let loose with a round house that took Knolls off his feet again. This time when he came back up, he charged, lowering his head, striking him solidly with his shoulder. Rain was rocked by the sudden blow, but Knolls slid against his bike parked beside the campfire. He and the Harley fell directly into the fire. Even as Knolls tried to lift the massive bike out of the fire, flames erupted from the gas tank of the Harley.

Knolls stared down at the brightly burning bike. "Oh, hell!" he snapped. "This smoldering hog belongs to Moses of the Screaming Eagles. You just demolished my president's bike!"

It was then that Jessie Dalton stepped silently from the shadows of the nearby trees. He lowered the hood of his black sweatshirt, his long, black hair settling upon his shoulders. Clad in jeans, boots, and a black leather jacket, he resembled a biker, but unlike the scraggly-bearded bikers before him, he was clean-shaven. He slipped out of his sweatshirt and draped it over the flames crawling along the hog's tank. "I," he said to Stone, "will repair the bike. Just see to the mad scrapper and keep him doing anything else foolish. He had to know attacking the president of the Outlaws would not end well."

Fifteen minutes later, the taillights of Rain's truck faded into the night. It had taken Rain, Stone, and Jessie to load the demolished hog into the back of Rain's truck. Someone was going to have pay for those damages, and Stone kept the peace by accepting Jessie's offer. The bikers rolled out of the Woods, following behind Rain's truck as it moved off down the service road.

For long moments after they had gone, Jessie stood there savoring the night sounds. Owl calls. The slap of a beaver's tail from nearby Salt Creek. A barking dog from a farm beyond the field. The rumble of a train near Dead Man's Run. The howls of coyotes in the distance. A fox nimbly stepped into a patch of moonlight, then turned and bolted into the trees.

Thinking how this could have ended, he sighed in relief, then retrieved his dirt bike at the edge of the Woods and headed back toward Havelock.

Chapter Thirty

By the time Rain dropped Reason and Collin off at the Nelson house in Havelock, red dawn seeped through the eastern sky. After receiving a warm greeting from Bummer and Tiger, the boys headed upstairs and out to the Loft. Plopping down on the mattress there, for the next five hours the two boys slept the sleep of the dead. When they woke up, Reason let Bummer and Tiger out in the backyard to relieve themselves. Collin said, "Did you hear Stone mention Bobby Cooper's helmet? After Rain found the helmet at the Nightmare, he went out to Fairview and put it on Bobby Cooper's headstone. Daniel Kane stole it. For bikers, it's like the missing Holy Grail. It makes me wonder if bikers believe in God or not."

Reason looked to Saint Patrick's half a block to the east, where an illuminated image of Jesus dominated an enormous stained-glass window. He said, "God was pretty desperate when he used me to save Judge Sully's dog. Can't get much more stranger, right? When I was a kid, all I ever heard was that God was mad at me whenever I screwed up. Detentions at school. Probation with court. Breaking curfew. Getting stoned. Getting blitzed. I screw up a lot. I figure God was plenty mad at me most of the time."

Collin said, "To keep you clean and sober as your partner in sobriety, I owe it to you after Logan jumped that train down at the train yards. You hauled my sorry butt home from the yards every time I went there. I don't think God is as mad at you as you think, Reason."

He stopped and picked up the morning newspaper, and said, "A ten-thousand dollar reward is being offered by Judge Sullivan for the safe return of his dogs. But we'll need transportation to ride out to this warehouse to find the judge's other dogs. Four hours till sundown. Besides our bikes are trashed. How we gonna get there?"

Reason said, "I'll borrow Boone's 250 Kaw."

Bummer and Tiger barked. Reason passed through the living room and opened the door. Jenna Kane stood there. "Is Boone here?"

Jenna's long, dark hair fell past her shoulders. She wore faded jeans and black boots. *Biker boots,* he thought. *And that tattoo on her upper left arm? A panther fighting an eagle. Bandits wear those colors.* Reason also noted Jenna's tanned, smooth skin, her deep dimples, and the slight cleft in her chin. She also had a rounded nose and pouty lips that looked more accustomed to wearing a frown than a smile.

Jenna walked up onto the porch. "I was scheduled to go to court. The Den is trying to blackmail Judge Sullivan, demanding he send me to the mental hospital. Mental patients don't make credible witnesses. I was trying to get Danny out of the Cosgrove complex when Jack shot and killed Brooks. I should have never given that deposition. All it has brought me is trouble."

Reason asked, "All this time I've known you and Danny, I always understood that your dad lived across town. How come neither one of you ever told me Daniel Kane is your dad?"

Offering him a sheepish grin, she said, "Danny and I often talked about it, but with Rain Nelson being your dad, we figured you would disown us as friends. Bandits and Outlaws are total enemies."

Startled by the thunderous roar of a Harley filling the air, Reason stared in alarm at the biker coming up the street. As the rider drew closer, Reason studied the small, muscular bald man with the red goatee. He'd assumed Daniel Kane would be an ogre who made Stone or Knolls look like dwarfs. But the man appeared to be a foot shorter than the two bikers. Though he had enormous shoulders and a barrel-like chest, Reason figured his short arms with their many tattoos would be a handicap in a brawl. Kane dismounted from his bike and said, "Moses lost his hog because of your dad. He wants compensation. He knows about the missing dogs of Judge Sully. Whoever gets that reward, Moses wants a share. If you need help with the Den, I want half of that reward to offer you protection. I will be keeping my daughter safe until Jack is arrested. Why does the Den want to silence Jenna's testimony? Didn't you and Danny witness the shooting of Brooks, too?"

Jenna said, "I'm the good witness, who would be more credible in court. Unlike Reason and Danny, I don't have a record at juvy nor have I ever been to treatment. To a jury, those things matter."

Looking over at Collin, Reason said, "As if Danny and I don't really matter. See? I told you. I'm such a loser."

***

Reason borrowed his brother's bike, planning on finding this warehouse where the dogs were supposed to be. With Collin clinging to him on the back of the seat, Reason took them flying down Superior Street on the 250 Kaw. "Hey," Collin said, pointing over his shoulder, "ain't that a cop coming this way on a fully-dressed Harley?"

Two blocks from the Superior Street bridge, the cop spotted the boys speeding away down a trail leading onto Bloody Mary's land. Bringing his cycle to a stop, the officer wondered if he should take his Harley down the narrow path. He eased out on his clutch and rolled forward. Three minutes later, he careened down the slope of the Fat Lady's Nightmare, and lost control of his massive 1200 Harley Davidson.

At the far end of the Nightmare, Reason glanced back to see the cop hit the ground hard. He cringed as the man's heavy motorcycle crashed on top of him. Collin said, "But we can't just leave him."

The Harley had died, and gas was leaking out of the tank, forming a puddle around the man's trapped form. He frantically pushed on the bike, then ripped off his helmet. Reason could see the cop was an older man with a buzz cut. Watching him struggle to pull himself out from under the heavy bike, Reason turned the bike off.

Big Mike looked relieved as the two boys approached him. "Thanks, guys," he said. "I can't lift this beast by myself."

Collin asked, "Are you okay? Is your leg broken?"

Big Mike grimaced. "Don't think so, but I'm definitely stuck."

Taking positions on either side of the cop, Reason grabbed onto the handlebars and Collin slipped his hands beneath the tank. Mike placed his own hands beneath the seat. Heaving upward, Reason strained with all his might to raise the huge machine. Collin and Mike pushed on both the seat and the gas tank. Slowly, the Harley began to move, yet just when it seemed they were going to succeed, Big Mike slipped and collapsed. "Son of a bitch!" he swore as the bike settled back down on his leg once more. He lay there in the gas-soaked mud, looking like he might faint. Yet as the boys renewed their efforts, Mike planted his hand beneath the seat and heaved upward. Grunting and straining, the three of them raised the Harley upright. While the boys kept the bike from toppling over, Mike clambered to one side of the trail. Collin slipped the kickstand down so that it wouldn't crash back to the ground. Big Mike pulled himself to his feet and began massaging his injured leg. "If you tell this story to anyone, leave out my name. Last thing I wanna hear from my fellow cops is that Big Mike Tory crashed his Harley out at Bloody Mary's!"

"Tory?" Reason asked, puzzled. "Beef's dad? How come Beef never talks about you?"

"My oldest boy," Mike said, "doesn't speak to me on account of what happened to my youngest son, Bobby. He was always trying to outdo his older brother. Myron claims it was his idea to hop a dirt bike over that ravine. Bobby just beat him to it. After I moved Beef, your dad, and his brother, Jessie, to Havelock, I remarried. My wife already had two boys of her own, and they kept their name, Cooper. *The* Bobby Cooper, who tried to jump that ravine back there. Yes. I steered Beef away from the Outlaws, but I couldn't keep Myron from starting his own club. Nor could I stop Bobby sailing out over that ravine. Sometimes, boys do the most foolish things."

When Big Mike left them and rode away, the boys decided to abandon there quest to find the warehouse. It would be dark soon, and they wanted to approach the place in the daylight. Bad things happened after dark. At the entrance to the Nightmare, Reason and Collin parked the Kaw.

The path dipped before them and snaked down a steep hill, passing between a stand of cottonwoods. The ancient giants grew so close to the trail that their gnarled branches formed an emerald cavern. Sunlight trickled down through their lime-green leaves, and a lemony haze seeped into the glade below. In the deeper shadows beneath the trees, dust motes floated through shimmering gold columns.

On either side of these pillars of light, small, winged shapes hovered above the trail and morphed into monarch butterflies, their orange and black wings backlit with a magical brilliance.

The passageway seemed like an enchanted grove graced by summer sunlight. But the boys knew with Pigman's to the north and Bloody Mary's to the south, it was unholy ground for sure.

Chapter Thirty-One

Reason headed down into the cavernous greenery. There, he found dozens of small mounds of earth. Planted at the head of each mound was a wooden grave marker. "Bloody Mary's graveyard!" he said. "It's where she's buried her victims!"

Collin said, "Why would she place flowers on their graves if they were victims? Percy? Billy? April? Cassie? Gus?"

Reason studied the rest of the clearing. A wooden arbor marked the entrance at the far end. Beyond that, a cobblestone path wound up through a grassy lawn, disappearing between rows of apple trees linking the clearing with Mary's two-story house. He said, "This is creepy. We're standing in front of the graves of a bunch of dead kids!"

Collin said, "Mary's goats. The old lady has lived out here for years, with no electricity, no plumbing, no telephone, her only companions are her goats. Many heartless kids have driven out here, and fired bullets into the harmless goats grazing in Mary's yard."

Looking down at the graves, Reason said, "Percy. There was a story I heard about Mary and Percy walking in the parade during Havelock Days. Mary dressed him up in a shirt and a straw hat. Percy had strutted beside her in front of the crowds. Just one happy goat, looking quite ridiculous in his hat and shirt, unaware that his life was soon going to end when some cruel kid shot him. I don't know how any kid could kill a defenseless goat. I couldn't even grasp that concept. Such cruelty is not in my nature, and yet over the years, I cycled past her house, spotted her seated in her rocking chair, and flipped her off. Giving her the finger seemed like a fitting salute. And for that, I now feel rotten inside. I'm not as bad as those kids who shot her goats, but I ain't much better."

The boys gasped out loud when a firm voice said, "Good afternoon, boys." They turned back around to face the elderly lady stepping beneath the arbor. She was tall and her long silver hair sharply contrasted with the black dress she wore. It was her green eyes, however, that Reason immediately looked to. Mary said, "Why, you're the boy who crashed his motorbike. Clarence has your motorbike all fixed up. It's parked up by my barn."

Reason warily followed Mary beneath the archway of the arbor, leaving Collin standing there in the goat cemetery. Reason fell in beside Mary, and together they walked up past her house, and over to her large red barn. He was totally bewildered when he saw his 250

Kaw parked there. Although the tank was badly dented, the handle-bars were fixed and the clutch handle had been replaced. Mary said, "You should be more careful. You nearly sucked up all the frog poop in my pond!"

Reason laughed. He couldn't help himself. There he was standing beside the terrible and awesome Bloody Mary, and she was joking with him. It was just so bizarre. She didn't lecture him about trespassing. The old lady he'd thought all these years to be a shotgun-toting witch, seemed normal. "Thanks," he said, glancing over at the apple tree beside the house and the black helmet wedged between its branches. It was the chain securing the helmet to the tree that prompted him to think, *Is that Bobby Cooper's helmet?*

***

By the time the boys returned to Havelock, the sun had set. As they entered the Nelson house, Reason kneeled down, fending off slobbery kisses from both excited dogs. The dogs rubbed up against him, then bounded into the kitchen and headed toward the backdoor.

Reason said, "Collin, let them out for a squirt."

"Sure," replied Collin.

Reason stared down at the coffee table in the living room. He looked down at Tiger's collar, the newspaper article about Judge Sully's missing dogs, and the information packet to be delivered to Judge Sullivan. "Check this out," he said. "All of these things on the table are related. Now, I wish we could rescue Sully's female lab and her pups."

They were startled by a loud pounding on the front door. Bummer let out a bark. Tiger let out a playful rumble. "Quiet!" whispered Reason as he crossed the living room. Bummer obeyed and took up a protective stance to one side of the door. Reason inched his way toward the front window. Loud voices came from the porch outside. "If he's got Judge Sullivan's dogs, we'll just nab them, Moses!"

Moses? Reason thought. *Oh, great!* He peeled back the curtain and peeked outside to see Stone and Knolls, and a man with shaggy blond hair and a thick mustache. Furious pounding caused the door to rattle. Reason whispered, "Collin, you stay here with the dogs."

Collin latched onto Bummer and Tiger as Reason slipped quietly out the back door. He crept around to the front of the house, where he discovered the three bikers still on the porch. He walked around

114

to the porch. He came within ten feet of the bikers when Nate Holland stepped up behind the other three. He did not see Reason as he said, "The girl doesn't have to die, just be labeled a mental case who wouldn't make a credible witness. By nabbing the dogs, we put that Judge Sully in check. By taking the dogs, dad was trying to force Sully to send that girl to the mental ward to taint her testimony."

Stone looked over at his brother, an angry scowl on his face. "What does dad have you mixed up in Nathan? You guys stole that judge's dogs? What does Rain's kid have to do with this?"

"He's got one of the damned dogs," Nate snarled.

Moses said, "If the kid has the dog, we'll make sure the hound gets back to the judge, claim that reward, and get me a new bike."

"No, Moses," Nate growled. "The dogs belong to my dad. Stone? Tell them how unhinged dad has become, before he starts killing anyone who threatens him." As the four bikers began to argue, Reason turned to retreat to the backdoor, when Nate spotted him. "Get me the dog!"

Reason ran as Nate came charging after him. He could hear Nate's labored breathing only five feet behind him as ran toward the park. He put on a burst of speed and ran for the pine tree ahead of him. Springing into the air, he leaped up and clawed at the branch above him. He climbed up through the branches and didn't stop until he was ten feet above the ground. Nate, Stone, and Moses came running up. Moses growled, "You can't just stab the kid. I won't let you, Nate."

Stone looked at the knife in his brother's grasp. "Nate? Turn this down a notch. We were planning a talk with the kid about turning the dog over to us. Now, quit with the berserker fit you're having."

Moses was about to address Nate when Knolls appeared on the sidewalk. "Rain Nelson is comin' behind me!"

Moses and Stone looked to the dark-haired man striding down the sidewalk in the center of the park. High above them in the branches, Reason looked curiously at Rain trailing Knolls down the sidewalk. His dad was walking right into an encounter with the three bikers. He stopped and stood still for a moment, the long strands of his raven hair trailing over his broad shoulders in the slight breeze. "Reason?" he called.

"Up here in the tree!" Reason said.

Rain swiftly veered off the sidewalk and with a flurry of solid punches pummeled Knolls senseless. Moses and Stone wheeled to face him, Rain, Moses, and Stone collided, and broke into a furious fight, sending loud, meaty *thwacks!* echoing through the air. Reason watched in amazement as his dad stood there, rooted to one spot, swinging madly. The two bikers staggered back with each stunning blow he delivered, taking quite a pummeling. Rain took them both to the ground with a flying tackle. Hardly believing that anyone could take that much damage, Reason felt light-headed.

While the fighting continued, Reason spotted a police cruiser racing down the street to the east of the park. Moses and Stone ceased fighting with Rain, and guiding Knolls between them, hastily moved away toward the street to the west of the park. Rain said, "Reason? Stay put! I'll come back and get you once the cops leave!"

He then ran to the west, following the three bikers.

Reason wrapped his arms around the trunk of the tree and sat perfectly still, trying to blend with the shadowy branches around him. Nate stood below him, red lights flashing across his features. He raised his knife and stabbed at the air between him and Reason. "You screwed up, kid! My dad wants that dog. He'll be coming for him, too. If you think I am bad, my dad is bat-shit crazy!"

Reason waited until Nate ran to the other side of the park before he even moved. Stunned by the fight he'd witnessed he wanted to puke. Reason dropped down at the base of the tree. He staggered dizzily away from the pine tree, heading toward the shelter ahead of him. Once he reached it, he bolted for the alley to the north. Darting between two cottonwoods, he warily peeked around the wide trunk to see three cops move into the park.

Reason ran two blocks and collapsed on the front steps of Saint Patrick's church.

Chapter Thirty-Two

Police sirens wailed. Reason moved up the steps on shaky legs. Inside of Saint Pat's, Reason eyed the statue of Jesus beside the altar. As he entered the sanctuary, he found it illuminated by rows of candles situated on a table in front of the altar. The light cast by their flickering flames, danced upon the features of Jesus.

Reason smiled, knowing no one as incredible as God could inhabit a statue. It was there for those at Saint Pat's to focus on as they prayed, so he figured it was okay to do the same. As he faced Jesus, a rush of memories washed over him. As a little kid, Reason had always believed in God, and for years before drifting off to sleep, he prayed and believed that if he stayed in touch with God, all things would work out good in his life. But then, life became more complicated, things didn't always work out good. Bad things happened that there were no good reasons for. Reason quit talking to God at night. Eventually, he quit thinking about God at all.

He had no point of reference to connect to a being so far outside of his ordinary life. He'd lost that along the way somewhere. Soon, he ignored God for so long he was convinced there was a canyon between them. Reason began to get into trouble with the courts. It never seemed fair to him. All the professionals placed a label on his behavior. He was diagnosed with Attention Deficit Hyperactive Disorder. One therapist said he had Oppositional Disorder. His school psychologist reported that Reason also had anger management issues, low self-esteem, and severe depression. In the years between 5th and 8th grade, Reason believed he was messed up. He didn't feel good about himself, and he'd think, *With so many things wrong with me, how am I supposed to change? People call me a problem child, but none have a clue how to help me!*

Professionals encouraged his mom to combat Reason's behavior disorders by putting him on medication. When it became a struggle, his mom gave up battling against Reason's strong will. He suffered consequences for his actions and ended up in detention. Probation followed detention. But eventually, he turned to self-medicating, for when he was high he didn't have to think about his failures. He spiraled into kamikaze mode, hell-bent on self-destruction.

Only once during this downward spiral, did he consider talking to God again. Reason figured God must have heard his prayers, because Judge Sully showed him mercy, giving him on a suspended sentence.

The next prayer had been sent up after his friend Vince had died. Reason had lost all hope then, and after a botched suicide attempt, he'd asked God to simply to give him the will to survive. He figured God had heard that one, too. After all, he was still alive today.

But the real turning point had been the winter night he'd climbed up to the roof of the nine-story Mahoney Manor in a drunken stupor. He'd faced the sky and talked, believing someone was listening. And Reason connected with some force beyond him, that helped him believe there was a purpose for him being alive. He'd been a kid so totally out of control by then, that no counselor, psychologist, or therapist could get through to him. But there on that winter night, that force had gotten through. Reached him. Touched him. Changed him. That winter night, Reason came away from that experience, thinking maybe God had feelings, too. He quit ignoring him and checked in with him a few times a week, believing that, in God's eyes, he *was* worth more than he realized.

Staring up at the statue of Jesus, Reason heard a sound behind him.

When he turned around, Rain stood before him. In the shadows behind him, were Jessie and Gypsy. "You okay, son?" Rain asked. "You've stirred up a hornet's nest. Let's get you home safe."

Relieved to have their protection, Reason said, "How would you guys like to rescue Sully's dogs?"

***

Webs of lightning streaked through the night sky as Rain drove them out to the country. The clouds west of Lincoln resembled cotton candy mountains, and after another brilliant flash, those same clouds transformed into a herd of white stallions. The four of them peered at the Morton building two hundred yards away from them. The large metal building was situated behind an old farmhouse. Rain had contacted Officer Tory, but they were not going to wait for him. Jessie tried three keys on the ring before finding the one that slid into the lock on the building's door. He turned the key and opened the door. "Holy Jesus!" gasped Gypsy, staring at more than a hundred cages lining an entire wall of the building. Dogs in the cages wagged their tails. Several more began barking.

Rain said, "There are cold-hearted bastards all over the country who steal dogs, then sell them to research facilities. I bet Jack and Nate are in that kind of business."

118

Reason walked over to the female black Lab and kneeled in front of her cage. He opened the cage door, watching her reaction. Soon, he was having difficulty keeping eight pups from breaking out of the cage. Gently pushing the pups back into the cage, Reason felt tears in his eyes. He could hardly believe that anyone would be so cruel as to subject these dogs to the unspeakable horrors of a research lab. It overwhelmed him, for he kept thinking how heartbroken he would be if Bummer was in their place. Reason looked out the office window to see headlights. The patrol car stopped ten feet from the building. The engine died, the driver's door opened, and Beef Tory stepped out.

Peering through the window at their boyhood friend, Rain and Jessie headed to the backdoor of the building. Before following the two, Gypsy said, "We got you this far. We'll let you take the credit for this dog rescue. Don't mention our names to Beef, kid. Our biker protocol is setting in."

***

The next morning, Rain stepped inside the Nelson house. Tall and lean, his dark hair fell to his shoulders, and he sported a neatly-cropped beard. Pointing to the newspaper lying on the coffee table, he said, "Read this Sunday morning news!"

Reason looked down to read:

Fifteen-year-old Reason Nelson, had quite an adventure in the country west of Lincoln last night. When a rainstorm threatened to ruin a summer camping trip, the Havelock teen sought shelter at a farm. Inside a warehouse on the property, Reason discovered Judge Sullivan's missing Labradors and seventy other dogs! Officer Beef Tory reported that the dogs belonged to residents of the suburb of Havelock. Officer Tory phoned pet owners to inform them their pets had been found. This was an operation involving an underground lab which uses animals for research. When asked about the ten-thousand dollar reward, Reason said, "Accepting it would be like a ransom. I'm just glad to get Sully's dogs back to him."

Rain said, "Your mom and your brother are gonna wonder how you became Havelock's patron saint of lost dogs. Tiger, his mate, and his pups are now back with Judge Sully?"

Reason said, "Beef took Tiger and his family back to Sully's place. He called me afterward, saying that Sully's little girls cried when they got their dogs back. It choked me up inside.

Chapter Thirty-Three

A soft knock came from the front door. Rain pulled the door open. A small, bald man stood on the porch. "Rain!" he growled through his thick, red mustache. Daniel Kane met Rain's studious look with one of challenge. He folded his thick, muscular arms before his chest. "Jenna says your oldest boy works with troubled kids. How come he can't seem to fix her? Last night, I grounded her to her room. Two hours later, she was gone! Is she pregnant?"

Reason was amused by Kane's concern about his daughter. It wasn't something he expected. He figured that bikes, beer runs, and brawls would be more important to him. It surprised him that Kane might actually be a good dad, despite the fact he was the leader of the Bandits. Kane cursed as a dozen Harleys roared down the street.

"Friends of yours?" Rain asked.

"Not hardly," answered Kane. "This is not good."

Moses and ten members of the Screaming Eagles parked their cycles in front of the Nelson house. The biker president climbed off his bike and started up the sidewalk toward the house. "I'll cut to the chase," Moses said. "That reward is going to pay for my new Harley."

"Did you read the paper?" asked Rain. "My son turned the reward down. He's not accepting Judge Sully's money."

Moses said, "Four grand. Otherwise, there will be war."

In the street, Knolls shouted, "Moses! Company!"

Reason watched as Big Mike Tory pulled up on a fully dressed Harley. The big cop parked his bike in the street. Mike removed his helmet, placing it on the seat of his 1200. Turning to face Moses, he sternly said, "You causing problems here, Myron?"

Moses looked down at his feet. "Don't make an ass of me, dad."

Mike said, "You're fairly capable of doing that on your own."

Reason noted that Mike had addressed Moses by *Myron?* In the street, Big Mike stood facing Moses. Reason watched in amusement as the huge biker looked like a little kid being scolded. Kane followed Rain up onto the porch, saying, "I don't know what would be more pathetic. Having a creep like Moses for a son? Or having a cop for a dad? He's Moses of the Screaming Eagles. But when we was growing up he was Myron Cooper. Bobby, who died out at the Nightmare, was his little brother. Since his death, father and son have been at war."

The President of the Screaming Eagles had a reputation for being savage and brutal. It had never occurred to Reason that he might be the son of a cop. He'd never thought of family dynamics with guys like Moses or Kane. He'd just figured they had gone from being bad kids to even worse men. When Mike finished speaking, Moses and his bikers rode off down the street. Mike walked toward the porch.

Rain walked down the porch steps, offering his hand. Big Mike shook it. "Rain, good to see you, son. I figured you might of had something to do with rescuing all those dogs. But, what's Kane doing here? Do you know he stole Bobby's helmet off his headstone?"

Kane said, "I had nothing to do with that nonsense."

Reason looked to Big Mike. The sorrow he felt at the mention of Bobby overruled any anger he might have been struggling with. He eyed Reason. "For rescuing those dogs, Jack is gunning for you. Judge Sullivan wants you in protective custody."

"Pops," Rain said, "I'll take care of my son. Kane's daughter is at the Emerald. I'll be taking her to a safe house. Arrest Jack, Pops, and lay this thing to rest."

***

Shortly after Big Mike left, Rain drove Reason to the Emerald Pub. They were met at the door by Billy. The old Irishman razzed Reason about his shaggy hair. Reason ignored Billy's comments. Billy was tall and scarecrow thin with wavy wisps of snow-white hair curling up on the collar of his three-piece suit. At first glance, he appeared to be an ordinary businessman. But Reason only to had to lock gazes with the Irishman to determine he had the temperament of a territorial lion king. Reason had known early on that he and the old man would never be friends, even if the old Irishman was his grandfather.

Billy ushered them into his office. There seated on a couch in one corner of the room was Jenna Kane and Rose Nelson. Billy lit his pipe. He blew three perfect smoke rings before saying, "Reason, your dad's taking you and Jenna to a safehouse until Jack is arrested. Since the night Mary Partington pulled you out of her pond, she's been asking about you. You afraid to go out there?"

"No," Reason lied, his stomach doing flip-flops at the thought of spending a night at Bloody Mary's house. Rose said, "Sorry you all had to get involved in this. If I would have just kept my mouth shut, none of the rest of this would have happened. I am the one who arranged a meeting between Beef and Jenna. Now prosecutors need her testimony to put Jack away."

121

"Did you find my little brother?" Jenna asked her.

Rose said, "Boone is escorting him back to treatment."

Jenna said, "Unfair. My dad is pissed that Danny is using drugs. He doesn't want me to testify against Jack. And now, I have to go into hiding? Just not fair."

Billy snorted, "Call it Cosmic Injustice."

He picked up a notebook from his desktop, and said, "Here is a police record of the Cosmic Injustice suffered by Mary Partington. Believe me, your fate might look crappy, but it's nothing compared to the Hand of Fate Mary Partington got dealt. Before things started to go wrong for her, she was just a teacher. Not a demented old lady."

Billy read, "Oct. 25: Mary shot with .22 by kids. Mary received a wound to her stomach. Oct. 26: Trespassers in yard. Nov. 4: BB's shot through windows. June 13: Man sleeping in car in front yard. June 18: Mary interrupts young couple making out behind barn. June 18: Mary robbed at gunpoint. June 19: Intruder tied Mary up and ate her food. Nov.16: Two carloads of kids caught trespassing. Jan. 16: Grass set on fire on front porch. Jan.17: Window shot out. Jan. 20: Bullets shot through windows. June 12: Trespassers throw rocks at house. Mar. 26: Trespassers in yard. Mar. 31: Window shot out. April 1: Stones thrown through window. April 2: Bullets fired through east window. April 4: Rocks thrown through north window. April 8: Girl enters Mary's bedroom and steals flashlight, shines it in Mary's eyes. April 16: Vandals overturn outhouse. July 10: Trespassers yell from car. Oct. 25: Trespassers dump trash. Oct. 26: Mary kills Eldon Hill with one blast from her shotgun. Sheriff takes Mary's shotgun. And after that, kids were convinced she had shot a young boy playing a harmless prank. But he was a 27-year-old ex-mental patient, and he was climbing through her kitchen window! She defended herself, and then became known as Bloody Mary, a shot-gun-toting witch!"

Reason and Jenna were subdued by what they had just heard in regards to the lady. "Cosmic," Billy said, "Injustice."

At this, Rain raised a hand to Rose and said, "Rosie?"

Ignoring his outstretched hand, Rose said, "Make sure our son is safe, Rain. We'll deal with when we were us, sometime later down the road."

Chapter Thirty-Four

When they arrived at Mary's place, she stood there on her porch, staring curiously at Reason and Rain now focused on the apple tree next to her front porch. "Bobby Cooper's," Reason said, tapping the black helmet chained to a branch of the tree. "The one someone snagged off of Bobby's grave."

Mary came down off of her porch, using one bony finger to point to the helmet. "Clarence tried once to hack saw through the chain, but that proved to be quite a chore. So we just left it there in my tree."

Rain looked puzzled. "Clarence?"

"Pigman," Reason said, casually.

Mary said, "But long before you boys were born, Clarence Higby worked as a farmhand for my father." Mary stared thoughtfully at Rain and then at the branch. "We need it, Mary," Reason said. "It's a long story. Just trust me."

Mary slowly looked to her apple tree. "There's a saw in the barn. Careful not to cut yourself." Mary then turned, opened her screen door, and stepped back inside with Jenna. Reason followed Rain over to the barn. Rain opened the door and walked over to an old workbench situated beneath the loft. He found a saw and picked it up.

Minutes later, taking the helmet with him, Rain drove off.

Mary stepped outside. Reason couldn't get over the fact that he was being welcomed by the notorious Bloody Mary. He kept gazing at her in wonder as she ushered them into the parlor, then went to the kitchen. The room was filled with antique chairs, looking like it had been frozen in the late 1800's. Reason figured Mary was living totally in the past. She had only kerosene lamps to illuminate her house, with no electricity. Then, sunlight streamed in through the front windows, making the place bright and cheery.

Mary stepped out of the parlor leaving Reason there with Jenna. When she returned, she carried a scrapbook of newspaper clippings. She said, "In 1866, Havelock was nothing more than a railroad stop for Lincoln, capital of Nebraska. In 1886, the town was deeded to Albert Touzalin, vice-president of the Burlington Railroad. He named it in honor of his boyhood hero, British General Havelock. In 1890, the town of Havelock became official. In 1892, railroaders worked in the Shops, including your great, great grandfather, Reason. Thanks to John T. Nelson, and a company of Irish railroaders, the Burlington Shops placed Havelock on the world map.

"That was a hundred years ago, son. But you can be sure your family helped establish Havelock. It was on account of all those Irish Pubs that the suburbs of Uni Place and Bethany didn't want Havelock to be annexed into Lincoln by religious folks who didn't approve of folks drinking. You see, in 1893, Havelock Methodist Church was established one block to the east of Saint Pat's Catholic church. And then the Lutheran Church at 70th and Platte. The site of that church was a hemp mill with its fields supplying marijuana to make rope. Why, workers there always thought it was odd that birds would eat in the hemp fields, then began flying erratically, sometimes straight down to the ground!

"In 1929, Arrow Airport became the world's largest manufacturer of airplanes. Arrow is where Charles Lindbergh used to land his plane! He would then stop in at the California Lunchroom to have coffee with Patsy. Charlie was a pleasant fellow. In 1929, he flew in to watch the first nighttime football game played under the new lights with 2,600 fans attending. History was being made. Ballard Field was the first lighted stadium west of the Missouri River and Havelock the third high school in the nation to have night football!"

Mary paused, then said, "Look at these articles of current events. The article that appeared in the newspaper over a year ago when you rescued that poor boy on the park shelter roof when you wrestled that gun away from Vince's brother. Vince's mother and I were friends. Poor boy died so young. Struck and killed by that car, now buried out at Fairview. And because he dabbled with drugs, her other boy is locked away in a mental hospital, west of town. That poor mother has suffered a lot over the years. But so, too, did these other mothers. Tragedy seems to haunt this small community. Five of these children died from overdosing on drugs. Two died in senseless car accidents. Two others committed suicide. What a waste of life. Who knows what they would have grown up to be?"

Chapter Thirty-Five

When Jack Holland and eighty of the Den rode their Harleys down the center of Havelock Avenue, it sounded like a thunderstorm had erupted. Jack's colors on the back of his vest depicted a Norse Viking wielding an axe. On the twin blades of the axe, flames spilled down to form the words *Elder's Den, MC, Chapter 8, Lincoln, Nebraska.* Jack rode point down the center line, while the rest of the gang rolled down both lanes on either side of him. The procession began at the west end of the avenue, on 60th and Havelock, and proceeded past Castles pub, the Mortuary, the Joyo theater, Wolfe's Ace Hardware, Norma's Café, Arnold's Tavern. Business owners stood looking on warily at the horde of bikers. Sons and daughters of railroaders who had manned the shops through the years, they were descendants of Irish immigrants, who had come to the small town back in the 1800's, tough folk who made Havelock the town it was today.

Jack pulled even with the Emerald Pub, when a tall, lanky, white-haired figure stepped out in the street twenty feet in front of him. Billy Connors stood there dressed in his usual three-piece suit. His long white hair curled down about his collar, and his thick white mustache fluffed out on either side of his mouth as he gave a slight growl at the sight of the bikers screeching to a halt before him. Billy said, "I'm telling you, Havelock's off limits to you."

Jack revved his bike as he inched his way to within five feet of the old Irishman. Letting out a long sigh, Billy reached beneath his suit jacket, and the old Irishman pulled out a rather large .44 Magnum pistol. "Here's the deal, you and your gang ride outta here within the next three minutes, and I won't blow a hole in you!"

The gun caused Jack some concern, but it was the gall of the crotchety old man that had him totally bewildered. He had a notion to ride over him, but he could tell by the steely glint in the old lion's eyes that he wouldn't hesitate to put a slug in him. Billy thumbed back the hammer on the pistol. "Dad!" called Nate, seated on his bike behind him. "He's Sinn Fein. He's off-limits. Respect him, Jack. We don't need trouble with the Irish."

Jack and Billy were locked in a stare down. It was like the lion facing the bear. A challenge had been given, and it wasn't in either man's nature to back down. But some spark of intelligence flashed in Jack's mind, and he decided his best alternative to moving forward was to shut down. He did so and sat there in the middle of Havelock

Avenue. Behind him, the other Den members followed his example. In the silence that followed, Jack said, "Now what are you going to do, old man?"

"Stay the course," Billy flatly stated. "Ten seconds left."

Which was not what Jack was expecting. He had foolishly called the old Irishman's bluff. He never realized what sort of man Billy Connors happened to be. Jack nervously glanced back to his men, searching for some sign of hope. It came a moment later, from in front of him, not from behind as a thunderous roar filled the air. Big Mike Tory rode his fully-dressed Harley down the Avenue from the east. Behind him followed a group of Screaming Eagles. As Pops brought the entire procession to a stop ten feet behind Billy, the Eagles shut down their Harleys, and when Mike turned his own bike off, a second wave of explosive thunder came from the intersections on both sides of the Den parked there in the center of the Avenue. Moses appeared on his hog, leading twenty Eagles down the south side of 62nd Street. A block to the west, Daniel Kane rode up with thirty Bandits, boxing in the Den and leaving them nowhere to go. "Put that gun away, Will Connors," Big Mike said. "Jack gets your point."

At a stiff nod from Jack, the Den members in the center of the street struggled to turn their bikes around, then kicked them to life, and with bitter glares at the Bandits and Eagles they rode out of Havelock. Mike approached Billy, asking, "How did you manage a peace between the clubs, Irishman?"

Billy said, "My grandson is the culprit on that one. I'll let his dad tell you about that helmet he reclaimed out at Mary's place."

Rain walked out of the Emerald, carrying a red backpack. He made his way to the middle of the street where Moses sat. Rain reached into the backpack to pull Bobby Cooper's black helmet out. Moses stared at the helmet that had belonged to his younger brother; the one he'd been wearing when he tried to jump the Nightmare. Moses said, "All this time we thought Kane stole this off Bobby's headstone. It's why we've been at war with the Bandits."

Rain handed it to Big Mike.

"Sweet Jesus!" he gasped. "Is this Bobby's? Oh, Lord, where did you find it?"

Rain told him, and Mike stood there, remembering his younger son. Rain gave Moses a stern look and asked, "Are we even now?"

Nodding silently, Moses said, "We are."

* * *

On Mary's farm, Reason and Jenna were taking a walk with Mary down by her pond. "Back in my day," Mary said, "we would have ice skating parties on the pond, and once we climbed down yonder bank, and skated down Salt Creek all the way to Waverly! Those were happy times. I had seven brothers and sisters, and all of us grew up and moved away from this old farm. Only I came back to live here after my teaching stints in quite a few small towns. God only knows why my troubles with wild hooligan kids has plagued me ever since. Earl Eldon Hill was a young man who had his share of mental problems. He was only 27-years-old the night I ended his life, but as a child he had grown up on a farm.

"Unlike most kids now days Earl had both a father and a mother. But his father was a bit overbearing, which I think is where his problems first began. I needed to know about the troubled young life I was responsible for ending. All these years, friends and family have tried to tell me it wasn't my fault. But I pulled the trigger that night. I killed a young man, and who knows how bright his future might have been? When I get to regretting the night I took Earl out of this life, I think of all the children I've taught over the years. I did my best to better the troubled students who passed through my classrooms. I just wonder if I could have helped Earl if he'd been one of my students. Only this wasn't an isolated incident. Kids had broken into my house many times before. The moment I heard glass breaking downstairs, I picked up my shotgun and went to investigate. When I got to the kitchen, he was halfway through my window. I was just so frightened, I fired my shotgun. Sheriff Karnop claimed it was a justified shooting. Funny thing is, after all the searching the police did that night, no one ever recovered Earl's car keys for his Ford Fairlane parked in my driveway. Earl Hill wasn't alone that night. Someone else ran away from here with those car keys! Someone who has kept quiet all these years!"

They walked in silence then around the pond, making their way to Mary's graveyard. By the time they reached the arbor entrance, the sun was setting, a bright red fiery ball that hovered above the skyline, casting shades of brilliant pink on the trees surrounding the small grove. Mary peered down at the graves of her goats shot down by cowardly kids.

"Percy," Mary said, "used to march in the Havelock Days Parade. I used to dress him up in an old shirt, a pair of jeans, and a straw hat.

He was one of the first to be shot. By the time I'd get outside the damage had been done. I heard their laughter as they drove away. Angry is how I felt. I then just felt awfully sad. I guess it's why I keep tending their graves. A hurt like that never goes away."

Chapter Thirty-Six

At Mary's place, Jessie Dalton approached her front porch. Reason, Jenna, and Mary were seated there in old rocking chairs. Jessie sat down on the dusty porch steps, reminded of his boyhood days when he, Rain, and Beef used to tell stories on the porch of the General Store there in Sprague. All three of them had taken such different roads after leaving that small town near the Bluestem. Rain went to prison. Beef became a cop. And Jessie, a private investigator.

Mary smiled at him and said, "I was hoping you were out here tonight, watching over my house. I'm just glad I could help with these runaway children. What happened to Jack?"

Jessie said, "Beef Tory is arresting him soon."

Gesturing at the kids, he added, "You'll no longer be their guardian, Mary. Beef will pick up Jack and get him off the streets."

"Do I still have to testify?" Jenna asked.

Jessie said, "Once Jack is arrested your testimony will be crucial, Jenna. Reason? You might be asked to testify, as well."

"Fine," Reason said. "Putting Jack away is a good thing."

"I am glad you feel that way," Jessie said, fixing Reason in his sights. "Then you won't be opposed to the meeting I arranged for you to have with Judge Sullivan? There is still talk among law enforcement that you had something to do with the theft of his dogs. I want to clear you of any lame accusations on that account."

Thirty minutes later, Reason sat inside Judge Sullivan's chambers. Jessie stood there, his raven hair hanging in a braided tail down his back. *Uncle Jessie* as Reason called him. Boone would soon serve as his street contact for his investigative agency. Jessie, brother of his father, same father, different mothers, was proving to be a strong advocate. Despite not having a dad in his life, Reason considered himself lucky to have Jessie on his side.

Judge Sullivan, an older man with white short-cropped hair, gave Reason his undivided attention as he said, "You see, your honor, this started when Jenna went to get her little brother out of the Cosgrove complex. Jack of the Elder's Den killed Brooks. The Den tried to have Jenna committed to a mental institution so that she could no longer be a credible witness."

Sully peered at Reason. "I'm pleased to say, there's hope for you. Why does juvenile court scare some kids into staying straight, while others just don't care?"

"Court," Reason said, "scares every kid. But once a kid goes to court, it takes so long for a consequence to be handed down by the judge, they forget why they went there."

"What's going on inside the head of a kid," Sully asked, "who constantly keeps violating his probation?"

Reason said, "The kid who violates his probation quits realizing how badly he's screwed up."

Sully asked, "Why do you think kids like to get high?"

Reason said, "Getting high is appealing. You feel good when you get high. Or who would bother doing it? Once I started using either weed or alcohol, they both became habit forming, and the more I put into my system, the more I wanted. Before long, weed and alcohol were controlling me. I got tired of being under their influence."

Sully asked, "Is there any hope for a kid who consistently gets into trouble with the courts?"

"Kids who don't connect with themselves," Reason said, "they've been doing bad for so long, they no longer know how to change. Me? I had Mom, Boone, Vince, Collin and Jenna all trying to connect with me, yet I pushed them all away. Eventually, I made a decision to change. I might have a great support system with all their help, but the final choice came down to me. I guess that's the secret every kid needs to learn. Because really, a kid's destiny is always in their own hands. They either chose to get in trouble. Or chose not to."

****

That summer was a tough one for Reason. One week into summer vacation, Mary fell ill and had to be moved to a nursing home. Two nights later, some unknown vandals set her front porch on fire, and Mary's house burned to the ground. Despite efforts to keep the fire a secret that Mary never need know about, some reporter wrote about the fire that destroyed a historic landmark, and Mary inadvertently read the article in the newspaper the next morning. Folks at the nursing home claimed Mary was depressed for days afterward, but as she faced all adversities in life, she got over it and moved on.

When Reason learned about it, he had been sorely tempted to either get drunk or stoned. He kept trying to convince himself that after all he had suffered, he really deserved a mental break from harsh reality. Just one bottle of strong liquor or simply one joint would take care of that for him.

The next night, Danny Kane showed up at the Nelson house. He had a full bottle of whiskey in hand. Reason accepted the bottle he offered him. "If I do drink this," he said out loud, causing Danny to stare at him curiously, "I'll blow a whole two years of sobriety!"

Three times he brought the bottle to his lips, fumes from the whiskey wafting up into his nostrils. And three times he lowered the bottle, without drinking from it. He looked at Danny. "What's the difference between a kid who fails to stay clean and a kid who succeeds? They both get knocked down, but only one gets back up. The secret is: Fall down eight times, get up nine! When I first started using it made all my problems fade away. Who would ever smoke up if it didn't help to eliminate pain? But the more I used the more addicted I became. I found myself wanting to stay high on a regular basis. I found that staying wasted was too appealing to me. It became my constant goal. It snaked its way into every corner of my life, getting me to do things I wouldn't normally do. Breaking laws. Violating probation. Breaking curfew. Cutting off those who cared about me. Addiction treated me as it did everyone who had ever been addicted since the dawn of time. It treated me like its victim, rising up over me like a tyrant insisting that I stay high. Smashed. Stoned. Wasted. Bombed. For when I was drawn to the Valley of Oblivion, I no longer had to deal with life."

He walked to the side of the porch and poured the whiskey out.

Chapter Thirty-Seven

Reason rode out to Mary's place on July Fourth. He was five days away from his 16th Birthday, and he wanted to test ride the 250 Honda that Boone had given him as an early present. It was unusually mild that summer morning. A strong breeze blew in from the north, carrying with it the smell of fresh silage from the fields beyond the old farmstead. As he rode down the country road that ran past Mary's place, he noted that some moron had destroyed her mailbox with a close range blast of a shotgun. The battered metal box, filled with hundreds of tiny holes, hung there on a post beside her driveway. Reason braked a few yards away from the blackened ruins of what had once been Mary's house. The stone foundation remained, but the timbers were a heap of black husks. Reason could smell the acrid stench of burnt wood.

Mary, he thought, *I'm sure this house held lots of memories for you. You grew up here when you were a little girl, then came back here to live when you were done teaching. But even though your house is gone, you can rest in peace now. No more kids will ever come out to harass you. No, that's a chapter that's closed forever.*

A moment later, he parked his bike and walked down the path that led to the small grove. He stepped into the goat cemetery, the breezes blowing through the wild tangles of his hair. He stood there, soaking up the silence, wondering if there was a place beyond this earth where his friends who had passed could actually know that he missed them. He opened his eyes and looked down to the gravestones of goats long since buried before him.

Birdsong filled the air in the woods. In the field to the north, a tractor growled. Above the grove, a hawk spiraled through the unseen currents. It was joined by a second hawk, and as the two raptors wind-danced through the country skies, Reason peered up at them. As they faded from sight, he looked in amazement at a rusty double-barreled shotgun leaning against the arbor. There, growing out of both barrels were two red roses, contrasting sharply with the greenery around them. He thought, *The gun Mary shot Eldon Hill with? But the forest has claimed it, and the two red roses sprouting from its barrels are a beautiful sight in a place where Mary suffered so much pain.*

He finished his time there at the goat graveyard and retraced his steps to his cycle. In a matter of moments, he opened up his throttle, speeding along the twisting trail until he came to the switchback leading around the gully of the Nightmare. Reason shuddered to think of how Bobby Cooper had failed to jump that forty foot gap and died when he crashed in Salt Creek below. He whipped his way through the switch-back of the Nightmare, heading onto the path where Pops had crashed his own bike that day they had rescued him.

When he reached Superior Street, Reason had just set his sights on the Woods ahead, when he spotted Jack Holland seated there on his Harley in the center of the Turn Around. For long moments, he held a stare down with the President of the Den. Reason spun around and sped away in the opposite direction. Jack followed behind him. He headed across Superior and down the trail leading back to Mary's place. But the biker stayed close behind him. Reason hit the dip in the trail that had taken Big Mike down that day last summer. He came up and off the seat, clinging to his hand grips to keep from wiping out. When he landed, he gunned the bike over a set of berms, then shot away, heading toward the Nightmare a block ahead.

Reason was tempted to jump the ravine. It was a mad idea, but if he could do it, he would be a legend for long years to come. Bobby Cooper had died trying to jump the Nightmare, and no one had been crazy enough to ever make the attempt again. But Reason thought if he could pick up enough speed, he'd launch himself over the gully, soar through forty feet of air, and land on the far side.

He peered down. The needle on his speedometer hit 40, then 45. He glanced back to see Jack twenty feet behind him. He looked to the sharp drop-off thirty feet in front of him. He just hit 65, when at the last possible second, his lame-brained death jump was cancelled by the black wolf suddenly appearing directly in front of him.

He skidded around the Nightmare, just in time to see Jack hitting the drop-off at sixty-miles-per-hour. The biker president cried out in surprise as man and machine soared ten feet out into the air. As the bike fell out from under Jack, he thrashed wildly, dropping at a high rate of speed into the gully below. Sixty feet below the high ridge, his Harley landed with a slight explosion. Jack landed his neck twisted at an awkward angle as he plowed into the dirt embankment a foot away from the waters of Salt Creek.

Reason nodded gratefully at the wolf looking down to the dead Jack Holland below in the creek. "You knew," Reason said, "that I would have failed that jump, didn't you?"

Offering him a warm look, his blue eyes glowing brightly, the black wolf turned and loped off into the trees along the high bluff.

Reason stopped at a gas station halfway back to Havelock to call the police. Thirty minutes later, Big Mike met up with Reason on the trail leading back to the Nightmare. The big cop was riding his 1200 Harley, and as Reason explained what had happened earlier, he looked apprehensive about taking to the narrow trail stretching ahead of them. The irony was not lost on Reason. Pops had lost his youngest son out at the Nightmare. Now, here he was going to investigate another fatal crash in that deep ravine.

Big Mike said, "Things could have gone the other way with your encounter with Jack. You're lucky to be alive."

Reason kept his bike at a steady speed. He was still disturbed that Jack had died. He realized he was responsible for the horrendous crash. Jack had been following behind him when he plunged off the high ridge. Despite the fact that Jack had meant him harm, Reason had heart enough not to want the man's death hanging over his head. Yes, he killed Brooks, but had he finally reaped what he had sown?

When they reached the Nightmare, both Reason and Pops parked their bikes to one side of the trail. They then walked to the lip of the steep cliff. Mike radioed in for an ambulance. Together, he and Reason stood on the high bank overlooking Salt Creek.

"The trouble with living on the edge is," Mike said, "eventually one falls off. A person can't go through their entire life spitting in the face of destiny, speeding recklessly down the highway of life without any regard to Stop signs. Some folks never slow down enough to make something positive happen for themselves. Always going to be a wild horse that can never be broken. Throughout history, there's always been outlaws, yet the truth behind those legends has been washed away. So that by the time that kids today hear of outlaws like Billy the Kid, Jesse James, and John Dillinger, they don't get the fact that all those outlaws were psychotic sociopaths.

"The same goes for gangsters trying to establish themselves by wiping out rivals, sending a bullet through an enemy while passing by them in a car! Those outlaws are way beyond normal. Something's not right in their head. Someone who steps that far over the line needs to get themselves back in order. Whatever circumstances in their lives set their feet on the wrong paths can never justify how they misread their moral compass. Life has to make sense. It can't be lived by those who think killing, stealing, and having no regard for human life is okay. Somewhere along the path, a person has to draw a line they'll never cross. And whether they believe that there is a God keeping track of all their deeds. Or whether they live by following their own conscience, they have to live a life that makes sense. When things no longer make sense, then a person needs serious help. That speech could be given to just about any delinquent out there. I wish I could have delivered it to Bobby before he crossed that line of no-return."

Chapter Thirty-Eight

The three of them stood on the open plains of the Cheyenne River rez in South Dakota. The thunder of an approaching herd of horses rocked them as more than three hundred of the steeds emerged from thick clouds of dust only two-hundred yards ahead of them.

Rain Nelson narrowed his eyes. He looked sideways at Ben Black Bull. The Lakota man did not seem concerned about the approaching horses. There was an air of calmness coming from him as he shook back the long strands of his raven hair. Standing between Rain and Ben, Reason fidgeted nervously. Wiping sweat from his palms on his jeans, he tucked them into his pockets and glanced worriedly at the roiling clouds of dust on the horizon before them. He wondered if they had been wise to follow the Native onto the open plains. The stampeding horses were coming their way. In the next few minutes, if they weren't turned, the three of them were going to be run over by the herd of horses.

The horses were running full out, too, a force of nature with the power of a thunderstorm and nothing could stop their forward movement. Rain and Reason looked behind them to a bluff rising up from the dusty plains. It would serve as a safer place to stand then the wide, open plains they were on. Father and son thought about asking Ben if they shouldn't wisely retreat to the sanctuary the small rise in the land offered before the oncoming horses trampled over them.

Ben looked to the two dogs taking up protective stances five feet in front of them. Bummer, Reason's Shepherd, and Harley, Ben's newly adopted Rottweiler, stared straight ahead, their teeth bared.

Ben said, "Harley? Bummer? Let them know we are here."

The stout and solid Rott immediately lifted his blocky head and peered at the lead horse of the oncoming herd. Reason thought the dog would bark, carrying on in excited yips and yaps to draw the attention of the wildly racing steeds now closing in on them from less than two hundred feet away. But Harley simply stared at them, and Reason assumed the Rott used a strange telepathy to warn the horses that they were about to run them over. And it appeared to be working. The lead horse turned swiftly, his movement of veering over in front of the rest of the herd causing the entire mob of madly running horses to wheel smoothly away from them.

Bummer let out a ferocious bark. Reason kneeled beside both dogs and hugged them in relief, grateful that at the last possible moment, the two dogs had kept them from being trampled. He watched the steeds as they raced away to the east, splashing into the sun-glazed river that cut across their path. Dappled here and there with the rays of the setting sun to the west, red, gold, and pinks sprouts of water shot up and around the horses as all three hundred leaped up onto the bank on the far side, then thundered away to the grasslands beyond.

Rain and Reason sighed in relief. Ben looked to the three Land Rovers coming their way down a nearby dusty road. He said, "The holy men of the Cheyenne are coming. They will be grateful that you've returned these relics to them. They will just be grateful to get them back. Trust me. They will be like little kids at Christmas time when they see this white buffalo robe and this sacred pipe."

A month ago, when Rain suddenly appeared at the Emerald, he had asked Billy Connors for the map he'd kept in his safe all these years. Before Billy handed it over to Rain, he had called Jessie, Beef, and Reason and invited them to a sit-down at the pub. The three of them had talked Rain into doing what was right with the Native relics.

Rain had retrieved the relics hidden in Quarry Oaks. He had then driven them out to Wounded Arrow, Ben's dog rescue ranch. Both surprised and saddened to have the artifacts placed with him, Ben made arrangements with the Cheyenne Tribal Council in Lame Deer, Montana. The hand off of the relics would take place among the holy men at the Cheyenne River rez in South Dakota. They were coming to them now. Their vehicles crested a rise in the road.

Ben said, "The Cheyenne are a prominent Great Plains tribe. Cheyenne is derived from the name *Sahiyenan* that is a Dakota name, translated as *people alive*. They once lived in Minnesota, but due to conflict with the Ree and Mandan, they migrated to the Black Hills. In 1832, they divided into two groups, the Northern and the Southern Cheyenne. In 1858, the Cheyenne joined in the Indian Wars. Sand Creek Massacre. Colorado War. Little Big Horn. The US government forced them to move to a rez in Oklahoma. The Northern Cheyenne relocated to a reservation in Montana. The Treaty of Fort Laramie of 1868 created the Great Sioux Reservation covering parts of six states, including both the Dakotas. The Cheyenne River Indian Reservation was created in 1889. Chief Sitting Bull lived here at the boundary between the Cheyenne River rez and the Standing Rock rez. In 1890, the US became concerned that Chief Sitting Bull was going to lead an exodus off the rez. Hundreds of Indians gathered on the Cheyenne River rez, preparing to flee. A force of 39 Indian policemen were sent to Sitting Bull's residence on December 16, 1890, to arrest him. The US Army sent Buffalo Bill to speak with the great war chief, but before he arrived a battle started in which 18 Natives were killed, among them Sitting Bull and his son. Sitting Bull's half brother, Spotted Elk, led 350 people off the Cheyenne River rez. The next day they were attacked by 500 soldiers in the Wounded Knee Massacre. 300 Natives were killed, including women and children. Survivors settled on Pine Ridge or returned to the Cheyenne River rez."

Ben introduced Reason and Rain to the elders of the Dog Soldier society. The exchange of the items became official after holding a council fire. Ben honored Reason by having him gift the headman with a bag of tobacco, a traditional gift among Natives. Reason would never smell Captain Black again without thinking how humble he felt amongst the Cheyenne elders. It would be a memory etched in his mind forever. He teared up as he watched his father hand over the relics to the headman, starting with the Sharps rifle, then the Colt .45, the warclub of Buffalo Calf Road Woman, the sacred pipe, and the white buffalo robe with the peace treaty marked on it.

It was late into the night when the council meeting ended. The fire burned low. Reason watched his father look on as the buffalo robe was carried to a car for transport back to Lame Deer in Montana. Rain had done the right thing in returning the artifacts to the Cheyenne. As he stood there, Ben thanked him for bringing the affair full circle as the late Benjamin Black Bull would have wanted him to.

Chapter Thirty-Nine

It was past midnight. Ben drove them away from the meeting place there on the reservation. Reason in the backseat with Bummer and Harley, knew that all those years he'd spent in prison, Rain had a goal of retrieving those artifacts and making a profit off of them. It was monumental for him to give them up as he had. Reason reached over the seat and gave his father's shoulder a squeeze. Rain glanced back at him. Reason said, "You did good, Dad. Real good."

Suddenly, Ben braked so hard the two dogs slid off the backseat and landed at Reason's feet on the floorboards. Ahead of them a fireball lit up the night. Reason looked to the single car that had been the last to leave the council meeting. Two members of the Dog Soldiers had been tasked by the elders to transport the Sharps rifle and the Colt pistol to an undisclosed location. Three holy men had determined that both were cursed by a host of spirit creatures from the Otherworld. The holy men had handed the rifle and the pistol over to the two younger men, who were then instructed to destroy them. "Someone," Ben said, "detonated charges on the bridge ahead of us."

The two Dog Soldiers clambered out of their fiery vehicle in the middle of the bridge. A hooded figure detached himself from the shadows beyond the firelight. The Nomad moved up behind the two young Natives, a pistol in his hand. One of the men reached back into the car and retrieved the Sharps rifle and the Colt pistol out of the flaming wreckage. Even as they wheeled away from the red-hot heat emanating from the car, the Nomad double-tapped both Dog Soldiers in the head with his pistol. By the time Ben reached the bridge in his Bronco, the Nomad was racing toward his car parked in the shadows some distance away. He carried the rifle and pistol as he ran.

"You, fool!" Ben shouted. "Evil is not to be trifled with!"

Something strange then happened in the backseat with the two dogs. Seated between them, Reason was puzzled as Bummer and Harley looked through the windshield at the Nomad fleeing into the shadows. Reason could have sworn they were talking to each other as the shepherd turned his head to look directly at the Rott. They leaped over the seat and sprang through Ben's open door. Both dogs raced past the two fallen Dog Soldiers. They cleared the bridge and swiftly closed on the Nomad. Bummer sank his teeth in the Nomad's left butt cheek. He howled in pain, dropping the pistol. Harley leaped up, his large head slamming into the Nomad's chest, knocking him back against his Ford Tauras parked beside the road. The Nomad swung the Sharps rifle in a two-handed grip, forcing the dogs back so that he could scramble up on top of his car. There, he shouldered the rifle, thumbed back its hammer, opening its breech. Grinning wickedly, he then removed a cartridge from a pocket of his jacket. He shoved the large .50 caliber bullet into the chamber and cocked the gun's hammer. "No!" Ben cried. "You'll unlock the wanagi residing in that rifle!"

As Reason ran up to the Nomad's car, he immediately latched onto Bummer and turned facing the madman with the Sharps rifle. He stood in front of his dog and the Nomad pulled the trigger. The hammer fell on the cartridge in a gun that hadn't been fired in one hundred years. There came a loud concussion from the firing chamber and the stock kicked back into the Nomad's shoulder, punching him off his feet. A phosphorescent cloud of violet smoke drifted from the end of the muzzle. The wraiths trapped inside the cursed gun erupted into the night air. Exiting the ethereal plain, they took shape as a pack of wild-haired, mad children, who flew through the air like a murder of swift-winged crows, cawing and howling. They swooped right and left, their red eyes glowing.

Knowing they were in the presence of savage, blood-thirsty demons, Ben spread his arms to force Rain to back away from the terrors hovering in the air. One of the purple spectral beings let out a war cry and dove down at the Nomad. Then, one by one, the mad mob of demons descended upon the Nomad, tearing, gouging, puncturing through the skin of his chest. No blood came from his wounds, merely a dull green light for the attack did damage to the man's soul. Picking up the Sharps and the Colt, the Nomad raced away into the darkness. The mad pack of howling imps gave chase.

The sound of thunder erupted from the west. A large herd of brawny buffalo ran on a course that would take them directly into the Nomad's path. The white lead bull of the herd ran full out. Plumes of silvery mist erupted from his nostrils. Crystals sparkled in the beard of white froth covering his chin. Specks of multi-hued light dappled his entire body as the loud pounding hooves of over three-hundred bison reverberated through the air. The buffalo herd trampled over the Nomad, brutally pounding him, the Sharps rifle, and the Colt pistol into the dusty plains.

Rain drove away from the western part of the state where the buffalo used to roam by the thousands, taking his son and his dog back to the small suburb of Havelock. He felt good about the fact that the map he had picked up in the aftermath of the bus crash caused by Jack Holland when he was just a kid, had finally been used to recover the Native relics. The white buffalo robe was back with the Cheyenne and so, too, was the warclub of Buffalo Calf Road Woman and the sacred pipe. This pleased Rain. He had done the right thing after retrieving the map from Billy Connors. After waiting all these years to claim the relics, he had relinquished them to the Lakota dog handler. Earlier that evening Reason had commended him for not keeping the relics for himself. After all, he could have made millions had he sold them to an antique collector. That his son was proud of him meant a lot to Rain, but had Reason known the secret that he was harboring it would change his opinion of him.

Upon arriving back in Havelock, Rain said farewells to Reason. He offered him one last friendly wave as Reason led Bummer inside the Nelson house. He was tempted to follow his son inside to see if Rose might consider reconciling with him. And yet he knew he could not push her into a corner after she had cut him off while he'd been serving time for the murder of Daws. She needed time to heal.

Besides, Rain had another matter to deal with. The meeting had been set in place by Billy Connors. The Irishman had brokered a deal with an art collector, and he had made arrangements for her to meet with Rain at the Emerald Pub at 12 AM. Billy warned him he was playing with fire, but Rain had known that when he had come away from Quarry Oaks with the Native relics he had retrieved. Yes, he handed the artifacts over to Ben, but he kept the last one for himself.

It was a leather shirt decorated with beads and other emblems, marking whoever had worn it back in the day as a great war leader. Rain figured that since Ben had never mentioned the shirt that it would not be missed. He figured the buffalo robe was the greatest find at the quarry. It was worth far more than a simple leather shirt.

Chapter Forty

When Rain arrived at the pub, he carried the relic inside a backpack. Billy met him at the door. As the old Irishman escorted him to a large round table at the back of the pub, Rain noticed the sign that hung above an ornate oak door adjacent to the pub's massive fireplace. The sign read, *Here, there be Dragons.*

Billy had orchestrated this deal. Rain suspected he was about to be arrested for possessing the Native relic, for the art collector wore a brown uniform complete with a badge. She was a Native American with short-cropped raven hair and stunningly beautiful. Her dark eyes remained fixed on him as he sat down across from her. She said, "I am Cora Red Cloud. Sorry about the uniform, but my shift just ended at Animal Control and I did not want to be late for our meeting. You have the Ghost Shirt?"

"Ghost Shirt?" Rain said, removing the shirt from the pack.

"Or," Cora said, "War Shirt. Either way they are considered holy by my Lakota people. That one," she added, gesturing at the leather shirt Rain spread out across the table, "has a lot of medallions and emblems on it. It is obvious, it belonged to a great war leader."

Joining them at the table, Billy lit his pipe. Peering at Cora through blue smoke, he said, "Tell us about these War Shirts, Cora."

Running her fingers reverently over the leather shirt which would have covered a warrior's shoulders and hung down past his waist, Cora said, "The Big Bellies made rules for being a shirt wearer: 'Wear the shirts and be big-hearted, always helping others, never thinking of yourselves. Look out for the widows and orphans. Think no ill of others, nor see the ill they would do to you. Many dogs come to lift the leg at your lodge, but look the other way, do not let your heart remember. Do not give way to anger. Do all these duties gladly, with a good face. Be generous and brave. You will lead the warriors in camp, see that order is preserved, no violence committed against one another. See that all among the people has his rights respected. You must be wise, kind, and firm in all things. Never take up arms against your own without council. Man living alone can do as he pleases, if he lives among others he must bow his head to the good of all. Without strong leaders to see this done, the people will fail, the nation break up into small, defenseless bands.'

"Crazy Horse was a Shirt Wearer. It is said that he rode into battle through a hail of bullets, and each battle he came out unscathed."

Rain said, "You think this might be Crazy Horse's ghost shirt? And you believe it is endowed with magical powers?"

Billy blew two smoke rings before saying, "It might stretch your imagination to know that Natives and my Celtic ancestors believed in magic, big medicine, and enchantments. My Dragon Room has magic that would blow your mind."

No sooner had he said this, than Reason appeared out of the darkness of the pub's common room. "I heard that, Dad," he said, picking up the decorated leather shirt from the table. "I think we should just give this to the lady. Don't you?"

Before Rain could answer him, Nate Holland came barging through the front door of the Emerald. The big biker waved his pistol wildly as he crossed through the common room, his hate-filled glare locked on Reason. "You're gonna die, Reason!" he growled. "Your dad killed my grandfather, but because of you, I lost my dad!"

Nate lunged forward, shoving the muzzle of his gun directly into the leather shirt Reason held. He jabbed at him, pushing him so hard he stumbled down the hallway. When his back hit the oak door behind him, Reason raised his arms, the shirt still in his grasp. Nate fired five shots, each slug striking the leather shirt, forcefully driving Reason back and through the oak door. Engulfed by ethereal forces, Reason felt like he had been kicked by a horse as each bullet struck the leather shirt, yet not one of the lead slugs penetrated the Ghost Shirt. Instead, they evaporated in the magic of the shirt.

"My God!" Reason whispered in awe as fell back through a portal inside the Dragon Room. He found himself in a forested glade, the air around him thick with swirls of green mist. Stepping out of the mist, was the black wolf that had appeared to him so many times these past months. "Storm?" Reason said. "Where are we?"

He had not expected the wolf to answer him, and when it did, he nearly fainted in shock. "Storm?" the wolf said, amusement in his blue eyes. "My name is Shantigar, which no pun intended, is quite a mouthful. My close kin call me Shan. I am pack leader of the Black Wolves of the Green Vale Forest. At the beginning of our journey together, I was assigned to be your guardian by Creed the Wolf Lord. He has taken a special interest in you. Have I done well so far?"

Shaking his head in disbelief, Reason said, "A talking wolf? What the holy hell! And here?"

"Valasar," Shan said. "It is the realm beyond your grandsire's Emerald Pub. Here, the war between Light and Darkness has waged for thousands of years. In that battle, the wolves of my line stand with the Lion Lords of Rockhaven. Though not as numerous as the White Wolves of Masgar, my black wolves and I make a difference in the war." His big blue eyes going wide, Shan stepped back from the clearing. Reason heard him shout, "Beware, the Wild Hunt!"

A black stallion burst from the undergrowth to one side of the trail. The steed snorted as it raced past Reason then wheeled about, its rider tugging on its reins. Keeping pace with the stallion and its rider were huge, shaggy dogs. Reason looked up at the figure mounted on the horse. Bare-chested with muscles rippling beneath the dark-tanned skin of his chest and broad shoulders, a shimmering sword appeared in his hand. The rider laughed. Long, black hair spilled down around his face and his shoulders, unruly tangles that gleamed blue-black in the glow of the sword blade. "I am Creed Black Stag. I've come to gift you with a book from the Lodge."

Creed handed a leather-bound book down to Reason, who read the title out loud, "Monster Compendium."

Creed gestured at the book. "Read about your enemies, know their strengths and weaknesses, develop your skills and talents to defeat them. Your days ahead will be filled with quests."

"Are you," Reason asked, "an elf?"

"Summer Kin," Creed said. "The Elves of the Summer Country claim you have been chosen as a guardian in a battle that has been waged for ages. If I form an alliance with you, you will become a Champion of the Celtic Road. As Bard Chieftain, I declare you are destined one day to accomplish many deeds that will serve a greater purpose. Through gateways, you shall travel to begin your training. May the All-Father watch over you. Do you accept the role?"

Reason nodded uncertainly. "Yes," he said in a whisper.

Creed Blackstag and his wolf hounds were then gone and raced away into the Unseen Realm. Shan looked to Reason and said, "I will see you soon in the future. As for now, your father fears you have been killed. I suggest you return to the Emerald."

***

When Reason emerged from the Dragon Room, he carried the Ghost Shirt with him. Beef Tory had handcuffed Nate and was leading him toward the front door of the pub. Billy was attempting to console Rain who seemed to be in distress over the supposed loss of his son.

It was Cora Red Cloud who first saw Reason stepping out of the room. "Rain," she quietly said, "your son yet lives."

Rain sprang up from his chair, using the backs of his hands to wipe tear streaks from his cheeks. "I'm okay," Reason said, surprised to see Rain showing so much emotion.

Rain said, "But Nate fired his gun at point-blank range."

"The shirt," Reason said, "produced a force field, shielding me from Nate's bullets. Dad? We screwed over the Indians so badly. They suffered enough. I say, we give this Ghost Shirt to Cora, okay?"

Cora took the shirt from Reason. As she folded it reverently over her arms, she said, "The Morning Star will be given this Ghost Shirt. As long as no one objects."

She met Rain's steady gaze. He raised both hands, palms up. "I don't object," he said, disappointment in his eyes. "I had no right to take it."

Chapter Forty-One

During the years following his encounter inside the Emerald, with proper guidance and training from Creed Black Stag, Reason became a Ghost Hunter, delving into the Unseen Realm on quests that he returned from, carrying tattered books, rare parchments, strange potions, and swords that shimmered with a mysterious inner light. He named them jewel-blades, for each sword was shaded the color of the large jewel each had embedded in their hilts.

As he grew older, he often Gated out of town, stepping through the Dimensional Portal inside the Dragon Room. He was teleported to places all over the world. Creed went with him on these trips to hunt down entities of Darkness. It was Creed, too, who taught him skills, for to defeat these demons, he needed mad warrior skills in order to prevail.

Creed was protective of him, claiming it was dangerous work, and he had a real fear that one of these entities might follow an ethereal trail that would lead a malevolent apparition back to the Emerald. Billy Connors was always there at the end of such dimensional trips to deal with any contagion that may have infected Reason in the completion of a quest. Creed referred to the Irishman as a Mage Lord, and as such, Billy had healed Reason of several nasty viruses that left unchecked, could have spread beyond the pub. Through a black walnut staff he wielded, Billy utilized his Linear Particle Accelerator skills to annihilate any spores or toxic chemicals that hitchhiked back from any war zone Reason had traveled to. Creed claimed ghouls and vampires were infected with vicious spores that could infiltrate one's immune system. Undead, zombies spread another savage disease, and in most cases, resulted in a virulent strain of rabies, which left their victims stark raving mad lunatics.

Reason joined the Order of the Hunters, an elite force of Paranormal Investigators who tracked down and destroyed demons wherever they threatened the human race.

In Tel Avi, he eliminated a demon-inspired terrorist cell plotting a chemical attack in Israel. In Tehran, he assassinated two fanatic brothers who planned bombings in nearby Iraq. Both brothers were crazed Extremists being manipulated by a band of jinn who hailed from the deserts of Saudi Arabia. In northern Africa, he led a team of Hunters and took out an Extremist faction connected with Boko Haram, led by a warmongering demon whose devoted followers had killed hundreds in savage attacks along the African coast. In Bosnia, Reason and his Hunters eliminated a terrorist group determined to bomb a dozen schools, using children as targets of their attacks. It was his first experience with Child Soldiers, and it saddened him that such a thing existed. In each of these places, Reason prevented attacks in the physical realm by taking the fight to the spiritual realm. In his quests, he had learned that the evils in this world had a basis in the spirit world. To win against Darkness, there were demons to be dealt with properly in order to shut down savage and lethal attacks. Before Reason became a skilled warrior in the supernatural realm, he spent months in training.

He gated to Koyasan Monastery in Japan, founded by Kōbō-Daishi, Grand Master of Buddhist Teaching. There, he learned Dai-toryu, Japanese martial arts first taught by Takeda Sōkaku. On his second mission, he gated to the School of the Winds in Scandinavia where he learned Sword Skills. On his third mission, he gated to Buddhist monks in Tibet to learn the Way of Silence. On his fourth, he gated to the Vatican at Rome to learn the Way from the Brother-hood of the Rose. On his fifth, he gated to Israel to be trained in Hebrew verses from the Torah by priests of the Essenes. On his sixth, he gated to Iraq to learn the verses of the Quran to battle against the jinn of the Middle East. On his seventh and last training mission, he gated to a haunted Asylum in Switzerland. During this Hunt, he confronted creatures infected with viruses. His battles were many. Each victory he stopped evil from being spread. In his confrontations, his allies were priests, shamans, wizards, Templar Knights, healers, druids, and Mage Lords known as Servants of the Light.

Very few knew of his battles and deeds, for in his personal life he took a career in the field of youth work, trying and many times failing to get through to troubled kids. It often frustrated him, to be so skilled in slaying monsters and demons, and yet having no control over many of the unruly, defiant kids who were hell-bent to spiral into Kamikaze mode. Try as he might, he could not lead them from the path of self-destruction they seemed determined to walk.

***

Reason had just turned 21 when he lost Bummer. The great and loyal German Shepherd had come into his life when he was nine-years-old, and became a permanent fixture. He took the loss hard, too. The dog

had been his constant companion all eleven years of his life. Bummer
was going to be sorely missed. Reason produced a farewell poem in
Bummer's memory. Boone had his ashes stored in an urn. He'd taken
it out to Wounded Arrow. Ben had honored Bummer by placing his
ashes in his pet cemetery, complete with a granite headstone. He had
Reason's poem engraved on the face of the stone. On an autumn day,
Reason drove out to Wounded Arrow to pay tribute to his dog. When
he reached the grave, he broke down and cried, for there on the face
of the headstone was his poem. It read:

Bummer's Creed

The Lord looked down from heaven,
a puppy in his hand.
He said, "I'm sending you to earth,
an often troubled land.

Your presence will bring comfort,
to ones I love so dear.
When you snuggle up beside them,
they'll know that I am near.

I know it's quite a mission,
for a tiny pup to do.
But I'll be in your heart,
my love will flow through you.
You'll whine, bark and sniff,
you'll cuddle and you'll play.
You'll be a ray of sunshine,
on dark and dreary days.

You'll share that thought-filled stare,
that dogs are noted for.
You'll wag your tail and smile,
greeting loved ones at the door.

You'll be a most welcome sight,
at the end of weary days.
You'll grow from pup to dog,
sharing yourself through each phase.

And when the day draws near,
that I retrieve my precious loan,
you'll leave the world a better place,
through you, my love will have brightly shone.

For those who cared so dearly,
and gave you love so free,
will know you were an example,
of the love that comes from Me."

Chapter Forty-Two
Ten Years later

Ben Black Bull tried to catch 11-year-old Lucas Holland as he ran up to the 6th floor of the open-air parking garage. Both were winded. Lucas climbed onto a ledge and seated himself facing forward, close to falling sixth stories to the sidewalk below. He held himself by the tips of his fingers, his head aimed in the direction of the flight down. Slight breezes caused his shaggy blond hair to obscure his vision. He shook back wild tangles of his hair to see Ben Black Bull cautiously approaching him. Ben said, "Lucas? What are you—"

"Shut up!" Lucas snapped. "I'm already annoyed by my anger manager! Some kids shoot themselves. Some kids take sleeping pills. Some cut their wrists. I used to think they were stupid! Now I know why they do it. I just can't take this, so just let me jump!"

Lucas peered down to the hard, unforgiving sidewalk far below. "My dad, president of the Elder's Den, tried to drown my mom in a lake. Gypsy, warlord of dad's club, pulled him off her. Someone reported the fight to the cops, so they removed me from my home, placing me with a stupid cop and his stupid wife! They wake me up by shooting me with cold water from a spray bottle. They walk me to the school bus. When I get in trouble at school, they ground me. They grill me with stupid words. Laws and rules are what keep me in line.

"I must abide by these laws in order to survive.

"I break a law, I suffer a consequence.

"I have had no proper instructions on how to behave.

"I need to be reprogrammed.

"I am wired wrong. I have disorders.

"Only Guardians of Guidance can save me from my mad self!"

Ben's job that afternoon was to transport his 11-year-old client to Child Guidance. His caseworker told him before he picked Lucas up that his father's biker club had been arrested for destroying headstones in a small town cemetery. The caseworker also received death threats from these bikers. Her last words to Ben were, "Lucas comes with a lot of baggage."

Ben had remained respectfully silent on the ride downtown. He led Lucas to the session room, then sat in the waiting room. Ten minutes later, Lucas snarled rage-filled words from inside the room. The door burst open, and the kid went racing through the waiting room filled with startled parents.

By the time Ben reached the ground floor, Lucas was one block ahead of him. He followed Lucas on a six-block run in downtown Lincoln. The kid reminded Ben of a scrawny scarecrow. Long blond hair flopping wildly. Skinny arms flapping. Thin legs pumping madly. Faded jeans and tattered sweatshirt threatening to swallow him whole.

When Ben reached the 6th floor of the open-air garage, Lucas had climbed onto the ledge. Ben froze, not daring to press his luck with the volatile kid. Lucas's attention was suddenly drawn to the street six stories below, where a black Pontiac screeched to a stop. The driver opened his back door. A pit bull puppy and a large Brindle pit sprang out into the street. The driver gunned his car, leaving black smoke drifting through the air as he squealed away down the street.

Determined to do something about the dogs in the street below, Lucas ran past Ben to the elevator. Minutes later, he raced outside the car park to rescue the dogs. The little biker kid darted out in front of a startled woman driver who braked just in time to avoid running the pup over. The poor lady shrieked as Lucas pounded on her hood with both fists. He scooped the pup up into his arms. The biker kid who wanted to die, went into rescue mode, cradling the pup in his grasp.

Lucas read the name tag on the tiny pup's ratty collar: "Goblin," he said, watching the Brindle walk past him and onto the sidewalk, a low growl rumbling in his chest. Lucas lowered the rambunctious pup to the sidewalk and released him. Goblin head-butted the bigger dog, his small head connecting with his front legs. The dog lowered his head and allowed the pup to play bite his nose. Goblin plopped down, exposing his belly to the larger dog.

"Grunge," Ben said, joining them on the sidewalk and reading the tag on his collar. "As big as he is, he could hurt him, but the pup's showing he trusts him. That was lame, you wanting to jump."

"I know," Lucas sheepishly said. "But I really hate having cops as foster parents."

"Yes," Ben said, frowning. "You made that quite clear."

To change the subject, Lucas said, "You're one big Indian. You look like Wind in His Hair. My dad knows Rodney Grant. What are you gonna do with the dogs?"

Ben said, "I'll take them back to my dog rescue ranch—"

"A ranch for dogs?" Lucas blurted. "Can I see it?"

The dogs followed the two of them back to Ben's van. Goblin scampered happily across the sidewalk, springing up into Ben's outstretched hands. "Whoa," Ben laughed. "No aggression with this one. He's a happy little guy. Let's see if the grouchy bear wants to go for a ride." He placed an excited Goblin into the back of the van. Goblin danced from paw to paw to paw, letting out soft whines. He stuck his rear end up in the air, wagging his tail.

Grunge's lips curled back in a snarl. Ben said, "He'll ride with us, but he has absolutely no reason to trust either of us. See those scars? We have no idea what he's been through to break his spirit."

Grunge leaped into the van. Goblin licked him to greet him. Sliding the door shut, Ben said, "You best ride up front with me, Lucas. It might be pushing it to ride with the big cranky fellow. He'll need some warming up before he decides to be friendly."

As Ben drove, Lucas said, "Just did a book report at school. Pits are loyal. Since they got a bad rap because of thugs, pits know they have a lot to compensate for by being eager to please. Animal Control used to put pits to sleep, but now, pits are being sent to no-kill shelters. Cops are adopting them as service dogs. Pits are Staffordshire Terriers, part bull dog, part terrier, descendants of the English bull-baiting dogs that were bred to fight against bulls. When bull-baiting was outlawed, people turned instead to fighting their dogs against each other. Pits are seen as vicious dogs, but all dogs have a wolf-like attack mode they are born with. It's only after some cruel thug ramps their aggression meter past the point of no return do they turn a loving pit into a monster. Killer pits are man-made. Weak men turn to breeding hot-tempered dogs to entertain themselves. Yet Pit bulls have been famous. Pete of the Little Rascals. Billie Holiday's pit, Mister. Helen Keller's pit, Sir Thomas. President Roosevelt's pit, Pete. Sergeant Stubby served in World War I. Weela saved 32 people. D-Boy was shot three times to save his family from an intruder. Popsicle, a pup found in the freezer of a drug dealer during a bust, became one of the nation's most important police dogs. Popsicle went with his handler to work in Texas, where he alerted to drug seizures of seven million dollars. He was a gentle dog, for his handler said, 'Only we know he's a pit bull. Popsicle thinks he's a cocker spaniel.'"

Goblin sat there in the back of the van, listening to Lucas talking. It was Grunge who was being a spoil sport. *Humans!* he muttered. *Just think if this Indian is up to no good.*

Goblin said, *You always told me to read the aura of humans I met. This man has a bright shimmering coming from him. His heart reflects all the colors of a rainbow.*

Grunge growled, *If he is not a dog man, why does he smell like so many dogs? And did you see the dark aura of that kid? I felt hurt, anger, and defiance radiating from him. He is a very troubled little boy, for sure. And troubled young boys are cruel and hurtful. Watch yourself around this one, Goblin. He may just be tricking us. He could turn mean in a heartbeat.*

Chapter Forty-Three

As Ben drove, Lucas picked up the book on the console, studying the Native warrior riding through a score of whizzing bullets on the front cover. "Recently," Ben said, "I've been having dreams about the war chief. My uncle, Pete He Dog, suggested I read *The Strange Man of the Oglala*. Do you know how Crazy Horse got his name?"

Lucas said, "Because he was hopping mad crazy?"

"On the contrary," Ben said. "The Lakota war leader's name came to him through a vision he saw where his horse was spirited. The closest way to describe this was to say, 'His Horse is crazy.' It was said that in his first vision, the Oglala Lakota boy named Curly entered with his horse into the Otherworld, a realm beyond this one. In that realm, his horse danced wildly, and therefore, Crazy Horse, became his name. He fought against the Crow, Shoshone, Pawnee, Blackfeet, and Arikara. Sand Creek Massacre. Battle of Platte Bridge. Battle of Red Buttes. Wagon Box Fight. The Lakota lost 120 warriors, but Crazy Horse rode through a hail of bullets, not once stung by those angry hornets. Crazy Horse came out of all battles unscathed. His magic came from a single eagle feather, an eagle bone whistle, and a stone tied with a leather thong at his left shoulder. He claimed that each time he rode into battle he entered into the Otherworld."

Ben glanced over at Lucas, then looked back at the road, aware that he was reading him. He drove through Havelock, the suburb where Lucas's real home was, then to the country road leading to his ranch. As they approached the iron gate at the front of his ranch, Lucas looked up to the wooden sign, seeing the dream-catcher carved into it. A set of deer antlers dominated the sign, with words engraved in it: *Wounded Arrow, a Haven to Heal the Damaged Spirit.*

Ben explained, "I not only work with troubled dogs, I provide a haven for those suffering from PTSD. My dog ranch houses fifty of the most behaviorally disordered dogs on the planet. Each carries a load of hurt due to cruelties suffered. Dogs are the most empathetic creatures God created. They can feel what we feel. Dogs are able to read you like a book. It helps in the healing process, for most of these soldiers are humbled by the fact that a dog looks at them with no judgement. These dogs are simply looking to be loved, and when a damaged soldier bonds with a damaged dog, magic takes place. In America, kids out of high school serve our country going to war-torn places on the planet. They soldier their way through ambushes, firefights, hostile enemies. They live in compounds, while everyone else in the country wants to kill them. These kids grow to be men too fast. Many are impacted by Post-traumatic stress disorder."

Lucas studied the layout of Ben's rescue ranch. At the end of the driveway was his underground house, with a large, round door and two octagon-shaped stained-glass windows showing on the front wall. To the left of this underground dwelling, stood a large red barn with several dog kennels lining either side, with various breeds of dogs prancing around in these kennels. To the right of Ben's home was a fenced-in pasture, where several men were walking dogs on halters, leashes, and in some cases, full-faced muzzles.

"First question," Lucas said, "why the name Wounded Arrow?"

Ben said, "A Lakota village once stood on these grounds. A Native woman was having her baby, when a line of warriors rode in from a raid on an enemy camp. One of these warriors, Hard Forehead, had six arrows sticking in him, yet he still lived. This was Big Medicine. The woman named her son Wounded with many Arrows, and the name was shortened to Wounded Arrow. It is appropriate, for the many dogs and soldiers who pass through my gate, also carry many unseen wounds, yet the Big Medicine is they still live."

Lucas said, "Second question, how do you feed so many dogs?"

Ben said, "Lot of good-hearted people donate finances, and plenty of supplies each month, keeping this place afloat. They believe in dogs. They believe in those who serve our country. They are good people, who care about others more than they care about themselves."

"Third question is," Lucas said, "who does poop patrol?"

Ben laughed and parked the van. Slowly, he opened the side door of the van. Goblin scampered over and happily greeted them. Lucas caught him, preventing him from doing a nose-plant on the driveway. Grunge snarled. "Yes," Ben said to the big dog. "You have no reason to trust me. You have no idea what I intend to do to you. I can tell by your scars that someone has hurt you, treated you cruelly in your past. And I am sorry for that. I promise you your days of fighting are over. No more ring for you, Grunge."

Grunge continued to growl.

"That doesn't sound good," Lucas said from the porch. He picked up a leash he'd discovered on a nearby lawn chair. "You need this?"

"That," Ben said, "might help if I could get this fellow to trust me, but since he doesn't pose a threat to anyone as yet, I want to try something else. And it requires your help."

"Me?" Lucas asked, looking unsure.

"Yes," Ben said. "Pick up Goblin and come back over here."

Lucas did as he instructed. Grunge took Ben out of his sights. He instead focused on Goblin held in Lucas's arms. The pup whined as he communicated with the temperamental bigger dog.

Lucas raised Goblin up. "Come, Grunge," he softly urged the big dog. "Come join Goblin."

Ben said, "That is good. Talk calmly to him."

Lucas actually let out a soft gasp as Grunge sprang out of the van. He stood there for several seconds, holding Goblin up between them. "It's okay. No one is going to hurt you. Just come on over to the porch. That's where Goblin and I are heading. Join us."

Ben whispered, "Good job, Lucas. Nice work."

He noted Lucas blushed red. *This kid is not used to praise,* Ben thought. *Need to go easy on compliments.*

Grunge followed Lucas and Goblin to the round door.

"Go ahead," Ben said from his place beside the van. "Open the door. Set Goblin down inside. Let's see what happens next."

Readjusting Goblin in his grasp, Lucas reached out with his free hand and opened the front door of the underground house. He placed Goblin down on the landing and stepped back to allow Grunge room to get through the open doorway. Sniffing at the air inside, Goblin let out an excited, "Woof!" and scurried down a flight of three steps and vanished into the darkness below. Grunge snarled once at Lucas, then followed Goblin down into the large den below.

Ben's underground home was a cozy place. At the bottom of three steps was a den that stretched away in front of them. Goblin's nails made snicking sounds as he scurried across the slick wooden floor. Lucas crossed the room to examine the fireplace. It had a wolf painted on a shield above the mantle. The mantle was an oak plank with pictures of dogs on it. A bone-handled knife. A tomahawk. A rack of deer antlers dominated the entire wall above the oak mantle. The entire fireplace was surrounded by what looked like a grizzly bear's head shaped out of the stucco that formed the rounded walls of the underground home. The bear was snarling, the hearth and the fire pit deep within its gaping jaws.

Lucas left the two dogs standing before the fireplace while he explored the other rooms linked to the den by a long hallway. Two were bedrooms, and the third was a washroom. Everything was neat and tidy, with a hint of lemony scents drifting through the air.

Grunge came up behind Goblin, turning his big head this way and that as if preparing for a surprise attack by some unseen dog. Goblin could smell dog, too, but it was surely from the many other dogs this Ben fellow had allowed into his home.

Grunge rumbled, *This Indian has to have an angle. Look at me, a pit with such a dark reputation, yet this man treats me with respect. Something is not quite right.*

Are all humans not to be trusted? Goblin asked. *They can't all be cruel. Maybe some of them can be trusted.*

Chapter Forty-Four

Lucas froze there in the hallway, his eyes gone wide as he saw a true vision: A cloud of thick mist appeared. A wind rippled through the cloud. Ben appeared, his black hair trailing over his shoulders. He wore leather pants. His bare chest was covered in white chalk with a scattering of blue hailstones. A yellow lightning bolt ran down his left cheek. Ben stood before a bear pierced by dozens of arrows. The brute stood on his hind legs, snarling in pain. Ben raised a feather tinged with pulsating golden light. He waved it at the arrows protruding from the wounded bear. Each one vanished in a sizzle of flickering fireflies. When the bear was healed of his many wounds, it then turned and ambled away.

Ben said, "That is my mission here at Wounded Arrow, to heal the hurts of this world. When I was a kid up on Pine Ridge, my uncle Pete was a medicine man. He walked in the spirit realm. He drew his healing powers from a realm just beyond this one."

Ben sank slowly to his knees.

Grunge snarled at Ben kneeling there three feet away from him. He spread his arms wide. He stopped, his hands out-stretched, not wanting to intrude into Grunge's space. Lucas knew there was no way Ben could touch that angry pit without the big dog going into attack mode. Lucas wanted to warn him, but he remained silent for fear he might ignite Grunge's killer instincts, unleashing a storm of fury. Grunge was downright spooky. His teeth showed in a snarl. Saliva dripped from his jaws. He narrowed his eyes. In those eyes was a promise that he was going to do great damage. He had his rage meter torked way past normal during past fights he had been forced to endure. He had been ramped up to kill or be killed. The scars criss-crossing his head spoke volumes about all that the dog had suffered.

"I know you are hurting," Ben said. "I know you have absolutely no reason to trust me You are suspicious of my intentions. But I ask you to please allow me into your space that you are so desperately trying to defend. You place a barrier between us for no reason. You have had every bond that you formed with past owners broken most violently. It will take a lot to regain that trust if I ever hope to bond with you. I ask you give me a chance, Grunge, you big, broken-hearted dog."

Lucas stood there, staring at Grunge in sudden disbelief. One second, the large, fierce and furious dog was snarling and prepared to launch an attack, and the next, he fell silent as if considering Ben's words. Something magical was taking place there in the underground home of the Lakota dog handler.

Lucas whispered, "You really are a dog whisperer, Ben."

Lucas greatly envied the Indian kneeling there before a beast that could have savagely ripped off his face. Whatever medicine Ben was blessed with, Lucas wanted it, too.

Grunge growled one last time, then quietly fell asleep.

Leaving Grunge resting peacefully inside the den, Ben and Lucas took Goblin outside so as not to disturb the big dog as he acclimated to his new home. The sun had set and the sky in the west was filled with amber clouds, pierced here and there by fading rays of sunlight. A deep purple haze was creeping up out of the hollows to the east of the ranch, leaving the skyline in that direction dark and shadowy.

Ben was surprised to find a police cruiser parked outside in the driveway. A second vehicle, a black Blazer, had an emblem of a dog on its driver's side door. In bold gold lettering above the emblem were the words, *Animal Control*. The raven-haired lady at the wheel locked gazes with Ben for several seconds, and he wondered if he had met her somewhere before. "Lucas?" said the uniformed cop beside the cruiser. "Heard about your incident at anger management. What are you doing here?"

Ben said, "I can explain that, sir."
The cop glared at Lucas. "I asked him, not you."

"Do you see what I have to deal with?" Lucas asked, looking over at Ben. "This is my foster dad."

Stepping forward, extending his hand, Ben said, "Officer Yardley, I'm Ben Black Bull, assigned as Lucas's family support worker. We had a little trouble at his session. I apologize for not informing any-one we were stopping out here before returning—"

"Duly noted," said Yardley, a frown causing his thick mustache to droop down on either side of his mouth. Tall with thin brown hair, he held a steely look in his blue eyes. "Lucas, get in the cruiser. No arguments or there will be strict consequences. And when this is over, one phone call to your caseworker and you're getting a new support worker. This guy is out of line, bringing you here after your tirade at your therapist's office. Mark my words."

Embarrassed by Yardley's rudeness, Ben lowered his extended hand. Handing Goblin off to Ben, Lucas said, "What about him? You are going to keep him, right?"

Ben said, "Yes, and you are welcome to visit him—"

"No," Yardley said. "After I speak with his caseworker, you are not going to have a thing to do with him."

Lucas stood there sulking. His defiance disorder kicked in and he gave his foster dad a defiant glare. "What's this?" asked the slender, raven-haired lady as she exited the Blazer. Dressed in a green service outfit, she tapped her badge with one finger. "See this? During my years as an Animal Control officer, I've dealt with hostile dogs and cats, but I have never dealt with a belligerent kid. Tamp down the hostilities and climb in your dad's cruiser?"

Lucas snapped, "He's not my dad!"

"Lucas!" Yardley said. "Get in the car! This is a serious matter that involves you and this Indian! No offence, Officer Red Cloud. Would you prefer, *Native American*?"

The Lakota officer ignored him. Instead, she addressed Ben, saying, "I'm Officer Cora—"

"Yes!" Ben said. "Cora Red Cloud from Pine Ridge! Last time I saw you, you were the feistiest girl at the rez!"

Cora flipped her braided ponytail over one shoulder, and smiled. "I am still mean and sassy. It goes with the territory. The last time I saw you, you were champion of the school boxing team."

Ben laughed. "Been trying to forget you, ever since you knocked me out cold in that all-rez boxing match. It was embarrassing to wake up to that hooting crowd from the Ridge and Rosebud. I had to live with the humiliation of being beaten by a girl."

Cora said, "We've come far from the rez. It is ironic that the love for dogs Pete He Dog instilled in us set us both on a path to work with canines? Animal Control and Lincoln PD serve on a joint task force. Our goal: To shut down dog fighting in the state of Nebraska."

Cora removed a GPS tracking device from her belt. "I was tracking this pup this morning," she said, moving over to examine Goblin. She kneeled down, offering her free hand for the pup to sniff. After a sniff at her, Goblin wagged his tail, letting her know it was okay to pet him. Cora did, then held him in place while she ran the device over his shoulders. It beeped. She looked up at Ben. "How did you happen to find this dog?"

Yardley removed his handcuffs from his belt. "You're selling dogs for the fighting rings, right?"

"Yardley?" Cora said. "Before you go all Dog the Bounty Hunter on him, would you let me conduct my interview?"

Yardley offered Ben one last glare, then ushered Lucas into his patrol car, and drove away. Cora said, "Break-ins at pit bull rescue centers have resulted in the dog men acquiring over a dozen dogs for the fights in the underworld. Nate Holland came on our radar when a killer pit by the name of Grunge was to fight a hyaena from Africa. Grunge is a legend in the fight circles. I was contacted by a modern-day crusader, *The Dog Soldier,* a private investigator who has taken an unorthodox approach to dog men in a sting operation. He's also a DJ who runs the Native program *Smoke Signals* on the radio. He wrote the book, *Broken Spirits*, burned by dog men for the truth it exposes. He inserted GPS chips in a dozen shelter dogs, in the hopes that one of these dog men would take the bait. Holland claims he knows nothing about the pup. His kennels were empty. So, I tracked the chip implanted in Goblin here to you."

A cool wind blew down from the eastern hills. Ben turned to face it. The breezes ruffled his raven hair, sending wild tangles streaming over his broad shoulders. He savored the smells of leaves, grasses, and the scent of Steven's Creek winding its way past his ranch to the west. "Snow will fall tomorrow," he said.

"Rumor is," Cora said, "you have the ability to read dogs. So, you can read the weather now, too?"

"No," he said, grinning. "I heard it from the weather man on Channel 7 this morning."

Chapter Forty-Five

Lucas was mad all the way back home. He is already mad most of the time, but his foster dad never knew when to shut his mouth. Instead of backing off and giving him space, he poured it on, dumping gas on a fire. Needling him until he wanted to explode.

He glanced at Lucas in his rearview mirror. "You just can't handle normal. You're not wired right. It comes from your own parents and their DNA make-up. What do you expect? Their own wiring had misfires, that resulted in rage boiling to the surface. A man who beats his wife is not a man at all."

Lucas badly wanted to hit Yardley in his stupid face, to knock out his stupid teeth, to shut his stupid mouth.

"You know Paula and I put ourselves out for you by taking you in. And how do you pay us back? You get in trouble at school. Have you ever stopped to think how much we put up with?"

As he pulled into the driveway at the Yardley home, he added, "Don't mention this to Paula. She's been praying that you be removed from our home. She has begged God you be placed elsewhere."

That surprised Lucas. Tears came to his eyes, to think his foster mom prayed for him to be placed outside her home. His heart sank. He fought back the urge to bawl. "I told her," Yardley said, "all I had to do is make one phone call, and you would be gone."

What really set Lucas off, was when Paula, his God-loving foster mom, offered him a disappointed frown and said, "Throwing a chair, Lucas? Normal kids don't act like that. You are not normal."

Lucas clomped his way up the stairs to his bedroom, unable to hear her mumbled words. However, just before slamming the door closed, he heard her say, "Perhaps God in his mercy, will find a better home for you that will put up with your maniacal rages!"

Lucas slammed the door. He stormed over to his computer and ripped the keyboard from the cord attaching it to his tower. He flung it across the room, where it made a dent in the wall. He saw nothing for the next fifteen minutes, but red-hot fury rippling away from his body in visible waves. He thought about Super Heroes with special powers. Only thing is, his rage was power that would burn him alive. He slipped into his parka. Opening the window, he scrambled outside, snagged onto the drain pipe, and slid down to the yard below.

He was then gone, thinking God had answered Paula's prayers.

Cora cradled Goblin in her arms as they talked there on the driveway. Grunge stared warily at the uniformed officer. Cora said, "How could anyone throw a puppy like this into a fight ring?"

"Men who have lost their moral compass," Ben said. "I run a rescue ranch. So consider these dogs rescued. What about Holland?"

"The plan," she said, "was to use the chip implanted in Goblin to lead us to him. It was going to be a slam dunk with Holland in possession of the legendary Grunge. If all had gone as planned, we could have cited him and sent a strong message to other dogmen. Our plan was to shut down this dog man who has caused his share of suffering in this state. When I read about Wounded Arrow in the paper, I was not surprised to see your name as the owner, Ben. I know the training Uncle Pete He Dog gave you on the rez. I, too, have a great love for dogs. Grunge is scheduled for a fight this weekend at the Barn, where dog men carry on their blood-sport. He was to fight against a hyaena from Africa. A network of dog men will pressure Holland to show up with Grunge."

Ben said, "I have men and women who have served in the hell-holes of the world during their military service. All afflicted with PTSD they are combat-trained individuals. If Holland wants Grunge back, he will have to go through an army to get him."

"How about we give him an incentive to try? We post a message about your rescue of him on pit bull support groups on the Internet. Word spreads like wildfire. Dog men read posts to shop for dogs to steal. He's bound to see it. RICO is a federal law that provides for extended criminal penalties for acts performed in an organization. He transported Grunge here from Colorado, crossing state borders to commit a criminal act by forcing the dog into a fight. We can apply RICO to his charges, which would carry stiffer penalties."

Ben's cell phone rang inside his shirt pocket. He used his thumb to click on his phone. "Wounded Arrow," he said, then listened to Lucas's caseworker from Health and Human Services. "Lucas is on run? He is no longer welcome at the Yardleys. Yes, my license is up to date? You asking for temporary placement? I've got an idea where he might be, but don't hold your breath."

Seconds before he bid Cora good-bye, Ben said, "Holland is the kid's last name. Any chance he and Nate Holland are related?"

Cora responded, "Ask the kid."

Chapter Forty-Six

Night had fallen and the winds were bitter cold. Ben sang an Indian song in a low voice as he drove us back into downtown Lincoln. He was preparing for battle. Goblin had seen the waves of red-hot anger drifting off the rage-filled kid. Maybe Ben knew just how desperate Lucas really was.

He stopped his van beside a tall parking garage. The moment he parked, he hopped out of the van, reached in and grabbed Goblin, and headed for the elevator. He stroked the pup beneath his chin as the elevator rose. When the doors opened, they were on the 6th floor, a long way from ground level. Ben stepped out, carrying Goblin past a row of parked cars. He stopped when he came to a wall intersecting the top floor. On the other side of that wall came a low mutter. Lucas was swearing into the wind, ranting at the fates. Ben set the pup down. Goblin took four steps that carried him around the wall and onto an open parking lot. Ten feet ahead of him, Lucas was seated on a four-foot ledge that ran around the entire top floor of the garage.

"Goblin?" he said.

Goblin met his sad-eyed gaze and felt such extreme sorrow in that look that he whined. It hurt that bad. Shimmering red waves floated away from him; rage-filled clouds drifted around and above him. He spoke and the words that came from his mouth were black smudges appearing for brief moments against the background of red vapors. "Get away from me! There is no hope! I am nothing but trouble!"

Each word he uttered flowed from his lips, creating tiny black particles that vanished within the red clouds swirling around him. Goblin barked. He barked again, trying to let Lucas know he wanted him to come down and off that ledge. Lucas reached back with one hand to gently swat at him, and as he did he lost his balance. Goblin stood frozen, watching as he tottered forward, then fell backwards off the ledge, landing on his back and hitting his head on the floor of the garage. He lay there, slipping in and out of consciousness.

And that's when Goblin saw a band of hooded figures appearing in the red vapors swirling around Lucas's prone form. Stark black against the red, they each reached out their hands clutching at him. The pup barked, for the ghost figures hovered four feet from him.

Ben's voice came from behind them as he said, "Those entities want his soul. They feed on his furious rage, his extreme sorrow, his determination to self-destruct. They feed on his apathy, his defiance. He is the perfect target, for he is damaged goods, and vulnerable to following their suggestions. His soul ripe for the picking."

At this, the spirit creatures bunched together, preparing to launch themselves at Lucas. Goblin let out a fierce bark. The dark entities howled in rage. The pup turned his head and *woofed* at Lucas. He had to wake up before they invaded his soul. If they were allowed to do that, Goblin knew Lucas would never be the same. Ben drew out a stone arrowhead attached to a leather cord beneath his shirt.

"Be gone!" he said. "Go back to the Otherworld!

"By power of the sun!

"By the power of moon!

"By the power of the stars!

"By the power of the Light!

"I command you to leave this child alone!"

The ghost beings wailed in distress and drifted away through the sky, hissing like mad cats.

On the ride back to Ben's ranch, Goblin dozed as Lucas cradled him in his lap. "Wanagi," Ben said, making a sound like *ahhgee,* "is what the Lakota call demons. They hail from the Otherworld. We live in a tri-fold world, past, present, and future, yet a thin veil separates us from the unseen realm. Those who can see the workings of this realm have the Sight. My Uncle Pete claims dogs see the spirit realm more keenly than we do. Goblin is attuned to both worlds.

"Lucas, you carry a load of anger inside of you that creates red-hot waves in the aura that surrounds you. I am no medicine man, like my uncle Pete, but I see the aura. You have gone on unchecked for so long that it has attracted destructive spirits to you. If you don't learn to control your rage, they will feed off your anger, lending their own madness to your fits. You are not a bad little boy. Simply troubled. You have suffered a deep hurt. Instead of allowing sorrow to leak out of you, the fires of rage explode inside of you. You have strayed outside of the Sacred Hoop. The Medicine Wheel is used by Natives for healing. It embodies Father Sky and Mother Earth. Wounded Arrow sits inside a giant Medicine Wheel created by rocks on my grounds."

"Too bad," Lucas said, "I couldn't live out here inside your Sacred Hoop, because maybe it might help me to get back inside my own."

Ben said, "Talk about that later. Right now I want to test a theory."

Chapter Forty-Seven

Ben stared at the aura drifting above the head of the big dog. A cloud of multi-colored vapors emanated from Grunge. He said, "I believe in the Otherworld, but unlike my Uncle Pete He Dog, I'm not a medicine man. You asked me if I was a Dog Whisperer. I don't know if my success at calming vicious dogs has anything to do with the whisperer skills. However, I was wondering if you had the gift."

Ben looked to the apparitions hovering above Grunge. Holding up the arrowhead, he sternly said, "Go, you spirits of darkness. Leave this dog alone. You have crossed the boundary between realms to cause great hurt. Leave this dog in peace. Go! Trouble him no more!"

The red specters obeyed him, drifting away into the fireplace on their swift flight back to the Otherworld. Grunge shook his massive head, bewildered by the sight of the vaporous beings leaving him. Lucas held his right hand out to Grunge, his fingers curled inward. The pit tried to growl, but his growl turned to a soft whine. Lucas said, "You've suffered pains few dogs have ever experienced. Those days are over. I will treat you with respect. I am your friend."

Grunge was so surprised at what Lucas did next that he went still. Lucas gently placed a hand on his head. His touch was feather light, yet he withdrew his hand a second after touching the big dog, merely probing to see how far he would be allowed to go. Lucas bowed his head, and touched the dog on the head again.

Grunge growled once. Lucas slowly withdrew his hand. "I get it. Too much, too soon. Thanks for not biting me. That would have put a damper on our relationship."

Despite how tense the situation was, Ben chuckled.

Leaving Grunge and Goblin resting near the fireplace, Lucas followed Ben out to the barn where the ranch's dogs were kept. Ben had called for a meeting with the leader of the volunteers there in the barn. The huge, blond man offered Lucas his hand. "Beef Tory," he said, shaking Lucas's hand.

Ben said, "My volunteers are men and women who served as Rangers, SEALS, Delta, and the four branches of US services. Each one trained in specific ways to defeat enemies. They are capable of protecting the dogs but I'm not sure I have the right to involve them in this. They don't deserve more stress."

Ben took a moment to introduce Lucas, and he made a big deal about him scooping Goblin up from the middle of the street. Beef gave him a high-five. Ben then told Beef about Cora Red Cloud's plan to catch the notorious dog man by using Grunge to entice him to trespass on the ranch. He concluded by saying, "If any of your vets are opposed to this, I would totally understand a three-day break."

Beef laughed. "My vets left out of the loop? They'll be on board."

On the walk back to Ben's home, Ben told Lucas, "Callie asked me if I would take you on emergency placement. If you are willing to give it a try, I'll call Callie and tell her you're staying."

"Will you teach me how to whisper?" Lucas asked.

"Don't know about whispering," Ben said. "But you can start working with Goblin tomorrow."

Lucas said, "What about Grunge?"

Ben said, "You might not have the patience. Every step with him will have to be measured according to how he reacts. He's a damaged dog. He needs a lot of stubborn love. That means never walking away from him. Grunge is more sensitive than most dogs because of what he's been through. He senses you losing your cool, you might damage him. Can you manage your temper tantrums?"

"I don't throw tantrums," Lucas said, flatly.

"Yes, you do," Ben said. "If things don't go your way, you turn into the Tasmanian Devil. Deny that and you'll never change. Grunge deserves better. If you want to heal him, first heal yourself."

Lucas didn't like Ben's words. He came close to throwing one of those tantrums. He stared at the ground defiantly.

***

The next morning, snow was falling. Lucas was hoping for a Snow Day, but even with near blizzard conditions, Ben dropped him off at BEST Education, a haven for suspended kids in the district. The director was a female throwback from the Billy Jack days, her intervention skills as refined as her talent for educating. She knew a lot about troubled kids. She didn't push and prod, especially if a kid was in a bad mood. She and her staff had been working with kids with behavior disorders for so long, take-downs were just a part of their day and blow-ups there had definite consequences. Lucas had blown through three elementary schools, and when he threw a chair through a window, special ed. coordinators sent him to BEST.

Lucas started out his school day with a pesky firefly hovering at the edge of my mind: He had been booted from the Yardleys because he was damaged goods. Too many bad thoughts came fluttering like a flock of starlings in his head. It happened quickly, too. Some kid pushed him. He punched him and the kid went into Drama Queen-mode and cried, "Assault!"

BEST's staff restrained Lucas and hauled him off to the Quiet Room, where he went into meltdown number seventy-five since he started his fifth-grade year. At the end of the day, Ben picked him up. He didn't say a word about the incident. He just offered Lucas a sad smile and told him he had a one-day suspension due to his blow-up.

That evening, Ben had just started a fire in the fireplace, when Officer Red Cloud knocked on his door. Lucas ran up the four steps to the door and pulled it open. He took one look at her standing there and hollered back down the stairs. "It's that animal cop!"

Ben said, "Invite her in. Get her a cup of coffee, please."

He greeted her as she entered the den, offering her a seat in a comfortable recliner near the roaring blaze. Cora took the chair he offered her. Lucas came from the kitchen with a steaming cup of coffee. He handed it to her, then planted himself on a footstool, looking from Ben to Cora, curiously.

"You like her, don't you?" he asked Ben, with a smirk.

A bit flustered at the question, Ben said, "We've known each other since we were kids living back on the rez—"

"Ben and I," Cora said, "are working together because dogs can't do what needs to be done to protect them. Besides, why are you here? Last time I saw you, you were headed home with Yardley."

Lucas said, "He and his stupid wife don't want me."

"Oh," Cora said, her tone softening. "I'm sorry things did not work out for you. I know how difficult it can be. I, too, was in foster care growing up. Besides, there is no juicy romance here. I have this thing about dating older men."

Cora laughed and Lucas decided he liked her, even if she was a cop. "Lest my young guest," Ben said to her, "thinks you drove all the way out to the ranch to flirt with me, why are you here, Cora?"

Chapter Forty-Eight

Cora said, "A snitch working with the Lincoln PD reported that the dog man took our bait. The message I sent out to all pit bull support groups indicated that Grunge was being held in your barn. The dog thief is headed here tonight. I have placed motion sensors at specific areas of your grounds. They'll alert us if he trespasses on your ranch."

Ben said, "My dogs guarded by an Army Ranger and two SEALs, might result in a trip to a hospital before this dog man sees a jail cell."

Cora said, "All he needs to do is step onto your grounds. Once he is cited, law enforcement can connect him to Grunge, and apply the RICO charges."

"So," Lucas said, "while we wait for him to trespass, tell me about that boxing match you had with Ben, will you?"

"Lucas," Ben said, "Officer Red Cloud has to return to work. She doesn't have the time to chit-chat with us."

Cora offered Ben an amused smile. "I can run surveillance from here. A hot cup of coffee, a warm blaze in the fireplace, a quiet fall evening, what could be more conducive to a storytelling session?"

Cora sat across from Ben in the recliner, while Lucas snuggled up beside Goblin before the fire, careful not to nudge Grunge who slept soundly beside them. Ben said, "That match is old news. How about a story of the Tall Man? Walking Sam? Dark People of Pine Ridge? On the rez of the Lakota, 241 attempted suicides happened in three months. The Tall Man appeared to these kids, telling them to kill themselves. Shadow People stalk the rez. In 2009, Walking Sam was blamed for many teenage suicides. At the Cheyenne River rez, a woman described Walking Sam as a big man in a tall hat. He had been picked up on the police scanners, but the police have been unable to protect the community from him."

Ben paused, then told his story:

"Sunsets on Pine Ridge were amazing. Autumn ones were the best. When that huge amber ball sank down in the west, it cast shades of deep scarlet, burnt yellow, livid violet, and vibrant pink across the sky. At 10-years-old, I liked watching sunsets from Uncle Pete's porch on the edge of the rez. I was a small boy with tangles of long, raven hair. When I smiled, I had dimples in both cheeks. The sun was going down in the west. I had been left in charge of Uncle Pete's brindle pit who had given birth to seven pups. Pete He Dog left me in charge of the momma dog and her litter. The only thing he left me with for protection was the stone arrowhead that dangled from the leather thong hanging around my neck. This talisman would shield me from the Dark Ones. It is endowed with big medicine.

"I had tucked the arrowhead into my T-shirt as I watched Pete disappear in a cloud of dust kicked up by his old Ford truck. I spent that next hour practicing with my BB rifle on the front porch. A yelp from the shed around the back of the house set my feet running, my rifle gripped tightly in my hands. I rounded the corner of the house to see a tall, dark figure moving away from the shed. He wore a long black coat and wide-brimmed black hat. He reached up, tipping his hat at me, then raised the squirming pup in the air and headed into the trees.

"Sighting my rifle, I pulled the trigger and fired. The copper BB nailed the man in the center of his back, sending a spurt of dust flying from his coat. The tall, dark man spun around, rage in his eyes. He was then coming at full speed directly toward me!

"I raised my rifle and fired again. This time the copper BB slammed into the center of the man's forehead. The man skidded to a stop not three feet from me. He sucked in a powerful breath. Still holding the puppy in one hand, he blew out his breath, sending the BB shooting past me. The Tall Man placed the pup down beside him. He then moved directly toward me, a long-bladed knife in his hand.

"Snick! Shring! Clang! filled the air as the knife was deflected. A figure appeared between me and the Tall Man. He had flowing black hair and wore a long, white leather shirt, adorned with many symbols. A yellow lightning bolt ran down the left side of his face, hailstones ran down his jaw. A small stone depended from a cord behind his left shoulder. A single eagle feather hung on the right side of his face. The Tall Man jabbed in a maddened frenzy. The Warrior moved like a swift wind, bringing his tomahawk into the play. It was Crazy Horse. The Tall Man's knife slid across his leather-covered chest, passing through symbols on the shirt. Each crackled with power, shielding Crazy Horse from taking any harm. The Tall Man swept past him his knife thrust at me. The tip of the knife passed through my T-shirt and connected with the stone arrowhead I wore around my neck. Bolts of purple lightning burst from the medallion. Scintillating tentacles of light wrapped around the Tall Man's hand. He screamed and vanished into the Otherworld. Crazy Horse fixed his eagle-proud gaze on the arrowhead I wore. He said, 'That arrowhead belonged to Sitting Bull, Tatáŋka Íyotake. Why did you save the pup?'

"I said, 'He needed saving.'"

Ben peered into the fire after he finished his story. Lucas and Cora remained quiet out of respect for Ben.

Ring! They all jumped at the sudden ringing of Cora's cell phone.

Chapter Forty-Nine

Ring! echoed through the den, waking up Goblin sleeping in Lucas's arms. Cora removed her cell phone from her belt and answered it. A crease appeared on her brow as she listened intently to whoever spoke to her. She disconnected the call, snapping the phone closed.

"We've got a hit!" she said. "Someone just tripped the motion sensor near the creek leading up from the north side of your ranch!"

Lucas was the first one to his feet, but Ben placed a hand on his chest and gently pushed him back down beside the fireplace. "You stay put," he said. "Guard the dogs."

It was snowing as Ben and Cora exited the underground house. Huge drops of the white fluffy stuff was falling from the sky. They had slipped into jackets before leaving the den, but only Cora's had a hood, which she pulled up and over her head to keep from getting pelted directly on the head by the furiously falling snow. Snow flakes gathered on Ben's head and shoulders as he trudged through the torrents of white flakes coming down around them.

The barn stood like a massive black ship before them. As they approached it, Ben looked over at Cora. "Are you armed?" he asked.

Cora said. "Animal Control officers don't carry guns."

Ben said, "Then how do you expect to arrest these low-life thugs? You want us to throw snowballs at them?"

Of course, Lucas did not listen to Ben. He wasn't going to be left out of all the excitement. But, he wasn't going out there unarmed. After pulling up the hood on his sweatshirt, he snatched the war club from off the mantle. Grunge stared at him curiously. Goblin let out an anxious whine. "It will be okay," Lucas told them as he made his way to the landing at the foot of the steps leading up to the door. "No one is coming to take you guys away from here."

He darted up the stairs and opened the door. The moment he stepped outside he was hit by a cold blast of wind and snow pellets. They stung his cheeks like tiny icy bees and he cursed softly. Slipping and sliding on the snowy ground, he could see Ben and Cora kneeling down not thirty feet in front of him. Beyond them in the distance, he could barely make out the bulky shape of the barn. It was a white-out created by the sudden snowstorm. In between him and the barn, Ben flicked on a flashlight. Even through the fiercely falling snow, the lemon-yellow beam of bright light illuminated the barn door as a small company of vets met Cora and Ben as they reached it.

Lucas heard a sudden noise behind him and glanced back to see a man sprinting toward Ben's underground home. Lucas raised the war club and charged. As the man reached for the handle, Lucas whacked him hard, swinging the club down and connecting with his head. The big guy sank to his knees in front of him. And there on the guy's bald head was the tattoo of a dragon. "Uncle Nate!" Lucas said.

Nate glared up at Lucas, cursing with flecks of spit flying from his lips. Nate Holland shoved him against the door, then took off running toward the snowy field to the east. Lucas ran after him. Nate sprinted through the falling snow. Lucas tried to stay right on him. He could barely see through the flurries ahead of him. He felt the ground beneath him shudder as a figure in a fringed leather jacket slid out of the falling snow. He was a *ginormous* Indian, his long hair whipping wildly about his shoulders. He wore war paint on his face, half black, the other white. He reached down taking the war club from him. "Fear not," he rumbled. "The Dog Soldier has come!"

He glided toward Nate as if he were performing a graceful dance. The giant Indian swung the war club up and under Nate's chin, lifting him off the ground. He flew backward, then fell on his back and did not move.

The Dog Soldier was then swallowed by the winter storm.

Chapter Fifty

Officer Beef Tory handcuffed Nate and escorted him to his police cruiser. As Ben led the way back to his home, Lucas watched as Beef's cruiser moved away through the snow flurries. "What will happen to him?" he asked.

Cora said, "Trespassing citations. But if our investigators get him to talk, more arrests can be made in the dog men circle."

Five minutes later, Lucas sat wrapped in a blanket before the fireplace. Goblin snuggled in his lap. Grunge lay sprawled before the crackling blaze inside the hearth. Cora asked, "What do you think your uncle was up to? As vice president of the Elder's Den, are he and your dad involved in the dog fights?"

"I don't know," Lucas said. "One second, I was chasing him and the next thing Crazy Horse came!"

Ben entered the den, carrying a tray of cups and a teapot. Lucas accepted the cup of hot chocolate Ben offered him. He sipped it slowly, nibbling on the tiny marshmallows inside the drink. "So," Ben said, "this Indian magically appeared?"

"Yes," Lucas said. "His face was painted black and white. He had long hair and he was ginormous?"

Ben said, "It wasn't Crazy Horse. He wore a dusting of blue with white hailstones on his face. That is well-known. He was average height, not a giant Native Incredible Hulk."

Lucas said, "He called himself the Dog Soldier."

Cora stared in disbelief. "He's the private investigator who chipped Goblin with the plan to shut down Holland. He's working special ops behind the scenes. Colton Lone Wolf of Pine Ridge runs a radio program, *Smoke Signals*, popular on many reservations. Wolf speaks of Crazy Horse, Sitting Bull, the Ghost Dance, Wounded Knee. If the courts don't take those dog men off the streets, the Dog Soldier will."

***

Morning sunlight shone through the bedroom window. Lucas threw off the covers. As he hopped out of bed, Grunge gave him a warning growl to let him know he was sprawled beside his bed. *Be nice,* Goblin said. *After all, he shared his room with us last night.*

Grunge stood up. *Just letting him know, not to step on me. He's a hyper little squirrel, and I don't like being trampled on.*

Goblin said, *Don't be such a grouch. Mellow out.*

Ben met the three of them at the kitchen doorway. "Imagine," he said, "these fellas need to go squirt. Would you let them out, please?"

Lucas led the dogs up the stairs and opened the door for them to take care of business. Golden rays of sunlight caused the white snow to sparkle and shimmer. Grunge checked out the entire front yard, running up and down the fence line some fifty feet from Ben's home. Goblin followed him to see country roads on either side of them. *Don't worry,* Grunge said. *I'm not leaving. Just checking out how remote this place is. We are way out in the country, which suits me fine. Race you back to the house!*

Goblin stumbled, tripped, and fell nose-first in a snow drift, trying to keep up with him. Grunge actually laughed when he looked back to see the pup covered in snow. Goblin had never heard Grunge laugh before. Something had changed about him, and he liked it.

Ben said, "Cora called this morning. Your Uncle Nate was cited for trespassing."

"What about the big charge?" Lucas asked as he scrunched in the snow with his boots. "That RICO charge? Any luck with that?"

Ben frowned. "The city prosecutor did not convince the judge that Nate transported Grunge into the state. The charge did not stick. He was out of his league last night. His encounter with the Dog Soldier had to take the wind out of his sails."

Goblin could tell Lucas was a little shaken up after his encounter last night. He listened to him talking about this Dog Soldier saving him from Nate.

What's up with them? Grunge asked as he stared curiously at Ben and Lucas kneeling between the house and the barn to examine footprints in the snow. Ben studied the scorch marks running away from the dog barn. The Lakota dog handler was spooked.

"What," Lucas asked, "made those tracks, Ben?"

Ben rose to his feet, looking down at the burn marks in the fresh-fallen snow. Grunge joined him, his ears pricked up, the fur on his neck standing up, as well. The big pit sniffed at the scorched snow, *whuffing* out a sneeze at the strange marks. Ben said, "I wouldn't want that up my nostrils either."

Lucas looked at the arrowhead dangling from the leather thong at Ben's neck. "That story you told about your boyhood, lets me know you use magic when you work with the pits out here at your ranch. So, what is your secret? Is it that arrowhead you wear?"

Chapter Fifty-One

Ben said, "I have a gift to transform them from aggressive fighters into even-tempered dogs. Some are adopted out to good families, where they become forever dogs. In the past five years, I've taken in three-hundred dogs. Scarred and emotionally damaged pits rescued from the notorious dog men. In the dog fighting circles, I am well-known as the champion of lost causes, willing to shelter pits who had the goodness beaten out of them."

He used two fingers to lift the arrowhead, bringing it out beneath his shirt. "Uncle Pete gave me this. I learned the prayers, the dances, the oral history of the Oglala Lakota under the watchful eyes of Pete He Dog, holy man, but during one of my times in the sweat lodge, I had a vision that changed my life, causing me to channel my energies to rescue the dogs who needed my services here at Wounded Arrow. Before I became the owner of this ranch, I was adopted by Ghost, the pit pup I saved from the Tall Man. Ghost was my hero. I had other heroes, too. Crazy Horse. Sitting Bull. Black Elk. In my vision, the warrior and two medicine men of the People were playing with Ghost. It was a humbling experience to see those legends actually play wrestling with my pup. The Bull said, 'Little Brother, fight on. On behalf of the dogs who have no voice, be their champion.'

"When I shared my vision with Uncle Pete, he said, 'An arrow-head that allows you to see into the Otherworld? Crazy Horse saving you from the Tall Man? Not one legend appears to you in a vision, but three? Do you know how blessed you are, nephew? Stay upon the Red Road and serve these troubled dogs that cross your path.'"

Ben reached down, placing two fingers in the black indentures in the snow. "Footprints. Someone with burning shoes left this scorched snow behind. There is something here that cannot be explained."

He removed a pinch of herbs from the medicine pouch he wore around his neck, then scattered them to the four winds, singing a low, soft prayer. He stood there, his dark eyes fastened on Grunge. "What do you think, boy?" he asked.

Grunge focused on the hillside in the distance. He took off across the yard, running past dogs in their kennels alongside the barn. He skidded to a halt at the base of the snowy hill just beside the wooded grove of spruce trees at the edge of Ben's property line.

Ben told Lucas, "Bridge-building is the key to saving most, but for the more vicious dogs, even bridges are not enough. In those cases, I make the decision to put them down. It costs me dearly each time I come to that crossroads. It takes something away from me each time I drive them down the road to Doc Morgan's place. It breaks my heart when I am forced to send a dog to the Beyond. But there are just some dogs that cannot be saved. The more aggressive dogs have been hurt beyond repair, their spirits broken. It is best to send them on the River of Stars to connect with the All-Father."

Ben smiled sadly and said, "You sure you want to hang in there with Grunge, even though a decision may need to be made when he cannot be tamed? Among my volunteers, military folks, bikers, and police officers have been completely dedicated to helping with these damaged dogs. But many could not take the heartbreak of mercifully ending a dog's life. I've seen some of the toughest men break down and cry when the end time came for a dog that could not be changed. It is a fact of life, some dogs have been too badly hurt to save."

Goblin looked up at Grunge. *Did you hear that?*

I told you not to trust this dog handler, Grunge said.

Goblin shot back, *Sounds like it is you who needs to make an attitude adjustment, Grunge. Couldn't you hear the pain in his voice when he talked about the point of no return with vicious dogs? He's going to give you a thousand and one chances to prove yourself!*

Even as Goblin said this, a small, shadowy boy moved down the snowy hillside before them. It appeared he had slid out of the tree line from where he had been silently watching. The dark-haired kid stared curiously at Ben as he bent down to study the black footprints in the snow. The kid floated inches above the ground, his black shoes leaving traces of dust behind him as he drifted toward them. Goblin could see that Lucas and Ben could not see him.

The kid stopped a few feet away from Grunge, his glowing blue eyes fixed on his scorched tennis shoes. "They were still on fire last night," he said. "At night is when the accident happened. I relive the fire each night around 2 AM. They start burning the ground wherever I step. I came here last night looking for Kipper. Have you seen him? A gray pit, one blue eye, one brown. He ran off during the fire."

Grunge whined when he realized the kid was searching for his lost dog. The boy turned his gaze on the distant barn, his blue eyes filled with tears as he sadly said, "You in there, boy?"

Something strange then happened. There, on the top of the hill, stood a tall man, dressed in a long, black coat and wearing a wide-brimmed hat. He snarled, "Don't interfere when it is none of your business! My Grandson and his dog are long gone, Black Bull! Both burned up in that fire long years ago!"

The old man spun around, his long, black coat fluttering behind him as he made a hasty retreat down the trail.

"Who was that?" Lucas asked.

Ben said, "Robert C. Kooper, AKA Koops."

Lucas said, "Looks like he was following these tracks, as well. And what was all that talk about his grandson and his dog?"

Ben said, "A sad, sad story. One I will tell you another time."

Chapter Fifty-Two

Later that same day, Ben drove into the suburb of Havelock to have what he called his monthly "Bored Meeting." The play on words was because Ben's meetings with potential investors was the most boring part of his job. He got all spruced up, wearing a dress shirt, a vest, and a tie to present himself as a professional dog handler to impress board members who invested in Wounded Arrow. They supported the work Ben was doing with dogs. He claimed he would rather spend an hour with a foul-tempered dog than an hour staying awake at a board meeting.

He had only been gone for fifteen minutes when Grunge began pacing restlessly back and forth between the fireplace and the stairs. Still deeply curious about the footprints, Lucas spotted Ben's arrow-head necklace dangling from one of the antlers above the mantle. He placed it there each time he'd removed it.

Lucas reached up to remove it from the antler tine. He stood there examining it for several seconds before slipping the thong over his head and letting the arrowhead dangle from his neck. He heard a soft crackle as something magical ignited. He cringed, thinking he was going to be blasted right out of the universe for breaking Ben's trust. Any second now, he was prepared to be punished by a backlash from the Otherworld.

Still pacing at the bottom of the stairway, Grunge looked back at Lucas and gave a soft growl. That's when Lucas saw sight traces of colors drifting like slow-moving clouds on the periphery of his vision. "Kipper?" he heard faintly, coming from somewhere outside. "Kipper? Kipper! Where are you, boy? Come back to me!"

Grunge darted up the stairs to the doorway. Goblin followed him. Lucas threw on his coat, then stopped. He just didn't feel right about wearing that arrowhead without Ben's permission. And he did something he ordinarily wouldn't bother to do. He removed the thong from around his neck and placed it back on the tine of the deer antlers. He turned and ran up the stairs. The moment he let the dogs out of the underground home, they shot across the yard and ran to the hillside where those footprints ended. Just within the tree line, those scorched footprints continued on a straight course through the woods.

Grunge bulldozed his way through branches in his path, plowing them out of his way. Toward the edge of the woods, Goblin began to flounder in the deep snow, so Lucas scooped him up and carried him out of the trees. They had traveled nearly six-hundred yards from the edge of Wounded Arrow, and the footprints continued on.

Ahead of them, Grunge had stopped, staring at the ruins of a barn burned to the ground. Some distance away from the barn lay the ruins of a house. It, too, appeared to have burned down. Lucas read the lettering on the rusty mailbox, *Kooper Steading. No Trespassing!*

"Ironic, ain't it?" a deep voice said.

Lucas wheeled around so fast that Goblin spilled from his arms and dropped to the ground at his feet. Even without his war paint, Lucas could tell it was the Dog Soldier. He wore his black hair in one long tail down his broad back, and he was dressed in a blue parka and camouflage pants with high-top boots. His face was rugged and worn, yet his dark eyes were alive with amusement that he had startled him.

Grunge let out a growl and turned around to face the man.

The Dog Soldier said, "Ironic. Two places out here in the country. Wounded Arrow, a place to heal dogs. Kooper Steading once owned by a foul-minded breeder who sponsored fights there in his barn."

Annoyed that the man had moved through the woods so stealthily, Grunge curled back his lips as he stood beside them. "Hush," Lucas said, preparing to place his hand on the big dog's head.

"I wouldn't do that," the Dog Soldier said. "He's in an agitated state on account of me. No need to rile him up."

Goblin darted past Grunge and greeted the big Indian with a lot of whining and wiggling his butt. The Dog Soldier started to pick him up yet stopped. "With your approval, big guy, may I pick him up?"

Grunge walked warily toward the Dog Soldier, sniffing at him. Lucas was impressed. It appeared Grunge trusted the man. When he scooped Goblin up into his arms, Grunge turned, no longer concerned by his presence. "Out here exploring?" he asked, his dark eyes fixed on the blackened hulls of the buildings. "Lucas, right?"

Lucas nodded. "Colton Lone Wolf, right? Cora and Ben knew each other when they were kids on the rez. And now, he has the hots for her."

Wolf said, "Black Bull's set his sights high if he has a relationship with my niece planned."

"Oh," Lucas said. "Cora is your niece? Sorry if I offended you. I was just being—"

"Funny?" Wolf said, purposely interrupting him.

Lucas was greatly relieved when a laugh rumbled deep within his chest. Wolf said with a grin, "Just razzing you, kid."

This is a bad place, Grunge said. *A lot of dogs died here.*
Goblin whimpered, *I know.*

"Dog fighting," Wolf said, "is cruel. I speak out against it on my radio show. I wrote a book, *Broken Spirits*, depicting the sad truth dog men don't want to get out there. Even with Michael Vick, there is still a large underground network out there. Just after my book came out, the cops busted four major fighting rings and saved hundreds of dogs from the dog men of Omaha. Five years ago, an angry mob swarmed onto this steading, carrying torches and threatening to burn down Wounded Arrow Dog Ranch on the adjoining property. Ben had just started up his operations, and the owner of Kooper Steading stirred the mob into a frenzy. Before they spilled over onto Ben's ranch, one of those torches ignited the explosives stored in Koop's barn. And the barn and house burned to the ground. The sad part of the story is, Koop's grandson Danny died in the fire. He and his pit puppy Kipper."

Chapter Fifty-Three

Wolf warned Lucas not to enter the ruins of the barn, but he moved forward despite his fretting. As he walked into the shambles, he scuffed up the charred floor, uncovering the outline of a trapdoor. Lucas opened the door. Wolf said, "Here, put this on."

He settled Goblin at his feet, then withdrew a leather cord from beneath his parka. He tossed it to Lucas, who caught the cord in one hand. The leather cord was attached to a small black and white feather. He slipped it around his neck and settled the three-inch long feather inside his shirt. "Ever heard of," Wolf asked, "a talisman?"

Lucas patted the feather beneath his shirt. "You mean like silver bullets against vampires? Or garlic? Like Kryptonite that weakens Superman? That kind of talisman?"

"Yeah," Wolf said, "That is an eagle feather, once worn by one of the original Shirt Wearers, American Horse. It is a sacred item. In the coming days, I think you're going to need it."

"Thanks," Lucas said and walked down a set of steps leading into a stone cellar. It looked like an underground fort. In one corner there was a cot and a stuffed chair, and in the other a big army footlocker. He opened it and found a collection of books *Big Red. Old Yeller. Savage Sam. Rin Tin Tin. Lassie.* Dozens of dog books.

"The story is," Wolf said, "ten-year-old Danny Kooper camped out in the family barn and a fire started."

Lucas continued to rummage through the dog books. "Danny must have loved dogs. He's left a library of books with dog heroes."

Lucas truly wanted to haul that locker out of there. But they didn't belong to him, so he closed the lid on that trunk. Wondering why Wolf had gone strangely silent, he climbed back up those steps and froze when he saw a huge, grizzled bear of a man, standing outside the barn, pointing a pistol at Wolf. Koops said, "Shouldn't have wrote that book, Chief. I ought to shoot you and both of your dogs."

Lucas said, "Mr. Kooper? Those are my dogs, not his. And it's my fault we trespassed. But we were following those footprints behind you. Sounds weird, but I think they belong to your grandson Danny."

Koops glanced down at the scorched footprints in the snow around him. "Danny died in the fire. He's gone. Both him and his dog."

Wolf said, "How strong is the bond between a boy and his dog?"

Koops scowled at him. "That fire snuffed out any bond the kid shared with that hound of his. Danny and his dog are long gone."

Lucas said, "What if his spirit is still wandering the earth in search of him. I heard Danny calling to his dog. Kipper."

Koops said, "What kind of Indian mumbo jumbo are you playing at, Chief? You need to be gone from my property. Vamoose! Scoot!"

Nodding silently at him, Wolf said, "He's right, Lucas."

Lucas walked over to stand beside Wolf. As Grunge went to follow him, Koop drew a bead on him with his gun. "Not you, big fella. You're scheduled for a fight this weekend. Stay, dog, stay!"

"No!" Lucas said, looking directly down the barrel of Koop's gun.

Koops cursed, fury in his eyes. "You don't trespass on my property and then sass me, kid! The big dog stays!"

Before Lucas could even respond, he a caught a glimpse of a ghost dog springing out of the cellar. He was merely a blur, his brown and black body fading in out of sight. A ghost of a pit bull pup that stirred up a cloud of dust specks that blasted Koops off his feet. He landed on the charred floor in front of Grunge, then scrambled back to his feet. He gave Lucas a crazed look and ran off toward the road at the front of his property as if the hounds of hell were nipping at his heels.

***

Wolf led Lucas and the dogs away from Kooper Steading. Big and brawny, he bowled his way through the undergrowth like a bull buffalo. Lucas and Grunge followed him. When Goblin fell behind, Lucas scooped him up and carried him. *That whirlwind,* Goblin told Grunge, *was Danny Kooper's dog. That cloud was created by the little kid's puppy. Where do you suppose the dog ran off to? Why, if Danny is searching for him, does Kipper run from him? Wolf said something about a bond between a boy and his dog. If that bond was so strong in life, why can't they be united in death?*

Lucas shifted Goblin about in his arms as he dodged a branch Wolf brushed aside. The leafless branch sprang back, forcing Lucas to dart to one side to keep from being swept off his feet. Goblin gave a little whine as Lucas set him down on the well-worn deer trail that cut a straight path through the last three hundred feet of trees before the Wounded Arrow property line. *That's not fair,* he said, *Lucas was just trying to help that kid find his lost dog.*

Fair? Grunge said. *Fair, little dude? I didn't want to be forced to fight. I did not want to rip and tear my way through dogs. I did not want to carry this rage. Nothing in this life is fair, Goblin.*

Goblin whined sorrowfully at Grunge's words. Lucas was telling Wolf about the vision Ben had that had him working with dogs. Wolf said, "I've been performing the Sun Dance for nearly sixty years, and the only vision I had was of a bear?"

"A bear?" Lucas asked.

"Yep," Wolf said. "This bear placed an arm about my shoulders and said, 'Stop drinking, Brother. Or you'll become lifeless as the bearskin rug you've had lying before your fireplace for the past forty years. Ben lucked out. Sitting Bull, Crazy Horse, and Black Elk came to him in his vision. All I got was a talking bear in mine."

Chapter Fifty-Four

Wolf gestured down at the deer trail they were on. "Stay on this, Lucas. It will lead you back to Wounded Arrow."

Lucas looked at him, puzzled. "Where are you going, Wolf? Don't you want to come and tell Ben about Koops?"

Wolf continued on down another deer trail. "That eagle feather you wear was my task for the day."

Wolf slowly vanished as he moved off into the black trees. Lucas trudged on, the dogs following close behind him. Ten minutes later, he was just drawing even with the opening between the trees that would lead to Wounded Arrow, when Grunge wheeled around. Lucas stared in alarm at the two bulky gray pits three hundred feet behind them. They were moving down the trail from the Kooper place. They were running full-bore. *Rooooll! Hoorool!* burst from their lips as their eyes locked on the three of them standing there frozen in the middle of the trail. Scooping up Goblin, Lucas turned and ran. "Grunge!" he shouted. "Run, boy!"

But Grunge was defiantly standing his ground, his hackles raised, a spooky growl rumbling deep within his chest. The two stocky pit bulls came on. "No!" Lucas shouted. He then felt a hand come to rest on his shoulder. He gasped in surprise as Ben brushed past him, a walking stick in his hand. "Stand down, Grunge!" Ben commanded, facing the oncoming dogs. The two pits were closing fast. Fifty feet away, then forty, then thirty, twenty, and at ten feet, Ben planted his walking stick in the ground. Still holding onto it by the leather grip, he kneeled in the center of the trail. Lucas knew he was going to get massacred. Those dogs were savage beasts, and they leaped the last five feet, prepared to viciously maul him when a brilliant blue aura materialized in front of them. It sparkled as it leaked from Ben, drifting like sapphire smoke, evolving into a spectral Ben, with his long hair blowing over his shoulders. The two charging dogs plowed into a field of force. Both bounced back and went tumbling down the trail. Grunge started forward, but Ben's spectral shape placed a hand on his chest. "No, Grunge, your fighting days are done."

Ben faced the two pit bulls. "I have no fight with you. Return to your master." The two pits stared earnestly at Ben. They sniffed at the blue smoky barrier in front of them. "Go," he told them. "Go away from here. Peace to you, Big Guys."

The pit bulls turned and trotted back down the deer trail.

Lucas followed Ben back to the underground home. The dogs curled up before the blaze in the fireplace, while Ben went into the kitchen to make dinner. By the time Ben exited the kitchen, two plates of tacos nearly spilling onto the floor, Lucas was more than ready to talk. After his third taco, Lucas's story came spilling out.

"The dogs and I followed the scorched footprints to the Steading. Wolf showed up. He gifted me with this," he said, drawing the eagle feather from beneath his shirt. "He claimed it belonged to American Horse. Wearing it, I was able to see the black whirlwind that knocked Koops off his feet. It was created by Danny's lost dog."

Shortly after dinner, Cora showed up at the ranch. Ben filled her in on the details of Lucas's day. He told her about Wolf's mysterious appearance, and how Koops pointed a gun at Lucas. Still dressed in her Animal Control uniform, she made herself comfortable in Ben's rocker. "Wolf said that feather belonged to American Horse?"

Finger-combing her long strands of raven hair back and over her shoulders, Cora said, "There were two Oglala Lakota chiefs named American Horse. Chief American Horse the Elder, son of Old Chief Smoke and cousin of Red Cloud, is renowned as a great warrior. The Elder was a war chief allied with Crazy Horse during Red Cloud's War. He was son of an Oglala Lakota chief and one of the last Shirt Wearers. After the Treaty of 1868, he was made a Shirt Wearer along with Young-Man-Afraid of-His-Horses and Sword. On September 9, 1876, the Elder was killed in the Battle of Slim Buttes.

"Chief American Horse the Younger, the son-in-law to Red Cloud, rode with him during the Sioux War of 1876-1877. After the death of American Horse the Elder, he assumed the name. The Younger was not related to the Elder. He was the son of Sitting Bear, leader of the True Oglalas. He claimed he killed Captain Fetterman in the Fetterman Massacre. The identities of American Horse the Elder and American Horse the Younger have been blended by some Oglalas who have never cleared up the tangle. After the Little Big Horn, American Horse the Younger became a scout for the U.S. Army. On May 6, 1877, Crazy Horse surrendered at Fort Robinson. Worried that his rage would spoil peace talks with the US Army, Gen. Crook rode to the fort, believing that a meeting with Crazy Horse would calm him. However, rumors Crazy Horse intended to kill him reached Crook, and he told several chiefs to arrest Crazy Horse. The chiefs said it would be better to kill him.

"On September 4, 1877, American Horse, Red Cloud, Little Big Man, and Young Man Afraid of His Horse moved to arrest Crazy Horse, only to find that he had fled during the night. On September 5, 1877, Crazy Horse turned himself in at Fort Robinson. He was escorted to the post guardhouse. Once inside, Crazy Horse struggled with the guard and Little Big Man and was stabbed with a bayonet. He died later that night."

Cora paused, then surprised them by saying, "I was descended from the Elder on my mom's side."

Chapter Fifty-Five

Lucas removed the leather cord from around his neck and handed the feather to Cora. She held it up in the firelight and examined it closely. "So how did you get yourself out the situation with Koops?"

Lucas offered her a sheepish grin. "You ready for this part, Cora? Because I swear to God it happened. I barely caught a glimpse of him as the ghostly form of a dog came racing up out of the storm cellar. A blur, fading swiftly, he stirred up a storm cloud of dust specks."

Ben looked to the eagle feather in her hand. He crossed the den to the bookshelf in a corner. "We know so little about the Otherworld, yet some believe spirits drift in an endless void, some with purpose, good or bad. Some involved in our fates."

He reached up and took a black and white photo from the shelf. Turning and retracing his steps, he handed Lucas the picture. "That boy is Danny Kooper. The pup beside him I gave him when I first started Wounded Arrow. Danny used to visit me. His mom and dad took in Danny's grandfather, Koops. He repaid them on the Steading by starting the fights two weeks later. And then came the fire. The ruins have set there since that night five years ago."

Lucas stood looking at the photo. "I saw that dog bolting out of the cellar. So, why did Danny come to your ranch looking for his dog? He could not reunite with the dog until he was released from the cellar. And who knows if Danny has caught up to Kipper yet?"

Tears suddenly welled up in Cora's eyes. Lucas looked over at Ben, totally bewildered. Neither one of them could figure what had been said to get this sort of reaction from Cora. A memory had been triggered. One that saddened her greatly. A great wave of sorrow washed over Grunge and Goblin as Cora shared her story. Sadness wafted from her in a swirl of waves. The dogs were engulfed in the raw emotions. "When I served in Iraq," Cora said, "US forces were required to eradicate packs of wild dogs roaming the streets of Bagdad. 58,000 dogs were destroyed."

Lucas gasped. "58,000? Is that true?"

Ben asked, "Eradicate? Does that mean they euthanized them or shot them? 58,000 dogs is a staggering number⫙"

Cora said, "Every day here in the States, thousands of dogs are put to sleep. Unwanted by owners. Abandoned. Kicked out on the streets. In Iraq, I was asked to shoot an entire pack of these dogs. I refused a direct order and was discharged, sent away from that war-torn land.

To come back to almost the same atrocious behavior here in the US. I dream of them often. All 58,000 dog souls lined up on a beach, waiting for an incoming ship to take them home beyond the stars. That is why I believe your story of a boy coming back to find his lost dog. I believe dogs have souls. I also believe some souls get lost along the way to the Beyond. Perhaps, this is the case with these dogs I see so many nights in my dreams. Perhaps this is the case with Danny and his dog, Kipper."

Goblin told Grunge, *Something is preventing that boy from uniting with his dog. Maybe it has to do with the way they died.*

Grunge said, *Maybe we don't want to find out. And these 58,000 dogs that Cora dreams about? Notice she did not answer when Lucas asked if they had been shot? She did not answer when Ben asked if they were put to sleep?*

Cora got up out her chair and approached Lucas. "Here," she said, "maybe Uncle Colton gave you this to accomplish a mission."

She gently placed the leather cord over Lucas's head and settled it down and around his neck, slipping the feather beneath his shirt. "Maybe he knows you are destined to play a role in bringing two souls together. Maybe you're supposed to be a special mediator."

Lucas stared at her for several long seconds. "Why me? I'm not a good kid. Souls are high-quality stuff? Special? Holy? Magical? I'm a unholy kid. A mediator? I am a raging demon most of the time."

Grunge let out a soft whine. Lucas looked on in amazement as the big pit slowly got to his feet and walked over to him. He stopped directly in front of him, his head cocked to one side, his big brown eyes fixed on his face, looking into his eyes. Letting out a soft whine, Grunge sat at Lucas's feet, not touching him, just being close to him. He simply sat there. "Whoa!" Lucas whispered, uncertain of what to do with the head of a 90-pound pit bull resting on his legs.

Grunge? Goblin said, peering at him. *What are you—*

Empathizing, Grunge said. *Told you this kid scared me. He's got a deep well of anger inside of him. What's the matter, Goblin? Didn't expect this from me? Ben and Lucas look at me as the one who needs to be rehabilitated. The fighting pit.*

The moment Lucas's hand came to rest on top of Grunge's head, tears welled up in Lucas's eyes.

Ben said, "Grunge thinks you've got worth."

Chapter Fifty-Six

After Cora left that evening, Ben was anxious to try out the gifts she had left them with. She warned him that Nate might return to follow through with his attempt to nab Grunge. To help prevent that, she had given them two sets of binoculars with night-vision lenses.

Night had fallen. Snow drifted down from on high. Ben led Lucas and the two dogs across his eastern field to a deer stand left there years ago. It stood on four steel-enforced beams thirty feet above the ground, and was fashioned with windows facing in three directions. A spiral staircase led up to the lofty perch.

While Ben carried Goblin up to the seven-by-ten foot building at the top of the stairway, Grunge followed behind Lucas. When they reached the landing at the top, the big dog sniffed warily at the open door before him, peering into the darkened interior suspiciously.

Ben reached around the corner of the doorway, and flicked on the light. The soft glow of a lemon yellow light illuminated the inside of the stand, revealing the bench situated before the windows. Lucas stepped inside, marveling at how far he could see even in the dark. To the west, Steven's Creek flowed past the property. To the north, the wooded hills connected the ranch with Kooper's Steading. To the east, a wide open field stretched away beyond the dog barn.

Grunge gave an airy *Huff!* He then walked inside the structure and leaped up onto the bench so that he, too, could see outside the windows. Ben placed Goblin on the bench beside the bigger pit, then closed the door behind them. He was quick to remove the two night-vision goggles from the backpack he had carried out to the stand. Offering one of the goggles to Lucas, he turned off the interior light. As Lucas fastened the goggles around his head and turned them on, he gasped, "Holy molie! These are really cool, aren't they, Ben?"

Ben peered through the window, seeing everything beyond in a strange greenish light. "They are cool," he said, amazed at how the goggles enabled him to see far off into the shadowy forest.

"What are those?" Lucas asked, peering hard at the green shadows darting through the trees about a hundred yards in front of them.

"Coyotes," Ben said. "They travel in a pack. Foxes travel in pairs, more than likely mates out on the evening hunt."

Something large and black moved through the birch trees near the river. Two of the creatures had antlers. The other five were does, having no antlers at all. "Herd of deer," Ben said.

An owl fluttered into view, gracefully flapping his wings as he sailed down and over the snowy meadow. He dipped quite suddenly, skimming the snow with his talons. Lucas said, "Oh, yuck!"

The owl latched onto a tiny gray-green mouse, then righted himself, the squirming rodent clutched in his talons. "Poor little guy," Lucas muttered. "Sucks being a mouse, right?"

Ben gave a chuckle. "They won't go extinct anytime soon. There are millions of them out there. Owls keep their numbers down."

Lucas readjusted his goggles and looked off to the bluffs to the east. There he saw the green shapes of bulky creatures lumbering at the foot of the bluffs. Ben said, "Buffalo. Sam Walker has a small herd to the east of my ranch. During the 1800's, millions of them roamed the Great Plains. Herds covered the prairie, fifty miles long by thirty miles wide. They nearly became extinct by white men slaughtering them. In Lakota, the word for buffalo is Tatáŋka. The Lakota consider the birth of a white buffalo to be the return of White Buffalo Calf Woman, the bringer of the Seven Sacred Rites. White buffalo are extremely rare. The National Bison Association estimates they only occur in one out of 10 million births. In 1833, a white bison was killed by a Cheyenne hunting party during a meteor shower, The Night the Stars Fell. The Cheyenne marked a peace treaty on its skin. Uncle Pete told me that long ago there was a famine. White Buffalo Calf Woman came to the Lakota and taught them seven sacred rituals. She gave them the sacred pipe. She then turned into a white buffalo calf and went running off."

Goblin let out a low bark as Ben and Lucas suddenly pulled the night-vision goggles off. Both let out gasps of surprise. Someone had ignited a campfire beside the dog barn, and the flames spiraling up into the air hurt their eyes. Peering now at the five figures pulling up lawn chairs before the fire that was getting brighter now that the wind fanned the flames, Ben said, "Beef and his vets end their day out here with a campfire. Nothing like sitting around a fire to soothe the soul. Holding fires, a dog snoozing beside you, no therapy better."

Lucas looked across the field to the distant fire. "Since these night-vision goggles allow us to see things we might not be able to see with our own eyes, aren't these talismans kind of the same. The arrowhead and the eagle feather? In some mysterious way, these two talismans reveal the unseen workings of the Otherworld, though if you told anyone else that, they would think we were nutty. Nutty or not, I know I saw the ghosts of Danny and his puppy. Just like you saw

Crazy Horse when you were a kid. So, I now know there are unseen things going on all around us. A whole spirit realm, right?"

Goblin had to agree with Lucas. There was sure something else alive in the realm just beyond this one. He could see small, squat forms of fire actually dancing around the ring of the campfire. They looked like fire-children playing a game. *Fire sprites,* Grunge said. *Saw them a lot back on Pine Ridge, when my master had his own fires. They don't mean no harm, just frolicking around the fire. Down by the river, you'll see water-sprites doing the same thing.*

Frolicking? Goblin asked, unable to take his eyes off the fiery sprites with wild shocks of flaming hair on their small heads. The sprites played ing a game of tag.

That's when both dogs saw movement beyond the herd of buffalo. There were two humans dressed in white creeping around out there. Grunge glared at the distant pasture. *You see them, too, Goblin?* he said, *Nate and his partner cutting right through the middle of that herd of buffalo!*

Chapter Fifty-Seven

Ben took long strides to make his way across the snowy field, his sights set on the campfire near the barn. Lucas and the dogs hurried to catch up with him. Ben said, "Those idiots just won't give up on trying to retrieve Grunge for that fight!"

They approached the vets sharing a fire near the barn. Beef stood up to greet them. The big bear of a man with his blond hair and red beard reminded Lucas of a modern-day Viking. "What's up, Ben?" he asked. "You don't look too happy."

Ben grimaced. "The trespassers are back. We just spotted them skulking across that field. They need a welcome they won't forget."

Beef gave a slight chuckle. He turned to share a knowing look with the other four men seated around the fire. "What say you guys? Want to get up close and personal with dog men?"

Staring out to the pasture nearly fifty yards distance, everyone at the fire looked to the milling buffalo beyond the fence. They were agitated and taking protective stances in front of four young calves in their midst. Ben said, "Buffalo are quite loyal. When chased by a pack of wolves, the males will lag behind the herd to defend the cows and the calves. I'd say those bulls are preparing to defend their own. Your Uncle Nate has stepped into a dangerous situation."

Suddenly, a large white shape appeared out of the night in the distant pasture. Nate's partner was a huge man, and he was running full-bore to reach the barbed wire fence at this end of the field. He had a bull racing to make contact behind him. Lucas took one look at the man his eyes wide with terror as he ran. "That's the Boar," he said. "Another member of my dad's club, the Den."

The Boar was only twenty feet from the wire barrier, preparing to hurl himself over it, when the charging bull shot forward and rammed his head and horns up and under the Boar's rather large posterior.

Screaming hysterically, the Boar was then airborne. The sudden impact of the bull lifted him off the ground, sending him sailing those last twenty feet so that he flew completely over the fence. The big man came crashing down, his butt meeting abruptly with the hard ground beneath his large frame.

"Arrest him?" Beef said. "Why not?" Ben said, and he and the five vets raced away from the fire and surrounded the Boar as he lay motionless between them. Upon seeing the Boar's spectacular flight through the air, Nate turned and ran back the way he had come, leaving his partner in crime. Behind him, Grunge sailed up and over the fence.

Nate vanished into the black woods running along the bluffs at the far end of the wide meadow. "He might outrun Ben," Lucas said to Goblin beside him, "but against Grunge he don't stand a chance!"

He turned and saw dim red lights out on the road. Although it was two hundred yards away, he saw a white van parked there. "Someone," Lucas said, "is waiting for Uncle Nate and the Boar."

Lucas decided to find out who it was. Goblin scurried along behind him. They cut across the eastern field and slipped into the line of trees running alongside the icy creek. The swift-flowing creek ran past them and continued on toward a culvert that lay beneath the road. Those black waters looked deep, and twice Lucas had to keep Goblin from rolling off the high bank and plunging into the creek below.

Lucas heard a thrashing coming from the pasture. He assumed it was Nate running from Grunge. He scooped up Goblin and stepped onto a deer trail. He saw the surprised look on Nate' face, and was then struck with his outstretched hands. The sudden blow was so forceful Lucas sailed backward for a good six feet as he and Goblin went hurtling from the high bank and plunging down into the creek. The freezing waters felt like ice piranhas biting viciously at Lucas in a hundred places.

He sank beneath the surface, yet kicked himself back to the top, sucking in a lung full of air. Pulling Goblin against him, he looked up to the high bank. Nate was standing there, windmilling his arms, trying to keep his balance and stop himself from falling over the edge of the creek bank. Then Grunge hit him from behind, and Nate sailed off the bank and into the creek.

Lucas thrashed madly to keep from being pulled under. He was simply too cold to make any noise as the currents swept him toward the culvert that lay beneath the road. And then Ben was there. Lucas clung to Goblin and despite the swift currents, Ben managed to drag them up onto the bank. They were greeted by Grunge. Ben rose to his feet, looking out to the middle of the creek where Nate was thrashing about. On the opposite bank of the creek, the Dog Soldier appeared, dressed in a winter parka. Wolf shouted to Nate, "Stand up, you fool! Put your feet down and stand up!"

Nate discovered he had floundered his way into three feet of water near the creek bank. He frantically clamped onto the big Indian's hand and Wolf hauled him up and out of the river and guided him up the snowy bank toward the road. They were met by Koops dressed in his long duster and his wide-brimmed hat. He loaded Nate into the van and closed the door behind him. He climbed into the van, started it and drove away, his taillights fading in the dark.

Chapter Fifty-Eight

Lucas, wrapped in a warm blanket, sat before the crackling blaze in the fireplace. Goblin and Grunge sprawled on either side of him. Ben offered Wolf his recliner, and served him a cup of coffee there before the fire. Ben had called Cora to report the Boar was badly injured from his attack by the bull buffalo. He had a broken leg and bruises to his rear end, and Officer Beef Tory had arrested him.

Wolf said, "For the sake of my niece, if the Dog Soldier decides to go all Billy Jack on those dog men, he would be wise not to inform her of his plans. Some very bad men are after this dog, and sometimes, bad men need to be dealt with . . . badly."

The fire crackled and blazed. Ben sipped at his coffee. Wolf stared into the fire. Lucas asked, "Who is Billy Jack?"

Goblin awoke to laughter coming from Ben and Wolf. *What's so funny?* Goblin asked Grunge.

Who knows? Grunge said. *Humans act weird at times.*

Wolf smiled. "Lucas, we are not laughing at you. It is just that we are feeling our age, when we think of the old Billy Jack movies. Now days, you have *Dances with Wolves, Geronimo, Thunderheart,* and *Smoke Signals,* unlike the classic movie *Billy Jack,* the Indian Bruce Lee. You should watch the old flick. You'd get a kick out of it."

At the word, "kick" Ben and Wolf laughed at once.

Told you, Grunge said, *Humans can be weird at times.*

***

It was Cora's story on the doomed dogs of Iraq whirling through Lucas's head that caused him to dream that night: *Lucas and Grunge trudged through the snow beyond the driveway. The frozen stream at the far end of the field shone like a silver snake in the moonlight. There was Danny Kooper his unruly dark hair messy. He was dressed in a jean jacket, blue jeans, and a pair of fiery tennis shoes. They sizzled as they touched the snowy ground, and flickers of tiny flames danced behind him as he ran toward the barn. The boy looked this way and that. "Kipper?" he softly whispered.*

Lucas felt a fierce, cold breeze rippling across the back of his neck. When he turned to look, he saw Danny fade to a red-orange glow, then disappear in a cloud of black dust from his burning shoes. Lucas came up over a hill. He looked down to the shoreline below. There were thousands of dogs gathered on an ocean beach. Beside them stood Cora dressed in a long, white leather gown, with beadwork that glimmered in the sunlight. "Do you carry the key? There are 58,000 dogs from Bagdad. I have been sent to see that these dogs make the journey home. But I must have the key to open the portal. Beyond the horizon a ship awaits them. But it cannot pass through the portal until it is opened. They suffered so much in this life. They are soon to pass on to a better place."

Suddenly, a little brown and white pit bull pup broke away from the others and ran to the top of the hill that Lucas had descended. The pup peered back down the hill, one blue eye and one brown now fixed upon him. He then turned around and darted over the hill.

Cora said, "He's a stray who came down here to the beach this morning. He was not with these other dogs when they arrived. I think he is looking for someone."

***

At seven AM, Ben rousted Lucas and the dogs from bed to attend the funeral being held there at Wounded Arrow for a German Shepherd named Rambo. Ben said, "Sending dogs on their way to the Beyond is a big deal here at the ranch. You share in the lives of Goblin and Grunge, but you must accept the consequences of the pain that bond will cause you. There will come a day when a dog's life will end. The sorrow of that passing remains with you forever."

The service was held in a small grove dotted with headstones of dozens of dogs who passed before. The pet cemetery was situated at the south end of the ranch in a section of cedar trees grown close to the road. Bundled up in his thick coat, wool gloves, snow boots, and a stocking cap, Lucas watched the company of vets walking down from the barn, then looked to the road where a long line of riders on fully-dressed Harleys turned off to enter Wounded Arrow. "American Vets," Ben told Lucas. "A large bike clubs with millions of members. Many had service dogs back in their military days. A fine showing for this dog's funeral. Rambo, a narcotics sniffer with a ten-year career, was a hero of the Nebraska State Patrol."

Sixty-two troopers parked their cruisers and climbed out of their cars in the frigid air before the grave site. Sixty American Vets trudged through the snow to join them. Beef Tory fell in line beside the vets. He carried Rambo's leash and an old rubber monkey that

197

had been chewed beyond recognition. He also carried a large silver urn. Beef joined Ben next to a granite headstone. Ben took pinches of sage out of his medicine bag, offering them to the winds, saying a prayer to send Rambo on his way. Beef broke down and cried then, and seeing that he wouldn't be able to compose himself, Ben kneeled and attached the urn to the top of the granite headstone. Beef continued to sob softly as he paid his last respects to Rambo. When the service ended, the troopers shook hands with Beef Tory. The American Vets did the same. As the officers and veterans left the ranch, Lucas and the two dogs followed Ben to the barn, where he pulled out a small plastic crate. "Take this to Beef, kid," he said, with a sad smile.

"Holy molie!" Lucas gasped as his eyes locked with the pit bull pup inside. "You are giving Beef a new puppy?"

Ben said, "Police departments find that pit bulls are extremely loyal to their handlers. With all the outcry about how vicious bully breeds are, this little guy is being placed with a capable handler."

The gray, green-eyed pup squirmed excitedly as Lucas removed him from the crate. And tears of relief ran down Beef's cheeks as he snuggled the pup against his chest.

Chapter Fifty-Nine

After the dozens of cruisers left the ranch, Ben, Lucas, and Beef were turning away from Rambo's grave, when the sound of thunder came from ten bikers on Harleys rolling down the road in front of Wounded Arrow. They were a scraggily lot, long hair and beards, and dressed in leathers. They lined up on the road and shut down their bikes. Lucas sidled up next to Ben, trying to hide behind him. "That's my dad!" he whispered.

Ben looked to a big man with long dark hair and a neatly-trimmed goatee. On either side of him, were two large men, one was bald with a shiny dome, the other's twin braids of raven hair trailed down his back. "Nate," Lucas said, "is vice president. Gypsy, the one with the braids, is warlord of the Elder's Den."

Nate casually put down his kick stand and dismounted from his bike. He shot a defiant glare at Beef standing beside Rambo's grave. Lucas remained hidden behind Ben. His dad had not seen him yet. Nate, however, passed beneath the gatepost, and saw him standing behind Ben. "Little Luke?" he said. "Your caseworker told us you'd been removed from the cop's home. So, this is your new home?"

Stone Holland slipped down his kick stand. He entered Ben's ranch, stepping around the headstones. He picked Lucas up, giving him a fierce hug. Behind the boy, Grunge stared up at the big biker, a wary look in his eyes. Lucas hugged him back, unable to get his arms around his thick frame. Stone wheeled around, setting Lucas down."Good to see you, Little Luke. Never expected to find you living with an Indian. No offense, you are an Indian, right?"

Ben said, "One-hundred percent Oglala Lakota to be exact."

He then extended his hand, saying, "Benjamin Black Bull."

Nate ignored the offered hand, but Stone shook it, saying, "Stone Holland, president of the Elder's Den, one-hundred percent Irish. I'm from the clan of Conn of the Hundred Battles. The coronation stone at Tara roared under Conn since Cú Cullen split it with his sword. The Hound of Ulster killed the King's guard dog. He then became the King's guard, sleeping at the foot of his bed to defend him against enemies. This Irish hero was much like a Dog Soldier. You know about them, right? They staked themselves out with a wooden stake and fought their enemies to the death. Cu Cullen, mortally wounded by a king's spear, tied himself to a stone as he stood off a horde of enemies, dying there against the stone."

Ben knew Stone was trying to manipulate him and being so cordial about it. He said, "Lucas needs to get to school."

Stone latched onto the back of Lucas's neck. "How about me and the boys get him to school for you?"

Ben kept his tone light. "Actually, you need to be approved to even have visitation with your son, Mister Holland."

Stone peered at Ben with a steely look in his dark eyes. "I like that you show me respect, Ben. The mister was a nice touch. But he's my son. Surely, you could bend the rules, right?"

Ben glanced out to the road, getting cold stares from the other bikers seated there. Nate eyed Beef with a menacing glare. All Goblin could see coming from Lucas's dad was a red aura.

Grunge? Goblin hesitantly said. *Is there anything you can—*

I got this! Grunge snapped, a slow rage burning in his eyes. He was all speed and motion, his stout legs propelling him forward, sending him directly at the biker. Lucas staggered, then fell to his knees, his outstretched hands connecting with Grunge's chest.

Grunge skidded to a stop, glancing down at the hands on his chest. *Not going to bite him! But I would like to sink my teeth in his dad!*

Lots of complications, Goblin said, *down that road. Best not.*

Suddenly realizing he was touching Grunge, Lucas lowered his hands. "Grunge had you in his sights, Dad. Please don't push this."

"That dog," Stone said. "The fight is tomorrow night. There's a lot of money riding on this boy. How about you turn him over to us?"

It was Beef then who said, "No, Stone, Grunge stays here."

Stone growled. "Beef Tory of the Outlaws, your days are numbered. Mark my words."

"Hold that thought," Beef said. He then flipped open his cell phone and punched a number in his speed dial. Seconds passed as the big cop spoke softly into the phone. Seconds later, he held the phone out to Stone. "He wants to speak to you," he said.

Stone took the offered phone.

Sullenly, he closed his eyes, listening.

Cursing softly, he disconnected the call and tossed the phone back to Beef. "Your day is coming, Beef. And the Irishman, Billy Connors, won't be there to save you."

Lucas flinched at the sullen look his dad shot at him as he started his own bike and rode off, followed by his bikers.

Tom Frye has worked for the past 45 years as an advocate for troubled youth. He began his career in high school, serving as a street contact for a runaway shelter. When residents at a detention center, asked for sequels to his stories, Tom knew he had discovered a way to connect with them. He has served as a mediator for his own truancy program, providing escorts to schools for alternative students. He once produced a substance abuse challenge course that impacted 15,000 at-risk kids. He believes, though, that his greatest accomplishment can be summed up by one troubled boy who wrote to him while confined: "Discovered your book today. It was like reading a letter you wrote directly to me. Thanks for giving me hope."

Check out his website:
www.tomfrye.org
Or send him an email and tell him what you think of the book you've just read:
authorfrye@gmail.com
The order of the Havelock Emerald series:

1.) Broken Red Road
2.) War Dogs at Wounded Arrow
3.) There be Dragons
4.) Thorns of the Black Rose
5.) Jewels of Kandahar
6.) Sons of Winter
7.) Fallen Heroes

www.ingramcontent.com/pod-product-compliance
Lightning Source LLC
Chambersburg PA
CBHW060414310726
48976CB00003B/1051